A WOMAN
OF
THE PEOPLE

D

D0815700

A WOMAN
OF
THE PEOPLE

Benjamin Capps

Afterword by James W. Lee

A ZIA BOOK

UNIVERSITY OF
NEW MEXICO PRESS

Albuquerque

Library of Congress Cataloging in Publication data

Capps, Benjamin, 1922–
  A woman of the people.

  (A Zia book)
  Reprint. Originally published: New York: Duell, Sloan and Pearce,
1966.
  Bibliography: p.
  "Benjamin Capps selected checklist": p.
  Summary: Captured by the Comanches at the age of nine, Helen dreams
of escape for more than fourteen years yet, when the time to choose
freedom arrives, she discovers no choice exists as she has become
absorbed in the Comanche culture.
  1. Comanche Indians—Fiction.   2. Indians of North America—
Captivities—Fiction.   [1. Comanche Indians— Fiction.   2. Indians
of North America—Captivities—Fiction]   I. Title.   II. Series.
PS3553.A59W6   1985   813′.54 [Fic]   84-11884
ISBN 0-8263-0782-5 (pbk.)

To Marie

CONTENTS

A WOMAN
OF THE
PEOPLE

1. West Toward the Setting Sun

The trinity river empties its clear water into Galveston Bay, a good harbor on the Gulf of Mexico. In 1854 the people who lived along the lower Trinity might enjoy many of the products of civilization, for they were in touch with all the world through ships and low-draft barges. They raised garden crops, rice, tobacco, and a great amount of cotton, and produced lumber in their sawmills from the forests of pine and hardwood that were native to the coastal hills. Here along the river, vegetation grew lush; Spanish moss hung on the trees; cane brakes stood tall and thick; sometimes an alligator might be seen sleeping in the mud at the edge of the water.

If a traveler moved northwest up the winding river, he found himself slowly moving into another world. The trees became fewer and smaller, without hanging moss. As the days of his journey passed, he might note that the air was drier. Less often would he pass one of the crude river docks. Finally, as he pushed against the slow currents, he would come to where the river wound through vast prairies of blackland, good for growing cotton, a land that had drawn some farmers into it during the past decade or two. About the western edge of this cotton land the river forked and spread out like the main branches of a tree.

At this point enterprising settlers had built a bridge across the Trinity, but a surge of angry red water had come down and swept it away; in the little-known country to the west sometimes violent thunderstorms dumped water on the land.

The traveler had come only two hundred miles of distance from the Gulf, but he had come more than seven hundred difficult miles by the tortuous path of the river. He had come away from a humid climate to a semiarid one. He had come to the place from which Western Civilization sent tentative probing fingers, along the forks of a river, into the interior of a continent. Out there lay a vast unknown. It would prove to be a rugged plains country where dust blew during the heat of summer and blizzards swept suddenly down in winter, an inhospitable land where the sparse vegetation had thorns and the water was bitter to the tongue. In 1854 it was almost trackless as far as the white man knew. Its native inhabitants were nomadic Stone Age people.

This area of the forks would be a good place for the traveler to turn back. Beyond here the crude and dangerous forces of a wilderness prevailed over the things of civilization. A few white people had gone farther—soldiers, explorers, hunters in the main, a scattered handful of settlers. Some of them were tough, bold people. Some were fools. Strangely, some were young and innocent, as tender as flowers that bloom in the desert.

Helen Morrison did not know that it was 1854. She lived in no complicated framework of time, but in such world as is known by a nine-year-old girl. In her family, her papa kept account of the days. Their calendar had run out the winter before, and they had not been able to get another one, and her papa had made one himself. He had worked three nights under the light of a tallow candle with pen and ink, using the back of the old calendar, since writing paper had to be saved for letters. Her papa had done the mysterious marking so that he would know Sunday, the Lord's day, and the time to plant seeds and other times that older people want to know. The most important thing about it to her was that it showed her birthday in about a month when she would be ten. Her papa had written it in: "Helen, B.D." And her mama was saving some white flour for a cake, if weevils didn't get into the can and spoil it. Her little sister Katy, who was five, had already had her birthday this year with a cake made out of the flour. And her big brother George had had one too, before they got the flour. George had said he didn't care. He had turned fourteen. She had thought he really did care and was only pretending, to seem older. But it was true that he was big and could do a lot of things, sleep up in the loft by himself, go out with Papa's rifle and get a turkey, or search out a bee tree and rob it and get stung and not cry.

Katy would cry at stubbing her toe or anything, but straighten up and laugh the next instant. She was a little tease. It was Helen's duty to look after Katy, help her dress, take her to the toilet, comb the tangles from her long blond hair, keep her from wandering off and getting lost. It was a lot of trouble, but better than not having a sister at all.

Being the middle child was troublesome. They would never let her do what George could do, because, as they said, she must remember that he was a lot older; and they would never let her do what Katy was allowed to do, because, she must remember, Katy was just a baby. She sometimes dreamed that among the neighbors that would come—which her papa was sure would settle this far out by next year—would be a girl her own age she could play with.

The neighbors would be close by. And a community fort would be built there on their own hill, or so her papa hoped. Sometimes at night she heard them talking after she and Katy were in bed. "All we can do," Papa would say, "is trust in the Lord and build a community fort when we get some neighbors. We've got the timber and the hill. I'd go ahead and start it, but they'll want to have their say." Pretending to sleep, she would hear them talk in low voices about the Indians. "I think the Wichitas are good people," he would say. "By themselves. But there's talk they trade with Comanches. Maybe they even spy for Comanches."

They never mentioned Comanches in the daytime. When they had lived on the Neches River, before Papa located his league of land, Aunt Melinda used to say to her children and to Helen, "You be good. You want the Comanches to get you!" But Papa and Mama thought it was a wrong thing to say. They never said it.

She thought about it sometimes, teasing herself with that forbidden secret, when she was lonely from being rebuffed by her brother and bored with her little sister's innocent play, when she was perhaps taking a little revenge for her little sister's more favored age. She would refuse to talk for a while, but would be saying to herself: There are things you wouldn't think are there. But they are. Comanches! There are really Comanches! ... They were vague things, a little like witches or bad fairies or trolls, but different, because her papa spoke of them in a low voice. She did not think of them to frighten herself, but because it always seemed they were a grown-up thing, secret, uncertain to her, but real and clear to older people. There were other ideas she savored in her private world: that she had hundreds of new and amazing things to experience in her life, that she might be the woman of a house, that she might meet unthought-of friends. That was mostly all wonderful and unending. But no thought could move her as that one she sometimes insisted upon to herself: You might not believe it, but there really are Comanches!

On that autumn afternoon it was cloudy and nice. Papa was clearing land a mile away beyond the hill. Sometimes they could hear the crack of his ax in the oakwood. He sent George home with the empty water jug. George had to saddle the mare and go look for the heifer, which had not come home the night before. The heifer was about to find a baby calf, and Papa thought it had happened and wanted her brought home to the lot. He wanted Helen to bring him the water. Katy begged to go until Mama finally said she could. Helen filled the jug from the keg, pushed the cedar stopper into the neck, and let the spigot dribble water around on the burlap cover of the jug, so the water would stay cool. "Now, go by the path, Helen," Mama said. "I'm afraid Katy will get on a cactus or something."

As she started, she saw George riding away on the red mare, Sweet Betsy, kicking his bare heels into her sides to make her gallop.

Mama called from the doorway, "Helen?"

"Yes, ma'am."

"Keep your eye on Katy every minute, now."

That brief backward look at her mama in the doorway showed only what she had seen many times: a familiar face, kind, anxious. But this was a time she would remember long, or try to. She would seek the face in her memory, even as it faded, and try to hear the voice again, and would never get the words back, only that they said something about taking care of Katy. Also, she would remember something of the look of her brother riding away, carefree but partly grown-up, kicking his feet into the sides of the red mare to make her gallop.

"Don't skip, Katy," she said. "Here, take my hand."

"No, I want to skip."

It would make no difference in the events about to happen that she disobeyed and left the path, unless it were some coloring of guilt that would remain in her memory of the day. It would make no difference, but her mama had said to go by the path among the last things she had said. Perhaps she disobeyed to feel big for a moment. Or it might have been that she was drawn to the hill because it meant the community fort and the neighbors who would come some day.

"You want to go over the hill?" she asked.

"Yes. Let's go over the hill."

"If you get a sticker, will you not cry and tell Mama?"

"No."

"All right. But you stay close to me, because I can't skip and carry this heavy jug."

From the rounding crest of the hill she could see the roof of the cabin behind them. Out to the left she could see a broad sweep of the West Fork of the Trinity River with its fringe of cottonwood and willows. Ahead she could see the oak timber with the opening in it where her papa worked. But something was wrong! She was aware of the sight and the sound at the same time. Where her papa should be, strange horses reared and plunged in a cluster. Dark, half-naked men danced and cried out with strange, reckless voices. She dropped the jug and grabbed her little sister's hand. "Quick, Katy, something's wrong! Run!"

She ran, heedless of any damage to their bare feet, almost dragging the smaller girl, who had not seen or did not understand. Then she saw other waving horsemen spill out of the timber toward the river and she knew there was no place to run. "No, get down, Katy! Hide! Get down flat!"

Nothing grew on the hill but grass and low weeds, mostly dry from summer heat. She spread out in the prickly growth with one arm flung over Katy, who was struggling, trying to see. From toward the cabin came a scream, not loud at this distance but almost unbearable to hear. It had fright in it and anger, as if it came from a desperate animal, and sadness. It seemed to linger in the air after it was gone. Though she had never heard such a sound from her mama, she could tell it came from that familiar throat and mouth. Something had to be done, but she could think of nothing except to pretend to hide. Katy was saying things and asking questions and trying to raise her head.

She heard the guttural voices and the thumping of hoofs coming near, even saw, out of the side of her eye, the dust they raised out of the dry grass, but still pretended to hide because there was nothing else to do. She knew they were over her. She put one hand over the head of Katy and the other over her own. But then she felt strong fingers on her shoulders,

and she was snatched up, as if she were small and light as a
doll, and was stood upon her feet.

Four of them were there, two mounted and two on the
ground. It seemed more, as if they covered the place. On their
faces and arms and chests were painted lines and circles of
muddy red and muddy yellow. They grunted and made small
cries as if they were excited and pleased, all making sounds at
once. One of them felt of Katy's hair.

The ride was like a long bad dream, beginning with a last
view of her home; she saw feathers from a mattress scattered
into the air and smoke rolling from a window. Then they
turned down off the hill and rode toward the lowering sun.
The brown arm that circled her in the saddle seemed as unyielding as a tree trunk. The Indian, against whose body she
was bumped by the motion of the horse, seemed as much an
animal as a man.

Katy was whining and sputtering in the arms of the rider
who carried her. Suddenly that Indian cried, "Hey!" and
slapped her on the side of the head. Katy had bitten his arm.
The other three Indians laughed at it and talked as if teasing
the one who was bitten.

She said, "Don't cry, Katy. I'm here." But the one who
carried her put his hand roughly on her mouth to silence her.
She was helpless, but she knew a thing they couldn't know. Her
brother had ridden in the other way from the house and was
mounted on the fast mare, Sweet Betsy. It was four miles back
to the Johnson place. If only he had not been caught and had
found out what had happened, he would ride back and tell the
Johnsons. She was anxious lest Katy say something about
George until she realized that the Indians would not understand it.

They rode straight toward the red setting sun. On a hill
they stopped and talked, looking back. She could see a loose
band of horses threading through the scattered oaks a mile
behind them, being driven by naked riders. Two of the riders

with her rode back toward them. The two carrying Katy and herself turned and continued in the direction they had been going. The sun was down.

As darkness came on, she worried that Katy would be even more afraid, and she worried that whoever was coming to rescue them could not find the way. They were going uphill, then downhill, across gullies, around clumps of trees, on and on through a dim country that seemed so big that no one could find his way in it. The stiff rawhide on the saddle hurt her legs. She was afraid that Katy would wet her pants and the Indian who carried her would be angry. She was determined not to give in and go to sleep; she must stay awake and do what she could to take care of Katy.

She slept without meaning to and woke from water splashing on her bare feet. They were riding across a stream. The horrible, impossible thing was still true. The horse scrambled up a sloping path on the other side, and when they came out from under the trees into the moonlight, she could see the other horse beside them and the form of Katy in the big Indian's arms, her yellow hair bobbing to the horse's gait. She was glad Katy was asleep. If only they wouldn't hurt her before George came with a lot of people to take them back.

Her legs were raw against the stiff saddle. She wanted to put her hands between her legs and the saddle to ease the rubbing, but could not because of the heavy arm that encircled her. For a long time she was half asleep, awake only enough to wonder when they would ever stop riding. When she came completely awake, they were stopped on a high place, and it was daylight.

The Indian dismounted. When he lifted her down, she could hardly stand on her sore legs at first. They took stringy meat out of a pouch and offered it to her and Katy. The meat was covered with rancid tallow. It didn't seem fit to eat. She and Katy held small pieces of it and watched the Indians eat. The two took a bag from the back of one of the saddles, untied a leather string from one end of it, and drank from it. The bag was made from an animal's stomach. One of them brought the bag to Katy and made signs for her to open her mouth and dribbled water into it. When he made the signs to Helen, she shook her head and clamped her mouth shut tightly. She didn't mean to eat or drink any of their things. He shrugged his shoulders and put the bag back on the saddle.

The two Indians let the horses graze while they walked around and made their strange talking sounds to each other and looked out over the countryside. Then one of them put Katy back on his horse. The other motioned to Helen.

"I want to walk," she said. She couldn't show him the raw places on her legs because she would have to pull up her dress.

He motioned fiercely.

"I want to walk. My legs hurt."

He lunged at her and jerked her up and sat her on the front of the saddle as before. He made some sounds as if scolding her. They rode straight away from the sunrise.

Before they had gone far, she was wondering whether she did right to refuse the water. That morning was longer than the night had been. It became hot, and she wanted a drink badly. It seemed strange that Katy was not crying or chattering or wanting something, but was sitting in front of the Indian rider as if she didn't mind. Thank goodness, she wasn't crying.

She wondered whether they would give her a drink if she asked. She could ask for it and point at her mouth and point at the bag behind the other saddle. Thinking of trying to make them understand made her realize how badly she would hate to ask them for anything. She said to herself, "I'd rather die than ask them." She remembered her papa saying a person could go a long time without food but must have water nearly every day in hot weather. If they offered her a drink again, she would take it.

They crossed endless hills covered with dry autumn grass and scattered clumps of dark oak shrubbery. Then, about noon, they came to the crest of a ridge, and the Indians cried out to each other. They yelled long sounds of greeting and kicked their horses into a run. Below them lay a small stream with big trees along it. Among the trees nestled a camp with brush arbors and fires and tied horses and Indians, mostly women and children.

She and Katy were picked off the horses and set down in front of them. Helen went to Katy and took her hand. The people grunted and croaked and jabbered and pointed. Most of them seemed pleased. The women had black hair, crudely cut and not well combed; they wore dresses of soft leather, and their shoes came up and covered their legs. The smaller boys, up to the size of Katy, had not a stitch of clothing on. The darkness of all their skins, the blackness of their hair and eyes, their crude and ugly clothes, such as they wore, made them seem all the same, like a crowd of strange animals. It was as if she had been snatched out of the world and set down in a bad place before a bunch of snakes or lizards or scorpions which were shaped like human beings.

A short woman with fat cheeks came through the crowd, and they parted to let her pass. She stopped with hands on hips and said, "You little girls talk the English?"

Her voice was strange, but her words were clear. The woman looked like the others and belonged with them. Helen was so surprised that she couldn't answer at first.

"*Habla español?* No? Come on, you talk the English, no? Yes?"

"Yes, ma'am."

"Ha! What's you name?"

"Helen."

"Ha! Ain't much name. What's you name, *chiquita?*"

"Her name is Katy."

"Ain't much name. My name Talking Woman. I talk all language, 'cept maybe not Apache and maybe not some more. No one learn Apache."

The Indian women shouted things to the one who could speak English. She answered them, then asked Helen, "Where you find funny clothes?"

She and Katy were wearing homespun cotton dresses that came down to their ankles and had half-length sleeves. They were plain dresses, but good. Katy's was dyed blue and hers was dyed brown. "Our mama made them."

Talking Woman told the others, and they laughed and jabbered.

"Why little one with yellow hair?"

"I don't know."

"You better tell."

"It just grew that way."

Talking Woman told the others, and they laughed and shouted to her in their language.

"How you like it this place?"

She didn't know what to say.

"You better tell."

She didn't know whether the woman was trying to be mean or what. She asked, "Are you Wichitas?"

Talking Woman laughed and told the others. Among the sounds she said was *Towyash*. They took it up and repeated it, *"Towyash! Towyash!"* laughing as if it were a joke. Then Talking Woman turned back and stopped laughing and made her shoulders and back straight and her face stern. She made a sign, drawing her brown finger across in front of herself, wiggling it in a motion like a crawling snake. She said proudly, "Komantcia!"

Several of them began chattering back and forth with Talking Woman. Helen said to her, "Me and my little sister are thirsty. We want to go down there to the water."

"You thirsty, you say?"

"Yes, ma'am."

"All right, go. Maybe you run off, you get whipped and tied up. You hear?"

"Yes, ma'am. Come on, Katy."

They went down on the sand and gravel and dipped up water in their hands to drink, while the Indians watched. Then they went back up where it was grassy and sat down together by a tree. She could feel two spots on the insides of her legs from the stiff saddle. It stung when she pressed them. No matter what they said, she wouldn't ride anymore.

"I want to go home," Katy said.

"We can't right now. Don't worry. I'm going to watch out for you."

"I'm hungry."

"Maybe they'll give us something. Don't be worried."

After they had sat still a minute, the Indians stopped watching them. There were about ten women in the camp and as many children, but only four men could be seen. The shelters were made mostly of four freshly cut poles stuck in the ground, with a roof of leafy branches. In some places a buffalo hide made the roof. Three shelters were made with only two poles with one connecting pole and a buffalo hide for a covering. Several cooking fires were scattered around, smoldering. Talking Woman stood by one which had a black kettle hanging over it.

Helen told Katy to sit still and walked over to the woman who could speak English. "My little sister is hungry."

"Ha! You sister hungry, no? What that mean to me?"

"She didn't have anything to eat for a long time."

Talking Woman took a forked stick and a polished horn and began to probe in the kettle. She came up with a rib bone which had a piece of backbone on the end and a good bit of meat. "Take it! Ain't hot. You want maybe I throw it in the dirt?"

She took it. "Thank you."

"You don't come around tell me. Maybe I hungry. No meat for all come around."

She took the bone back to the tree and sat down beside Katy. There was as much meat as they both could eat.

They sat there through the afternoon and watched the camp. Once two men caught horses and rode away. Later three men rode in leading pack horses loaded high with a jumble of things. Katy slept a while. It was sundown when the children came to tease them. First two girls came, about seven or eight years old. She thought they were girls; it was hard to tell. Their black hair was hacked off at the shoulders, and they wore a kind of skirt out of dirty-colored leather.

The girls yelled things at them and laughed. Helen thought it best to pay no attention. On the slope leading down toward the stream was a bank of crumbling clay. The girls picked up clods of clay and threw them.

"If you hit my little sister," she said, "you'll be sorry."

They laughed and screamed and got more clods. The noise brought the other children, boys and girls. They got clods and threw them. The pieces rained down. One boy swung his arm around and around, yelling, before he turned the clod loose. Katy began to cry.

"Stop it right now!" she told them. "Why do you want to be so mean? We didn't do anything to you."

They laughed at her words. One naked boy about five or six brought his bow and arrow. The bow was nearly as long as he was tall, the arrow the same length, a straight limb without head or feathers. He aimed it at them.

"Stop it!" she said. "You could put somebody's eye out with that."

He pulled it back with all his might, bracing his bare feet wide apart, aiming at Katy. He let fly. The arrow curved and went between them, striking the tree trunk. She snatched it up and broke it in two.

One of the larger boys shouted at the others and took the bow. He dashed straight at her. She threw herself in front of Katy. He touched her on the leg with the bow and ran back. They squealed and laughed and danced up and down. Another boy took the bow and did it, then another. They began to try to go around her and touch Katy. Helen stood up and threatened them with a piece of the arrow she had broken.

She heard laughter behind her and turned to see Talking Woman standing with hands on hips. The woman shook her finger at the children, and they began to leave. It was getting dark.

"Listen, little white girls," the woman said. "Buffalo Bones say warn you. You don't maybe run off tonight. He say you not give him some trouble. Too bad. *Comprende?* Don't go leave."

"Yes, ma'am."

"You maybe remember it. You go off, Buffalo Bones tie you up tight. You can't breathe. *Comprende?*"

"Yes, ma'am."

The woman went back, and she sat down beside Katy and put her arm around her. The camp looked different with the dark. Three fires had been built up, and she could see nothing but the flitting shadows caused by the flames. When a form passed between her and the firelight, she could not tell whether it was a man or a woman or an animal. The enlarged shadows of the forms jerked out among the trees and were stretched and broken by the dark foliage, and her feelings about the Indians were as mixed and broken as her view of the shadows and forms. Sometimes a murmur of voices rose in that strange, harsh tongue. A smell of spoiled meat was in the air.

The tree against which she leaned seemed a good thing. The spot of ground there by the tree seemed good. She knew what it looked like in the daytime. She had defended it. All the rest was unknown. How far had they come? A hundred miles? A thousand miles? She had no idea. But it was so far as to be a hopeless thing to expect to find anything more friendly than a tree trunk and a small piece of ground.

The sense of the deaths of her mama and papa came over her. She had known it, but kept it back. Even when she and Katy returned, they would be gone. They lay still right now, not breathing or seeing or feeling. Her mama would never again call her to supper or make her a dress or a birthday cake or tell her it was bedtime. Her papa would never again tell her to sit up straight or call her his "big girl." They lay still and cold right now, maybe cut up by these animal Comanches.

How could they do it? And laugh and have fun as if they were on a picnic. How could they do it? Such a senseless and needless thing, and not care. They didn't have to do it at all. They just wanted to.

She hated them. They ought to have something done to them to make them see what they had done, and stop laughing, and be sorry for what they had done. She hated them so much that she was trembling. Then the hate and the sadness became mixed together, and she was racked with silent crying.

She felt Katy stir beside her and made herself stop. That was enough. She must remember Katy was just a baby and had no one but a sister and a brother. She promised herself that she would not cry a bit more till she had seen Katy safely back. It was George's job to bring the Johnsons and a lot of other people and the Rangers. It was her job to watch out for Katy till they came.

Next morning more men were in camp. They were all walking around, eating and talking. Some buffalo robes were spread on the ground and piled with a jumble of things, cooking pots, a white man's saddle, some pieces of colored cloth. Helen saw the Indian who had carried her speaking with Talking Woman. She had been wondering how to get something to eat; then she saw the woman coming toward the tree.

"Little white girls, you come on. Buffalo Bones trade you now."

"My little sister is hungry again."

"I don't help it. Someone buy her, they give her food. Come on. Don't waste time. We go for home today."

At the word "home," a quick hope came to her, and for a moment her parents were still alive and everything would soon be all right. Then she realized that "home" meant something different to the woman. She took Katy's hand and led her.

"Listen, you girls," Talking Woman said. "I make you some good advice. I'm first wife Ute Killer. He war chief here, peace chief all Mutsani. So you maybe listen to me. You be nice.

Then you might be stay nice. Maybe Spitting Dog buy you. Little baby girl die catching the fever. So, *quien sabe?* Get on buffer robes, sit down nice."

There was nothing else to do. She sat down before all of them and pulled Katy down beside her. The Indians were talking and looking at them but didn't seem to be making fun as they had the day before. The one who had carried her seemed to be arguing with a skinny man who wore fancy decorations. One would speak and the other shake his head; then the other speak while the first shook his head. They were talking about Katy and a large brown horse that was tied to a stake in the ground. It was not an Indian pony, but a work horse with white hairs on his neck from wearing a collar and with a circle and an *X* branded on his shoulder.

A man who was taller than the others, with a stern face and a great beak nose, walked back and forth. Sometimes he grunted and spoke, and then all the others listened. It was easy to see that no one was arguing with him. He could be no other than the one the woman had called Ute Killer.

A woman brought another horse like the first, except that the new one had a colt a few months old, which stayed close by its mother's flank. The woman tied the mother horse to the same stake as the first.

Talking Woman came near and said, "Well, *Chiquita* with yellow hair, you lucky. Spitting Dog has make two horses for you, and Buffalo Bones say must make colt too."

"For you," Talking Woman said to Helen, "Ute Killer say little one grow up good *Komantcia*, fine *Komantcia*, but you old to tame. Might maybe to cut you throat. You too little make slave, too big make tame. What you say? Yes? No?"

She didn't answer. She couldn't tell whether the woman told the truth or was cruelly teasing. Why would they have brought her so far to cut her throat? But who could read their thoughts —if they had thoughts? She was determined not to cry, no matter what they did.

"You better tell."

"I don't know. My little sister wants to stay with me."

"Ha! Spitting Dog don't want. Well, maybe some think you be nice. So, you wait."

The skinny one walked back and forth arguing. He had rings of silver in his ears, and at his waist two dry gourds with feathers at one end. The gourds rattled a little as he walked. Finally he threw out his arms in a sign that he had lost the argument to Buffalo Bones and smiled painfully. All the others laughed.

The skinny one walked toward Katy. Helen had a feeling of hatred greater than she had ever felt before. She had never fought nor thrown tantrums nor lost her temper. But this! It was so unfair that even a stupid Comanche ought to be ashamed. It was not so much that she was afraid, though she was and she was having to fight against showing it. It was not even so much the danger that she and Katy might be taken to different places. It was just the way they were doing. Paying no attention. Katy couldn't even understand what was going on, and if anybody ever had a right to anything, a little girl that size had a right to let her big sister help her and take care of her. And she, Helen, had a right to do it. She had a right to have a say about it. They acted like it was a game. Something funny. They just thought they would do it because they could, no matter how hateful and mean it was.

She sprang up in front of the skinny man and screamed at him. "Stop it! You leave my little sister alone! Don't touch her! Don't you dare!"

He stopped and smiled a little, as if it hurt his face to smile. Then he started to go around her to Katy.

"Get away!" she screamed. "Get away!" She swung as hard as she could and struck him on the hip with her fist. It hurt her knuckles. She began to kick at him with bare feet, crying, "No! No! Leave her alone!" She became so excited and breathless that she could only say, "No!...No!"

The skinny man held out his arm to ward her off. She knew that Buffalo Bones was behind her, and then she felt his strong arms pin her and shove her down. She started to scream again, but his hand clamped over the bottom of her face. The skinny man stopped and called to a woman, who came and led Katy away from the spread buffalo robes.

All the Indians were quiet, watching. She felt the hopelessness of straining against the strong arms that held her, and she relaxed, waiting for them to do what they would. She was trembling, but not crying.

They began talking again in their strange grunting language. Out of the crowd came a man and a woman she had not noticed before. The woman was young and wore a girdle of silver conchos. The man was almost as tall as the one she took for the chief, but his face was different. His face was broad with great jaws and wide cheekbones and red-brown skin, smooth except for an ugly scar that curved from a spot below his mouth up to his temple. In his hand he held a hoop. The young woman spoke to him, but he only stared at Helen.

She felt his brown eyes look into hers. It was surprising, as when Talking Woman had first shown she could speak English. This man was not laughing or shouting or joking, but simply looking at her face to see what kind of person she was, maybe wondering what she was thinking. Or maybe wondering whether she hated them or was afraid. For a moment she was deathly afraid; maybe it was the scar, which showed that he had known violence and felt it. He was judging her. She hated it more than she had hated the laughter and teasing. It was as if a big, dirty snake were looking carefully into her face.

He gruffly answered some question the young woman had asked, then tossed the hoop on the robe beside Buffalo Bones. It was a plain iron hoop from a wooden barrel. Buffalo Bones turned her loose and picked up the hoop. The young woman took her hand. She understood that she had been traded.

She was given a cake made of rough-ground corn to eat that morning and could see that Katy, too, had been given food. Preparations were under way to move. Pack horses were being loaded. She was worried about going farther away from where white people lived. Already they had come so far that George and all the men who would come with him would have trouble. She couldn't fight them, but it might be that she could do something. She saw the woman who could speak English going toward the water hole and ran to her.

"Mrs. Talking Woman, I have something to tell you."

"Got no time. We go for home."

"But you better tell them not to move. I have a big brother, and he's going to bring a lot of white people with guns. If you all would turn us loose—"

"What? No one follows. Ute Killer knows."

"But my brother will! He'll bring the Rangers. You better not take us any farther."

"Ha! *Tehanita,* no be foolish. Be nice."

"You'll see! I warn you."

"Maybe you brother with yellow hair, like little pretty one?"

"Yes, he does. And he was riding our fast red mare."

"So? Some Kiowa man, War Dog, he with a yellow scalp tied to lance. He ride a red mare. Pretty mare horse, yes? Go back to Kiowas."

"No, it's not true!"

She shrugged and started on toward the water. Then she stopped and turned. "Little girl? *Tehanita?*"

"It's not true! I know it's not."

"Yes, true. You listen. You know how close you come maybe killed? I see you lie dead on robe at trading. Yes, close. Now you life hang like some fine, fine tendon holding weight. Lance Returner make a bit of iron for you, enough for some few arrowheads. That's all. Wife Blessed like you. She best wife for love. Maybe Blessed some foolish. Listen, maybe you be good *Komantcia,* maybe good slave, maybe dead. *Tehanita,* throw away foolishness. Be nice."

She said again, "It's not true," but the woman had turned her back and gone.

They began to move out. She feared briefly that she would

be forced to ride a horse, but found that she was allowed to walk. About half the women and a half-dozen children walked. She followed along behind the horses of Lance Returner and Blessed, who believed they owned her because they had traded a barrel hoop for her. Katy rode. An old gray horse was tied with two poles, which dragged on the ground, scratching and raising dust. Across the poles was tied a cane wickerwork basket, piled with a buffalo robe and other things. Katy perched on the rest of the load. The horse, like the pack horses and others with poles, was not led, but wandered freely with the loose-driven horse band.

Walking was not hard at first, though she saw that the others who walked all had their rough leather shoes. She had to pick her way. Out to the left of their course she could see a flat-topped hill that rose alone out of the nearly level plain. It seemed like a fortress built from layers of rock and earth of different colors, dark gray and red and light gray. The flat top had grass and oak shrubbery growing on it. She had never seen such a hill before. She thought it was probably the only such hill in the world. It was a place she could remember.

She would allow herself no doubt that Talking Woman had lied, that her brother would come and rescue them, and then they would be taken back where they belonged; but the flat-topped hill, standing alone in the hopelessly unmarked distances, suggested the idea that she might herself understand some of the puzzle of their captivity. It seemed a month since she and Katy had been taken, but she knew it was not. They had ridden, in a walk, one night and about half a day. The direction, when she had seen it, had been toward the setting sun. That was a direction that was always the same, west or south or one of those. Then soon after, the flat-topped hill, which she could remember when she saw it again. It might be that if she could escape with Katy and could find the unusual hill, she could start going away from the setting sun and meet her brother and the rescuers. Or it might be that after George and the other men came, she could help them by telling them,

"We must first go to the flat-topped hill, then a day and a half ride away from the setting sun."

Her feet were getting hurt. She didn't have time to watch out carefully enough, because of needing to keep up with the others. She was starting to get sunburned. The walking became hard. Bare places on the ground were too hot, and they made her feet tender, and the bunches of grass held hidden stickers. If she took too much care, she fell behind. She would have stopped and let them do their worst except for seeing Katy up ahead, now and then, perched on the drag.

Low dust drifted back from the plodding horses. It stuck on her sweaty skin, made her feel gritty and filthy. It made mud in the corners of her eyes. Sometimes a cloud passed overhead, bringing a rest from the heat; their shadows could be seen far out on the land, to be waited for and hoped for, to block out the harsh sun for a minute. She thought how she would give anything to stop walking and at the same time how she didn't want any of their help or their sympathy. Lance Returner and Blessed didn't even look back at her. A lot they cared. She thought one minute that she would show them she could walk as far as any Indian; the next minute she thought she must find some way to ease her feet.

In the middle of the afternoon they stopped to eat and rest in a grove of trees. She had no chance to speak to Katy. When they were ready to move again, she stood up, and her feet felt puffy, as if she had thick bandages on the bottoms. She stumbled that afternoon and hated Lance Returner and Blessed every step. It wasn't a fair test they were giving her and she was giving herself. The Indians who walked had shoes. And some of them who had walked in the morning rode in the afternoon. Before the day's travel was done, a weariness and aching had passed up into her legs and back, so that she stopped thinking much of her feet.

As they camped just before dark, Lance Returner and Blessed saw that her feet were bleeding. They pointed at them and talked about it. Next morning Lance Returner threw a lariat over the neck of a brown horse which had carried no burden the day before. He lifted her up on the horse, and she didn't protest. She grasped the mane at the withers and held on as the horse wandered along with the others. Later on the sweat of the horse stung the raw places on her legs, but she found she could bring her knees up and prop her feet on the horse's shoulders, and it was better. She had to watch carefully to keep from falling off.

Her face and arms and legs became sunburned. She did not keep count of the directions they went, or the days.

2. Winter on the Goodwater

THE HOME CAMP of Ute Killer's Mutsani Comanches that winter was in the rough country along a small stream which was called, so Helen Morrison would come to learn, Goodwater Creek. Across the divide above camp lay Badwater Creek, fed by a salty, gyppy spring. From the top of the divide could be seen a mountain shaped like a haystack, which the Comanches called *Dokana*. Much of the country was rough and rocky with red clay slopes dotted with scrub cedar, but grazing for the horses could be found on the prairies between the eroded brakes.

The camp, made up of some fifty lodges, straddled the clear, sweet stream. The dwellings were cone-shaped, covered with scraped hides, some decorated, some plain, and out of their tops stuck the small, smoke-blackened ends of lodgepoles. The ground was worn bare of grass between the dwellings and along paths in the edge of camp. Women worked in the open over cook fires. Small girls and naked boys frolicked along the paths. Lazy dogs lay yawning and scratching. Cottonwood trees shaded the stream, and a few large cedars.

The lodge of Lance Returner was near the center of camp. It was made up of a large tipi, where he and Blessed slept, and a small tipi, where Helen was given sleeping room with three others, two women and an old man with a drooping, sad face. These three, so she would come to learn, were Come Home Early and Old Woman and Story Teller. Come Home Early was the older sister of Blessed and the first wife of Lance Returner. Old Woman was the mother of the two wives; Story Teller, the father.

That first evening she lay in the small tipi, dividing her attention between her own hurts and the confusion of noise and movement that went on outside. First it was random cries and laughter of many people, then the drums began, and the singing. It might have been called singing because many hoarse voices repeated the same sounds, rose and fell together, followed the pulse of the drums, but it was like no singing she had ever heard. The sounds came from their noses and throats, fierce grunts that seemed to be beaten from their bodies as they stamped their feet on the ground. Some cries rose shrill by themselves, free of the regular up-and-down singing with the drums. Then the drumming and singing would stop for a time while one man's voice spoke loudly, beginning with proud clear words, but rising to quicker speech and to a frenzied screaming.

In the middle of it, Lance Returner came after her and led her out, limping. A huge fire burned to light the scene of the celebration. Many of the Indians stood or squatted in the background, watching. Out in front of the fire some poles were stuck in the ground; here the singers, decorated with paint and feathers, danced and sang. When she was brought into the light of the fire where they could see her, all became quiet. Katy was brought too, in a woman's arms, and put down. Then the one called Buffalo Bones came and made a screaming speech, waving his arms and pointing at them. When he stopped, many of them started grunting and singing again. She saw Katy carried out of the crowd, and she was led back to the dark lodge of Lance Returner.

For a week she lay most of the time on a robe, nursing her legs and feet, looking out under the lifted sides of the small tipi, wondering when the white men would come. Her sun-burned skin peeled off and one big toenail came off from having been bruised, then she began to feel like moving around again. She was wanting to find out what was happening to Katy.

She didn't know how much they would allow her to do. The women of Lance Returner's family let her go to the toilet place alone. They gave her food or let her take it when she wanted it. Sometimes they spoke to her, neither kindly nor unkindly, seeming not to mind that she couldn't understand or answer. She decided to test them and walked out away from the tipi to a point where she could see the camp better. They did not call her back. She could see women and a few children and many dogs, mostly short-haired and large and skinny. Some looked as much like wolves as dogs. They looked mean but paid no attention to her.

She had watched the camp nearly an hour when a boy about her own age came out of a tipi with a small girl. It was hard to realize the girl was Katy, for she had on a fancy little doe-skin dress and matching boots. The boy carried a cooking pot toward the stream, and Katy followed him.

She ran toward them, calling, "Katy!" and caught them at the stream. "Where's your blue dress, Katy?"

"This is my new dress. See?"

The soft tan dress had fringe at the shoulders and at the sleeves and down the sides and on the bottom. Tiny blue and white beads were sewn in bands to make a pattern at the top. The leggings matched the dress.

She wanted to scold Katy, make her take the clothes off, but she knew she'd better not. It might make some of them angry. Besides, Katy needed the shoes. And their good dresses ought to be saved to go back in. She, herself, should try to get an Indian dress and save her good one to go back in.

"Where is your blue dress you had on?"

"Back yonder. See my shoes?"

The boy was looking at her. It was hard to remember that he couldn't understand anything she said.

Katy saw her looking at him and said, "He's my brother now. That's what Talking Woman said. He's my brother."

"No! Don't say that, Katy!"

"Why not?"

"I'll tell you why not when we go home. But you don't say it." It was clear that her little sister did not understand any of it, what horrible thing had happened to her own mama and papa, and what these savages meant to do—keep them here from now on. Katy probably thought it was just a visit with some people who were a little different. It would be cruel to tell her now. There would be time later on when they were back safe.

"Just believe me. You mustn't say it. Do those people treat you good?"

"Yes."

"Do they hurt you or anything?"

"No."

"Well, don't you worry. I'm going to watch out for you, and George will bring some men to take us home. Can you get your blue dress and bring it to me? Do you know where it is?"

"Yes."

"Bring it to me. I'll keep it for you."

Katy went back to the tipi. The boy followed with his pot of water. They went inside. Katy came out with the dress and the boy came too, holding her hand.

She wanted to yell at him to turn her little sister loose; what did he think he was? But he didn't look like a mean boy, except that he was one of them, and all of them were beasts without any feelings. At least Katy didn't seem afraid, and that was good.

She folded the blue dress as small as she could, took it back to the place where she lived with the family of Lance Returner, and hid it under the robe upon which she slept.

The women began to give her work to do. They had a large rawhide box full of pecans. She was given the job of shelling them, a small pile at a time. This work she did out at the side of the lodge, sitting on a flat rock, using a stone the size of her hand, which looked as if it had come from the creek bed, to crack the nuts. The bits of nut meat she put into a leather pouch. It was slow tedious work, but they did not seem to worry that she was slow.

One day all three of the women of Lance Returner's lodge came to her while she was working, bringing two deerskins with the hair scraped off. They put the skins against her in different ways and chattered to one another. They had her hold her arms out and one would hold a skin against her while the other two stood back and looked. Finally they began to mark the skin with a piece of charcoal and by pinning it with thorns. They drew around each of her feet. She knew it meant new clothes for her, like those Katy had. She wanted them, but hated the way the women went about it, as if it were a happy thing to have clothes made. They would not change her with clothes. Every minute she wore an Indian thing she would hate it and remember that she was white and look forward to the time when she and her little sister would put their right dresses back on and go back where they belonged. She would wash the blue dress and her own the first chance she had and have them ready.

The dress and the shoes with tops that came up to her knees were finished in one day. They had no fringe or beads as Katy's had. She put them on and stood still while the three women went around her, chattering. She felt strange in the clothes, but was surprised that they felt comfortable. The leather was soft. At her first chance, she rolled her brown cotton dress as tightly as she could and hid it with the blue one.

The pecans had not been finished when they put her to work on the plums, a basketful so large that she could not carry it alone. Old Woman took her up on the rock ledge at the edge of camp for the work. The ledge was back away from the stream, about as high as the tipi tops. They pushed and tugged the basket up the rocky trail. On top was a broad layer of rock that led around the hill, mostly bare and smooth, cracked here and there with twisted scrub cedar.

Old Woman swept a place as large as a tipi clean with a cedar bough, then showed her how to take the seeds out of the plums. A ripe one could be mashed with the fingers and the seed would squirt out. One that was more firm had to be sliced with a small knife and the seed cut out. The seeds were thrown away. The pieces of plum, some of which were mostly peel, were laid out on the clean rock. Old Woman watched her a few minutes, then went back down to camp.

She didn't mind the work. It was a good place from which to see the whole camp. She got juice and pulp on her hands, but licked them clean. Flies came to light on the spread plums. She shooed them with the cedar bough.

Other women came to spread plums or to pound grass seeds in shallow holes in the rock some distance away. They paid no attention to her.

In a clearing at the upstream edge of camp she could see children playing with a ball, boys and girls younger than she, a few girls her age or older. They shouted and laughed as they kicked the ball back and forth. At the edge of the clearing, Katy stood, watching, noticeable because of her blond hair. She seemed a pitiful figure, standing there left out of it, too young to know that it was better to be out of it, that these were dangerous, cruel savages, for all their resemblance to human beings.

She dropped her eyes and went on with the plums, wishing she could have Katy up here with her. After a time, louder cries came from the playing field. She looked and saw that two of the children had fallen down and the game had become more lively. They were all laughing and running. Katy was still in the same place, but was springing up and down with little, stiff-legged jumps. She thought she could hear Katy's voice rising with the squeals and cheers of the players. Then as she watched, the ball was kicked by two children at once and bounded out to the side among the trees, past Katy, and Katy ran after it. She could hear her little sister's voice above the others. "I'll get it for you! I'll get it." And she did get it and ran back and heaved it onto the playing field among them; then waited at the side, showing by her little dance that she was hoping it would come her way again.

Helen wanted her up here with her. She wanted to put her arms around her and say, "Don't do those things. That's the thing they want you to do. They killed your mama and papa, and now they want you to like them. Don't do it. Hate them. It's all right. I'll take care of you. It's all right." It would be a cruel thing, but no more cruel than this pitiful thing she was seeing.

She turned all her attention to the plums. Sometimes a wasp came and tried to light on them. She would slash out with the cedar bough and drive it away. Two women who had been spreading plums a little distance away finished and went down off the ledge, leaving their fruit to the flies and wasps. A blue jay came and carried off a piece. She was alone on the ledge now, working and protecting her own plums.

A dog scrambled up the rocks and came toward her, a big skinny dog. It had short gray hair, the color of a wolf's, except for rusty patches of bare skin. She stood up with the cedar bough in her hand and said, "Git!" He looked filthy, and she hoped he wouldn't try to come closer. She would hit him if she had to. He eyed her, motionless, and she said again, "Git!" The dog dropped his eyes, sniffed the ground, then walked around her toward the other women's plums, which he sniffed all over. He looked back at her and went on to a bit of shade away along the ledge.

The nights were cold and some of the days were chilly. The yellow leaves were dropping from the cottonwood trees.

She was beginning to learn some of their words: "Come on," "Bring some water," "All right," "No," "Here, take it," "Stay back." Some few of them she learned from Talking Woman, but most she learned from the women of the Lance Returner lodge. They often put meaning into their words by motioning or handing her something as they spoke. The sounds were full of grunts and throat noises and trilled *r*'s. It seemed bad at first to learn their words and their strange ways of putting words together, but she realized she needed to know what they said.

Winter was not far off. She had been expecting George and the white men to come. As the days passed and nothing happened, she thought about it and told herself it would take many days for all the men to come together and then make their way to this place. She hoped they would come before bad weather and worried that, if they did not, they might have to wait till spring. Then one day she became aware that the whole Comanche camp was preparing for some big event. Knives of all kinds and hatchets were being honed on sandstone. Men squatted over small fires, sighting along arrows one by one, heating, bending, straightening them. Daily two or more men rode away from camp, and two or more rode in, talking and answering questions as if they brought news. She believed they must have seen the white rescue party and that a battle was in preparation. It might be that she could stop it, for while she believed that the Indians should be punished for what they had done, she thought it would be better to avoid any fighting if they would agree to turn over Katy and herself to the white people and give back anything they had stolen.

She went to Talking Woman, who was working outside the Ute Killer lodge. The fat-cheeked Indian woman was always willing to talk, though Helen could never speak with her without thinking of the cruel lie she had told about her brother.

She pointed at two men who were straightening arrows and asked, "What are they going to do?"

"Go for robe hunt," the woman said. "Get winter meat. Now buffer come, wait for *Komantcia* people past *Dokana*.

Good fun. Maybe you beg Come Home Early, you go, too."

That same night they danced with two big fires for light and four drummers and many singers. She watched from back behind the sitting old people and children. The dancers, dressed in their regular clothes, seemed to have a good time. They laughed often and called out to one another. Among the watchers, here and there, a child pranced, imitating what he saw, an old one nodded or patted hands to the drum sound. Away from the dancing area, the firelight was dim. She could not see Katy. All the people seemed happy, as if they had no cares at all, and she believed that Talking Woman had told the truth about what they were going to do. She went back to the Lance Returner lodge and went to sleep to the patient, continuous drum.

Next morning she found that she was to go with them. Lance Returner, Come Home Early, and Blessed were going. Story Teller and Old Woman were staying behind. It seemed that half the entire band was going, but as far as she could see she was the youngest. She was given a spotted horse to ride, bareback. She had a single rein to guide him, a rawhide thong tied around his lower jaw. They had risen early, and at sunrise trooped out of camp, riding down the valley of Goodwater Creek. The air was crisp. Frost sparkled on the grass.

She had decided the white rescuers were going to wait till spring. Still she hated to be separated from Katy. No doubt they would take good care of her. To know it was both a comfort and a source of bitterness.

She had no idea how far they were going. After a few hours they gained the crest of a long, grassy ridge, and from this point, because of the distance and variety of terrain, she received anew a sense of the vastness of the country. How could anyone know his way or find his way across it? It seemed impossible. Yet it was clear that Ute Killer, up in the lead, knew exactly where he was going, and from their confident voices and laughter Lance Returner and the others knew too.

Far ahead rose a rounding mountain. Away to the left the earth was broken and rugged with outcrops of rock in layers. The dark-green spots among the rocks were cedar trees. Out to the right and beyond the valley they had turned out of, the ground swept away in long swells, bare of trees, gray and yellow with fall grass. She had no idea whether this might be the route her captors had brought her along. It was the sense of distance that made it seem familiar. Neither could she judge how many hours of travel, or days of travel, it might be to some point she could see far away in the land. The flat-topped mountain, that key to the boundless mystery, might lie somewhere there. She described it to herself. When she closed her eyes, she could see it. As she rode, each time they came onto high ground, her eyes probed out to the misty purple horizon, searching.

The weather stayed cool. The ride was easy. One would have thought that most of them were going to a party rather than a hunt. Her horse was gentle and lazy. He would stop to graze, and she would have to pull his head up and kick him to make him keep up.

They camped early that night and pulled out at first light the next morning. In the middle of the day they were met by two men of the band, scouts who had left home camp several days before. They stopped to rest and eat by a water hole, letting their riding horses graze, hobbled, along with the loose horses they were driving. In the middle of the afternoon, they went on, guided by the two scouts, who rode beside Ute Killer. Dark came and they rode on. After some hours of darkness, a word passed back through the straggling riders, at which time the laughing and loud talk and singing stopped. They moved quietly for another hour, then came down a slope to where fires flickered under tall trees. Three other scouts were there before them.

After a short sleep it was daylight, and she could see that

their camp lay beside a broad river with sandy shores and islands of bare sand out in the stream. The water was muddy red. It didn't look anything like the West Fork of the Trinity, near which she had lived.

Some of the women pointed. She looked and saw upriver, almost within shouting distance, a dozen shaggy buffalo, grazing like cattle. Downriver, farther away, more trooped along as if going for a morning drink. Across the river a herd large enough to raise a pall of dust moved in the distance; they were like a dark-brown blanket spread out. When the men had grabbed a little food, they got ready quickly. All of them stripped down to breechclouts, though the air was cold. Each carried only his bow and bag of arrows and knife. They mounted, speaking in low, eager voices, and rode away in a bunch. As they left, about half the women were mounting. They waited until the men were passing over a rise out of sight, then followed.

She was left with Blessed. They worked that morning, mostly cutting and carrying limbs from willow sprouts along the river. Blessed gave her the job of making small stakes, or pins, cut square on one end, sharp on the other, by hacking with a heavy knife. When she had made one, Blessed took the knife with a little smile and showed her how to make one faster, hacking against a dead stump for a block.

When she had cut a small pile of them, Blessed came back and knelt on the ground beside the pile. Motioning for attention, the young woman drew a figure in the dirt, like a sand-glass for telling time with a line down through it. Then she began sticking the pins around the edge of the figure and along the line. She would frown as she stuck a pin at one place, look at it, then move it to another place around the figure. Finally, she seemed to get a pattern that pleased her. She nodded and quickly rose and ran along stooping, drawing nine more of the figures in the dirt. Two pins were left over from the first figure. She stuck them in one of the nine, and looked up smiling as if it were all clear and simple.

Helen could count to a hundred, and she could see that the young woman had used twenty-four pins around the one figure. It looked as if she wanted enough pins to go around all of them. It seemed silly. It made an awful lot of pins. But, since Blessed was friendly and agreeable, she would make them.

In the middle of the day the hunters came back, both men and women, leading their loaded horses. Their hands and arms were dirty with dried blood, and their faces. They seemed quite happy. When she had helped unload and open the great furry bundles brought by Lance Returner and Come Home Early, she thought she had never seen so much meat in her life. And every horse that had been ridden away that morning had come back loaded. There were broad rib slabs, great hams, rolls of thin meat, white chunks of leaf fat, kidneys, livers, tongues. The strong, sweet bloody smell and the sight of it all made her stomach sick.

That afternoon the women worked, slicing off long thin pieces of meat and hanging them on bushes and trees and on racks of limbs bound together with rawhide. They worked hard, chattering to one another, many of them eating bits of raw meat as they worked. She found out the use of the pins and the meaning of Blessed's pictures on the ground. They had been pictures of buffalo hides, whch were now spread, hair down, on the ground and staked in position, twenty-four pins to each pair of hide halves. Lance Returner and Come Home Early had brought the meat and hides of two large buffaloes. The men did not work that afternoon but lounged around smoking and talking and broiling meat, of which they ate great quantities. Some of them ate portions of entrails, raw or roasted. Come Home Early wrapped a long piece of small gut, which contained marrow, around and around a stick and tied it, then handed it to Lance Returner. He held it to the fire until it sputtered and browned and the juice dripped. He carried it around, eating off it as he talked to other men.

Helen ate marrow from a rear leg bone that had been

roasted and cracked open and meat from a broad slab of ribs that was propped up against their fire. She had learned to take food she wanted without asking.

The following day the hunters went out and again came back with horses loaded. The weather became warm in the middle of the day. As the women opened the great loads of meat and began to slice it and spread it with that of the day before, the flies came. They swarmed everywhere, small flies and big green flies. The women dashed about, flailing at the green flies. They went around looking, cutting off bits of meat where small piles of white eggs had been laid. The flies were so bad that they hardly had time to get the meat cut up. At last they raked up piles of dead leaves, wet them with water from the river, and flung handfuls on the cook fires to make smoke boil out all over camp. It helped, but they worked with watery eyes. As the sun began to drop and chill grew in the air, the green flies gave up and went away.

For three days the hunters brought meat. Trees, bushes, and meat racks were covered with flat strings of it, drying, turning dark. The fourth day they brought only skins and tongues and leaf tallow. Lance Returner got ten skins in all; the hair on them was long, dark brown, shiny.

The seventh day they set out for home camp with loaded horses. Helen rode the same spotted horse, this time not bareback but perched on top of four packs of meat rolled in green skin halves. The skins had become so stiff that they had to be dampened with water before they could be rolled around the meat, but the packs, with hair side out, made a good place to ride. It turned colder on the journey. The wind whistled out of the north. She rode cold and was glad to get back to the winter camp on Goodwater Creek.

For the first few days after they came back she was kept busy helping with the meat and had no chance to go find Katy. She worried that her little sister might have caught cold or

something. One day she saw that a game of kick-the-ball was
being played out in the clearing. She left her work and walked
out far enough to see the children plainly, thinking maybe to
find Katy watching. She saw no one standing to the side, so
started to turn away, but then stared with surprise. Her little
sister was there but not watching. Katy ran in the middle of
them, laughing and screaming and chasing the ball. She played,
and they played as if she were one of them.

She could do nothing about it. Even if she had lived in the
same lodge with her little sister, Katy was too young to work
and needed something to do. She didn't understand. Who could
blame her for wanting to play?

She found something even worse the next day when she
met Katy in the path. That boy, the one she had called her
brother, was with her. She asked Katy whether everything was
all right and whether they treated her well, and her little sister
answered as if she had no trouble in the world. Katy proudly
showed a doll she was carrying. It was a little girl doll made
of soft leather and had black fur for hair. It had a painted
face and beaded designs all over its dress. She wanted to snatch
it, tear it to pieces, and throw the pieces into the creek. She
hated it even more because it was a pretty piece of work and
because she could see Katy loved it. It was clear, too, if she did
anything to it, that stupid boy who was standing there grinning
would stop her. She handed back the doll and went on her
way.

The women made her winter clothes with buffalo hair inside,
even in the moccasins. They were the warmest clothes she had
ever worn.

One piece of work they did was of great interest to her
because they used her pecans and plums. The strips of buffalo
meat had dried until they were stiff and hard, almost black
in color. They carried loads of this meat up onto the ledge and
pounded it in the shallow holes until it broke down like meal.

It was whitish with a few red fibers in it. This meal they put in two large rawhide boxes. In layers they put it in, a layer of pounded meat, a sprinkling of pecans, a thin layer of dried plums, then another layer of pounded meat. When the boxes were full, they poured boiling tallow, rendered out clear, over it all and let it soak in.

As the winter wore on, she had less work to do. She had come to realize more the importance of learning the language. It wouldn't be easy for the white people to rescue them. It would take time. She needed to be able to understand the Indians' plans, where they were going and when, what they intended to do. Already she knew a lot of simple words, enough to follow directions when she worked and to get by around the lodge. Now she set out on purpose to learn as much more as possible. When she heard difficult words, those that seemed to have meaning she had not understood, she remembered them and went to ask Talking Woman the meaning.

The Indian woman liked to be asked questions about words. She liked to teach things and give advice. She had been born of the Penatuhka Comanches, those who were not enemies of the whites, and had worked for a white trader when she was young. Later she had picked up Spanish from the New Mexico traders, and having learned a few Kiowa and Wichita words, proudly claimed that she could speak all languages.

Helen learned from her that the new name they had given Katy meant in English "Sunflower." The name they had been calling her, *Tehanita,* meant in English "Little Girl Texan."

Talking Woman was also proud of being the first wife of Ute Killer, the chief. His lodge was the center of camp. Those most important lived near him. In his lodge lived No Name, a cranky old man who was the chief's father; Little Wild Horse, his son by Talking Woman, eight winters old; and Sweet Mouth, a young second wife, who was made to work hard by Talking Woman when Ute Killer was absent. Talking

Woman ruled the lodge most of the time and jealously cared for the fancy shield and lance of the chief. One tipi of his lodge served as a council room, and when the men gathered, even Talking Woman had to leave, for no woman could listen to the council. Some way, though the council was secret, the women knew all that went on. They knew who spoke for raiding Mexico next summer and who for raiding the Utes, who proposed moving home camp to Prairie Dog Town River and who to Trading River, who made a grand speech to the others and who disagreed with him.

Helen didn't like to visit Talking Woman when Ute Killer was around. She was afraid of him. He had the broad face of the others, but it was dominated by a beak nose which made him look like a cruel eagle. His mouth drew down at the sides, and the creases between his cheeks and upper lip were deep. His eyes, too, were set deep. His shoulders were rounded and somewhat humped, yet his bearing gave an impression of dignity and power. He seemed to rule those around him with his eyes and with his sure way of moving.

Weather that winter alternated between bad spells of cold and sunny days when the film of ice at the creek edge would melt by the middle of the day. On some good days she had to go with the women to bring wood or dig roots for eating. Other good days she spent time at the lodge of Ute Killer with Talking Woman or at the lodge of Spitting Dog, where Katy lived.

Spitting Dog had two tipis, as had most of the important men who lived near the center of the village, but one of them was used for all his holy things, and he and his family lived in the other. There were three wives and one old man, who kept busy most of the time making arrows or some decoration of feathers and beads. He was the only one, besides Spitting Dog, allowed to go into the tipi where the holy things were kept. Besides Katy, the only child was the boy she had said was her brother, one they called Burning Hand. Burning Hand didn't work much around the lodge. Often when the weather was good, he would go out with the chief's son, Little Wild Horse, to help in training horses or to practice trick riding or to have races.

Spitting Dog kept busy much of the time with his medicine. He would stay in the holy tipi hours by himself, and they could hear him in there mumbling or chanting and shaking his rattles. Most of the men were heavy set, but Spitting Dog was slender, even bony. He held himself erect, regally, and always wore decorations. When he was not making medicine by singing, his face was set in a permanent expression of puzzled pain. If he smiled, it could be seen that the smile stretched his face out of shape and would soon be gone. He was serious and spoke little, seemed always to be thinking of something important. He spoke hardly at all to Katy. At times he patted her on the head, absentmindedly, and allowed himself a little smile. He didn't appear to notice Helen when she was there. He didn't seem to remember that she had hit him with her fist at the trading.

During bad weather they lived huddled together inside the skin tipis. In Lance Returner's lodge, the warming fire was kept in the big tipi, where he and Blessed slept. Sometimes the north wind blew cold rain or sleet or fine snow pattering against the skin wall, and she sat long hours with them, Lance Returner, Blessed, Come Home Early, Old Woman, and Story Teller, listening to the winter outside. On those days they also let a dog come in, a mother dog with two pups. A small fire in a hole in the center kept the crowded room warm.

The air was close and smelled of unbathed bodies. They sat cross-legged with their robes about them, scratching lice and fleas, listening to the wind. She longed for better weather, but it was a comfort to have a warm, dry place.

She learned to adjust the smoke hole. Sometimes water dripped down it to sizzle on the fire, or, worse, wind blew the smoke back down to smart their eyes. She would go out into the weather and move the pole that was hooked to the smoke flap until she could see smoke coming out as it should. Then she would go back in and tie the door and wait until Old Woman grunted that it was all right. After being outside, seeing the lonely, barren winter countryside, the crowded room seemed a good place.

Living close to them, she began to see that they were each different in appearance and actions, quite contrary to her first idea that they were all alike. Lance Returner had a broad face with great jaws and wide cheekbones like most of the others, but his skin was smooth and deep red in color. The ugly scar on his cheek made him look fierce at those times when he sat silent and moody in the dim lodge. Other times one forgot the scar. He was tall and large. Sometimes he made grand motions as he spoke. His hair was well cared for; often both his wives combed it at the same time. It was greased and slicked down on top; then the two braids, which started at his shoulders, were wrapped in bearskin. They paid more care to his hair than to their own.

He was of importance in the band and always went to council. At times he would practice his speech beforehand, pointing slowly at the sky and the earth, waving his hands, pounding his chest, speaking in a voice he used only for important words. If a whisper or a giggle escaped one of the women while he practiced his speech, he spoke in sharp anger to Come Home Early and threatened to throw everyone out of the lodge. They were afraid of his anger, or at least were quick to obey if he seemed angry. When his temper was up, the great scar on his face looked white.

One could see the women were kin by the shapes of their faces, but they gave different impressions. Old Woman was ungraceful, somewhat dried up, but she was strong and tough. She worked hard and knew the best way to get things done. Come Home Early seemed equally strong, more sturdy of build, with fat arms and waist. She might have been thirty years old. Blessed was less than twenty, a graceful, slender, friendly, simple copy of them. Lance Returner bossed the lodge, but he seldom spoke to his wives' father, never to their mother, Old Woman. When he wanted something done, he told Come Home Early. Somehow she had a special place because she was first wife. Her mother would start to help her, usually ended by doing half the work while she advised the two wives. Both she and Come Home Early ordered and instructed Blessed in the work, but she did almost exactly as she pleased in her slow, lazy, friendly way. Blessed had the silver and the beads to wear, and if Lance Returner lay down in the daytime, he put his head in her lap.

The one who surprised her was Story Teller. At first he had seemed like nothing. His hair was white and wispy, hardly enough to draw into braids. Across his drooping face were scattered a few white hairs, which he did not bother to pluck, since he didn't care about his appearance. One eye was bad; it was filmed over and the skin around it drooped even more than the rest of his face. He was thin and stooped, and his spindly legs seemed hardly able to carry even his small weight. Usually he seemed sad and of little account, hardly alive. It was easy to overlook him. But when he told a story, it was different. He would fold his spindly legs underneath himself and cast his robe about him, holding the robe with one hand while he stuck the other out to gesture with. That hand would point or wave or thrust up as if commanding something to halt; it would draw mountains or level plains or winding rivers in the air. His voice would be harsh or soft, according to what he said; and his face would come alive to the feeling of his tale, showing anger or surprise or fear or sorrow or merriment. He would seem a beautiful girl or a great warrior. Sometimes a smile would draw all the sag out of his face; another time his voice would break and a tear would come out of his one good eye to wind down his face. He held himself spellbound as well as his child listeners. An endless number of stories seemed inside him, and he seemed to live only to tell them.

They were not made up by himself, but stories he had

heard, some quite old about the Little People or the time when the earth was new, others about true happenings. Story Teller was concerned with the truth. He would comment on the story or parts of it: "I know it was true, for I had it from the lips of three different men who were there." Or, "A brave of the Kwahadi told it that way, but he was known to exaggerate, so I expect it was less than that." Or, "The Kiowas tell it a bit different, but they are superstitious people." He told no stories in which he was the hero, nor did he draw lessons from a story, as did Lance Returner.

Sometimes Blessed stopped and squatted with the children to listen. The old man made no difference in his story whether he spoke to one child or a dozen or to grown people. Helen found that she could understand his stories even though she didn't know all the words. His movements and the look on his face explained the words better than Talking Woman could.

In early spring a Kiowa visitor rode into the camp. He rode a red mare. Helen heard them call his name in Comanche words and from the knowledge of the language she had learned, she interpreted his name: War Dog. The name struck her, for it had been part of the story Talking Woman had told, which she had told herself was a lie. She had remembered the details of the story and had pondered them often and had repeated to herself that it was all a lie—that there had been no Kiowa Indian named War Dog with a lance and a blond scalp on the lance and riding a pretty red mare.

She went down below camp where the Indian had staked his mount in a patch of grass near the stream. The mare was gentle. She said to it, "Sweet Betsy? Sweet Betsy?" The mare's eyes were like pools of dark liquid, and she could see reflected in them sparkles of light from the stream. The mare snorted gently through her nose and turned back to the grass. On her left hip was an *M,* her father's brand.

She went and buried her face in Sweet Betsy's neck and cried for her brother. Something inside her had known it all along.

There would be no white rescuers. It was up to her. They thought she was little and weak and would become one of them, but she would not. She would never forget who she was. Even if it took years, she was going back and take Katy, back where they belonged.

3. Winter When the Buffalo Hid

Helen Tehanita had come up on the gentle divide above the travel camp to pick prickly pear apples. She had not been told to do it, but having picked them with great trouble at times during the past two years, could not now pass up this field where the apples stood up thick and fat and red on the gray-green leaves. She had become a good worker on purpose, not to be more a part of their life, but to gain and keep their trust. Let them believe that she was a good Comanche, that she had forgotten her great grievance against them, that she accepted her life as it was and had given up hope of a decent life among white people. Let them believe it if they would.

This day without much work she had half filled her basket, a container woven of heavy grass that Lance Returner had brought back from the Mexico raid. She picked the apples skillfully with a tool made of cane, almost never getting any of the fine stickers in her hands.

She had learned patience and great respect for the long job she had set for herself. She had determined to learn Comanche ways so that she would have the ability to escape from them, but the more she learned, the more she found to learn. Those visitors now in the travel camp were Penatuhkas, and there were many other Comanche bands: Nawkoni, Tanima, Tenawa, Kwahadi, Yamparika, Kotsoteka, Pagatsu, Pahuraix. The Penatuhkas had some kind of connection with white people. They lived part of the time on something called a "reservation." That was the kind of thing she had to learn.

Understanding the nature and ways of her captors was hard. They believed that they were better and stronger and smarter than any other people, white or Indian. They liked to brag about what they had done and what they intended to do to such as the Lipan Apaches. It seemed false, yet they had gone against the Lipans and brought back scalps. They bragged about feats of horsemanship that seemed impossible; yet she had seen them riding in play, man and boy, and had seen them drop down to hang on the side of a running horse and shoot arrows under his neck. And she had seen two of them charge side by side on running horses, lean over, and pick up a grown man lying on the ground and pull him up on one of the running horses. Having seen some of the amazing things they could do, she found it difficult to judge their bragging, whether it were true or false.

During the two years she had seen some of the country they called their own, which she was trying to learn. She was wondering if the trouble were that she wasn't old enough, for as much as she had seen was all different, and its only common trait was its vastness. It was filled with landmarks that one never saw again and with paths made by buffalo and deer that led everywhere and nowhere. At least she had learned to ride in comfort. She could live most of a week on a horse and not mind it, as all the others seemed able to do.

After the winter on Goodwater Creek she had gone with a hunting party in the spring, then with a party that met a Mexican trader and exchanged robes and skins for silver ornaments, tobacco, knives, red cloth, and powder and lead for the few muskets they had. After that they had moved the whole Mutsani camp, carrying everything they owned by horse, carrying the old, such as Story Teller, and the young children

by travois, traveling for ten days to a new home camp on
the Concho River. From there she had gone with a party
to set up a raid camp from which the braves went out to fight
the hated Tonkawas. Later she had stayed at home camp
with Old Woman and Story Teller while the braves went on
an autumn raid to Mexico. Then she had gone on a winter meat
hunt as cold weather came and on a spring hunt as grass began
to green and leaves sprouted on the trees. They had made a
raid already this spring against the Lipans. Now they were
moving the entire Mutsani camp again, to a place they called
Wild River.

They had stopped here and made travel camp because a
good herd of antelope was nearby, also to visit with some
Penatuhkas who were in the area hunting.

She went forward to the crest of the rise with her basket of
fruit, seeing a patch of prickly pear with many good apples
standing on the leaves. She set her basket down beside one of
the clusters, wiped the sweat from her face, and looked out
at the country ahead. The twin peaks of Double Mountain
stood out there a day's ride away. Straight ahead of her in the
distance green foliage marked the course of a river. Between
her and the river, dust rose and hung in a line along the hot
ground, marking where something moved.

The strangeness of the dust pattern first caught her eye. It
did not look like that made by a bunch of running, scattering
antelope or wild horses; nor like Indian riders, nor buffalo, both
of which moved in groups rather than in a string. She shielded
her eyes with her hand. A small gasp escaped her when she
realized what she was looking at: a column of white soldiers.
They rode in pairs, and in the middle of the long string went
wagons drawn by mules. The blue of their suits was dimly
visible, and here and there a flashing of sunlight on metal
things they carried.

She stood trembling a moment, her mind a blank. It was too
wonderful to grasp. Then she sprang toward the distant
vision, hardly noticing that she upset her basket, but running

as fast as she could. At first her way was downhill, and she seemed to fly; she had no doubt that she could catch them and no doubt that she must. In a minute the ground became level, she lost sight of the column from the bulges of the terrain, and her mind started to work again as she ran. She had been a half hour's walk from camp and probably no one had seen her. What would they do, the white soldiers, if she could catch them? She was beginning to pant. What would they do when she ran up to them in her Indian clothes? Would they shoot her? If she caught up to them, shouting, "Don't shoot! I'm a white girl! Don't shoot! My name is Helen Morrison!" Now the ground sloped gently upward again, the running was hard, and she slowed in order to keep from wearing out her strength too soon.

Two years ago she would have trusted white soldiers; during the time since, she had heard many Comanche opinions. Now, as she ran, she was wishing it were just white men, not soldiers. But she was willing to risk the danger. She was gasping as she jogged onto the top of the next rise, but again she could see the dust of the white soldier column, and the sight gave her strength to run faster. She was flying again, though her heart was pounding and her breath came hoarse in her throat, when the thought came to her: What about Katy Sunflower?

The thought brought her up short. She slowed to a walk. Only then did she feel the sweat running down her body under her dress. She walked on as questions raced in her mind.

What would happen to Katy Sunflower after they found she had escaped? Would they kill her? Some of them would want to, but she thought Spitting Dog would stop them. She couldn't tell. If they didn't, how would she ever get her little sister away then? It was so far to where white people lived. Katy Sunflower was becoming an Indian, might become one hopelessly if she were left alone with them. Many times she, Helen Tehanita, had stood back and seen her little sister petted by the women of Spitting Dog's lodge and that boy, Burning Hand, and she had felt like crying as she whispered to herself,

"I'm losing her! I'm losing you, little Katy! Mama, I'm losing her, and I don't know how to stop it. I don't know what to do." She felt lonely and young at those times.

If she got to the white soldiers and asked them, would they come back and try to get Katy Sunflower? If they tried, could they do it? The Comanches were strong fighters. Would they kill Katy Sunflower before they gave her up? Would it be better to be dead than to be a Comanche Indian?

She trudged on to the crest of the next rise and could see the white soldiers again. They were farther away now. The low rays of the late sun shone on the dust and almost hid the soldiers. She had a hopeless, faint, desperate thought: If she went on, they might stop for the night, and she might catch up to them in the darkness. But the questions about Katy Sunflower were not answered. She felt a strong need for an older person to help her. When she tried to think of what her mama or papa might have said, she could only hear the words: "You can't go off and leave Katy." How she would ever win back her little sister or carry her away by force she couldn't guess, but she couldn't leave her. She could do nothing but wait and learn. As she stood watching, the white soldier column moved farther and farther away toward the distant river, until finally she could see nothing but a trace of dust. She turned back.

She had come a long distance. Her body felt tired all over, and her legs were heavy, but the sun was almost down. She jogged and walked alternately and came in the last light of dusk to the place from which she had started running. She found her overturned basket and picking tool. It was necessary to put her face down near the ground to find all the scattered fruit. When she finally got back to camp, it had been dark nearly an hour.

Come Home Early said, "Tehanita! You mustn't be out in the dark alone."

"I got some good prickly-pear apples," she said.

"But you mustn't do it."

Old Woman said, "The big cannibal owl, *Piamuhmpits,* will get you."

She got some food and ate.

Later that night she worked at a fire singeing the stickers off the apples one by one. Two of the Penatuhka visitors had come around to thank Lance Returner for antelope meat he had given them. He was sanding some arrow shafts which he had kept tied in a bundle and hanging in the smoke hole to cure during the previous winter. The two visitors watched him and sometimes passed him the pipe they were smoking. She worked within hearing of their voices.

One of the Penatuhkas said, "Well, Lee goes back to Camp Cooper, I guess."

"Our scouts say he heads that direction," Lance Returner said.

"Maybe the heat got him. Those people don't know where the good water holes are."

She realized they knew about the white soldiers and were talking about them.

The other Penatuhka said, "It's hot weather, all right, for traveling or fighting or anything like that."

Lance Returner asked, "Do you think that man Lee would fight?"

"They say he's a fighter."

"But you've never seen him?"

"No, but they say he's called the very best soldier the whites have. They say—"

Lance Returner laughed. "They say. They say. I say a Comanche warrior can whip two Rangers, and a Comanche warrior can whip about four of those bluecoats. Charge them. Cut them off from their wagons. They'd be helpless."

"So you think the Mutsani could take them?"

"Sure, we could. We'd have to play it smart. Send the women west, then attack. Keep after them like wolves after an old buffalo. Lead them away from water. Destroy their horse feed and their supplies. I wish they'd found us. We could have taught them a lesson."

"Then why didn't you?"

"Ute Killer's mind is on the Utes. We'll go up to Wild River and find a winter camp, then carry the pipe around to the Yamparikas and maybe a Kiowa tribe—anybody that wants in on the fun. Then we'll go visit the Utes. We're afraid the Utes will forget us and start thinking too well of themselves. We haven't danced under a Ute scalp for six winters."

"It might be better to visit the Utes than to attack the bluecoats under Lee."

"Ho! You Penatuhkas. You have listened to the whites too much. You forget what it is to be a Comanche."

The Penatuhka who held the pipe drew deep, then said thoughtfully, "The People grow fewer in numbers."

Lance Returner said, "With our alliances now we are stronger than ever before."

"But we grow fewer year by year."

"It's because the women drop their babies before the moons are finished. And because of the plague. And because we forget the old ways. The Kwahadi no longer number you Penatuhkas among the People."

"Who made the Kwahadi to judge us? We live the same as ever. Besides, we get plenty of presents from the whites."

"It is said you scout for them," Lance Returner said.

"We don't. They only give us presents because they fear us."

"Well, what presents we Mutsani want we will take. We'll never be friends with the whites. If you act friendly toward them, they want you to live at a certain place, and they want to count you. Our enemies have always overestimated our numbers. The worst thing that can happen is to let them count you."

The pipe had burned out, and the friendly argument was finished. Lance Returner invited the two visitors to go north with the band and take part in the planned Ute raid, but they would not.

The band traveled north through the hot dry countryside. They forded the River of the Arms of God and the various prongs of the River of the Wichitas. When they came into the valley of the River of Tongues, clouds began to darken the sky, and they met showers of rain. It was pleasant. They crossed the river and shortly afterward came to the camp of a band of Comanches called the Nawkoni, where they visited seven days. Both buffalo and deer were plentiful in the area. The Nawkoni people held dances and feasts in their honor and asked them to stay longer, but they did not have enough good grazing for their own horses and those of the Mutsani.

They moved north through the damp weather to Prairie Dog Town River. It was a broad, muddy torrent. Several braves and some of the boys swam it on horseback to test the currents. Among these were Little Wild Horse, the son of the chief, and Burning Hand, the slender son of Spitting Dog. They, like most of the boys, hunted every chance to show off their prowess on horseback. All of them returned safely, but some of the heavier men had found it necessary to slip from their horses' backs and swim holding to their horses' tails. It was decided that the crossing was too difficult for the old people and to carry across supplies and equipment. They made camp to wait for the river to slow and to construct bullboats from rawhide stretched over willow frames.

After four days they crossed. They pushed on across the forks of Wolf River, thence on to the broad Red River, where again they used the bullboats.

In the mind of Helen Tehanita had grown an idea from watching the sun and the rivers. She had begun to wonder whether it is true that all rivers flow toward the rising sun. She had seen that small streams may flow in any direction and that larger streams may wind about, but any stream large enough to be called a river seemed, if it curved or twisted, to turn again downstream toward the rising sun. If it was true, it was the kind of thing she needed to learn about the great country. If all rivers did it, then the West Fork River where she had lived did it. She and Katy Sunflower had been taken away from the rising sun when they were captured. It all seemed to say that if she ever found the West Fork River, she could go downstream and find where white people live. She had been looking ahead to each river and to the place they were going, Wild River, and the idea had proved true thus far.

As they broke camp, the first one across the Red, she helped Story Teller onto his travois and helped him get comfortable. The old man spoke seldom, seemed to daydream a lot, but she felt free to ask him questions. She asked, "Story Teller, do all rivers move toward the rising sun?"

He turned his drooping face to her and answered slowly, "That's hard to say. There are many rivers. I must think about it."

She turned loose the gentle old horse that pulled him and let it follow the pack horses. The old man said nothing when they stopped for noon, nor that night, but the next morning as she again helped him find a comfortable seat on the travois he seemed to suddenly remember her question and said, "It may be that all rivers flow toward the rising sun, or just to the right of it. Those I remember do. But I know stories about the People when they lived in the mountains long ago, and they had rivers, but I don't know which way mountain rivers run."

"Did you ever know a story about the West Fork River?"

"West Fork," he repeated. "That's a queer name. No. But remind me sometime to tell you about the river started by women with their tears when their men went off to war and didn't return."

He was not much help. He might have seen West Fork River many times but wouldn't remember it unless it had a story connected with it. She looked forward to Wild River. They moved on through a barren rolling plains country, crossed Beaver River, and came in a few days to the site where they would make winter camp. Wild River lay in a broad valley between low red bluffs and along its course grew patches of scrub cottonwoods. It flowed toward the rising sun. She was not sure whether she had figured out something important, but if she could learn enough such things, some day she would be old enough and wise enough to escape.

Ute Killer met delay in his planned raid against the Utes. First he carried the pipe to a band of Cheyenne and Arapahoe who were camped downstream. They were friendly, but some of them had been with the Comanche chief Mow-way when he was beaten by the Sac and Fox, and they could not be persuaded to follow a Comanche chief on a raid.

Then Ute Killer and most of the warriors visited a camp of Kiowas, who said it was too late in the year to go into Ute country, besides they had already taken their fill of raiding for the year. Finally, Ute Killer and his men carried the pipe to the Yamparika, a Comanche band that lived up on the headwaters of Wild River. The Yamparika had returned not long before from a raid against the Jicarillas, and now they were preparing for their winter meat and robe hunt. They would not go.

Ute Killer, Lance Returner, Wide Mouth, Buffalo Bones, Spitting Dog, and the other leaders of the Mutsani had thought so much about the pleasure of a Ute raid and had so strengthened their determination by talking to the other bands, that they would not give it up, though the time was late. It was the beginning of the Moon of Thin Ice. Cottonwood leaves were yellow. The party would consist of sixty warriors, none too young, none too old, no women. They would take two horses per man, make the long trip, strike hard and swiftly, and hurry back. Spitting Dog made medicine that the winter would wait for them. They danced the war dance and slipped away that same night to ride northwest toward the mountains.

Those left behind immediately began a struggle for food. The band had killed little meat during their summer and autumn travels other than what could be soon eaten. Buffalo were passing through the country in small bunches, moving south, but most of the good hunters were gone. The women of the Lance Returner lodge had no hunter at all. They had half an *awyawt,* or parfleche box, of sunflower seeds, a full *awyawt* of dried pear apples, and a few handfuls of mesquite-bean meal.

Two days after the raid party left, Come Home Early took Helen Tehanita out to see if they might get a buffalo. They rode out early in the morning. Helen Tehanita carried only their knives. Come Home Early carried a lance she had made by binding an iron spear point with rawhide onto a willow stick as long as a man is tall. They saw two buffaloes, which stampeded away at the sight of them; then, about noon, they came upon a large bull lying on the crest of a hill. "Get down," Come Home Early cautioned. "Stay behind me." They dismounted and led their horses slowly toward the animal.

When the buffalo bull began to rise, Come Home Early scrambled onto her horse and kicked him in the side. Helen Tehanita followed. Come Home Early gained on the surprised bull, though she was heavy for a rider and the horse was no trained hunter. She beat her mount on the rump with the lance handle and forcefully pulled his head over to make him come against the right side of the fleeing old bull. Meanwhile she was bouncing from side to side, about to lose her seat. By some luck she got her lance into position and thrust it into the bull's back, leaning her weight into it.

The bull bellowed and came about, to get his great horns toward the horse. As the horse dodged, Come Home Early fell to the ground. She was obscured by the dust of the hoofs for a moment, then the two animals moved on, the horse dodging and fleeing. When the enraged buffalo had chased the horse some distance, he turned and ran straight away. He disappeared over the next rise, still running, his tail in the air and the makeshift lance flopping to his gait.

Helen Tehanita came up to the woman and started to get down. "Are you all right? Are you hurt?"

"Get the horse," Come Home Early said, sitting up.

She caught the loose horse and returned. Come Home Early got to her feet slowly and felt of her legs and her back. She began to wipe the dirt from her face. She said, "I think we are in trouble."

"Are you hurt?"

"No," she said, though she limped badly. "I was thinking it even before we saw the bull. These buffaloes are stragglers. Where's the herd? It's not around here anywhere. I hope Lance Returner comes home soon. We need winter meat. I don't like the cold nights coming and no winter meat and the buffalo not in sight."

After the heavy woman was again mounted, they rode up to try to see the wounded buffalo, but could not. They followed for an hour in the direction he had gone, hoping at least to recover the iron lance point, but had no success. They went back to camp empty-handed.

Next morning Old Woman and Come Home Early whispered together, then Old Woman announced, "Today we butcher one of the twin colts."

Blessed said, "Oh, *Pia,* no! Not one of the sweet colts."

"Yes, one of the sweet colts. They still suck, and that mare can't carry them both through the winter anyway."

"Oh, no! Please!"

"Don't say 'no' to me, young lady. This is not your husband; this is your mother. I'll whip you so you can't sit down for a week. We're in trouble for meat. And don't pout! Get a rope. Get your knife sharp. We'll have fresh meat tonight."

With care, the meat of the colt lasted until Lance Returner came home.

Ute Killer brought his party back in a blizzard. The north wind struck in the afternoon, blowing fine rain, then sleet, and those of the camp had taken to their tipis. One laggard woman had been out gathering buffalo chips against the cold, and she hurried toward camp just before dark. She saw the returning party and ran among the lodges yelling, "The men are back! The men are back!" They spilled out of their shelters to greet the warriors in spite of the fierce wind, for they were not only returning heroes, but seemed saviors to those who had remained behind and were out of meat.

They brought two scalps, but had paid well for them. Their mounts told the story. They had left with extra mounts; they came back with so few that many of them had to ride double. Three horses had their manes and tail hair cut off in mourning for Fighting Eagle and Ride Away and the young brother of Wide Mouth, three braves left dead in the land of the Utes. Also, Ute Killer himself had a wound in his leg which made walking painful, and two other warriors had lesser wounds. There would be no scalp dance.

That night Lance Returner hunkered over the warming fire in his big tipi, steaming, solemn of face. They waited, still cold from being outside, for him to tell what he would about the raid.

He asked Come Home Early, "How much meat do you have?"

"We have none."

"Have you scouted to keep up with the herd?"

"We've done our best, but the herd has gone away somewhere. Are you hungry?"

"I haven't eaten in two days."

She put the sunflower seed before him, and Old Woman made him cakes from the last of the mesquite-bean meal. He mused as he munched on the food. "Some say it was a mistake to raid so near winter, but I hold with Ute Killer. If we don't hit the Utes, they'll hit us. They are our oldest enemies, and we know them. Our friends in this country ought to thank us."

He wouldn't tell much about the raid. Spitting Dog's medicine hadn't been good. They had been unable to surprise a single Ute camp. Then after they had stood and fought and taken two scalps, the Utes had tried to prevent them from leaving that country. They had found themselves cut off again and again. They had lost horses and men. Finally Spitting Dog had used his most powerful medicine, which was the help of a bear spirit, and they had been able to go at night and get out of Ute country. It wasn't a defeat; Lance Returner saw it as a hard duty that had been performed.

In two days the wind laid, leaving thin, scraggly drifts of sleet and dirty snow. Lance Returner led the band, all who could ride and work, out for a winter meat hunt. He sent scouts to comb the country. They found no bunches, only stragglers. Five days of cold riding and work delivered to them only seven buffalo, and there were forty-nine lodges of people to feed through the winter. It was too little to divide through claiming and gifts. It had to be portioned by the council. Though Lance Returner had led the hunt and had killed one of the seven himself, his part was only one forequarter, one hide half, and one large marrow bone.

After the unsuccessful winter meat hunt, they all accepted that the band was in trouble. They buckled down to the work of living on little, and they wasted nothing. The rolling prairies out of the river bottom had no trees, only sagebrush and shinnery, cactus and sand grass. There were no mesquite beans, but there were roots, called *yehp*, which would serve for food, but were hard to find since they were marked by only a short dry stem above ground. Out across the prairies the women would spread, hunting *yehp*. Helen Tehanita spent many cold days at it. Out of the river bottom nothing broke the force of the north wind, and when she thought she had found a good root, she would have to beat her hands together to drive away the numbness so that she could use the digging stick to dig it up. After a day on the prairie, she and the other three women might return to the warm tipi with no more than enough food to feed those of the lodge one day.

Spitting Dog had been in bad favor in the band since the Ute raid. They would have asked someone else to make medicine for meat, but he had more knowledge of it and more magic objects than any other. In the Moon of Howling Wind, they appealed to him, and he led them in the antelope surround ceremony. He set his helpers dancing two days while he chanted to draw the antelope. Then with his magic sticks, which were dried legs of the antelope, he made elaborate passes which would prevent the animals from running away. Then he sent two runners in a great circle with the sticks while he chanted and prayed. When they returned, he sent the hunters around the circle; he continued to sing to keep a single antelope from escaping. The circle closed in, and not a single antelope escaped, for none were inside it.

Spitting Dog blamed it on their lack of faith in him. After that failure he confined himself to watching for signs from ravens, which sometimes will tell from their actions where the buffalo hide, and to asking his live horned frog, *kusehteh-mini,* which was supposed to run in the direction of the buffalo. The horned frog, placed on the cold ground, would only blink sleepily and not move.

Helen Tehanita worried about Katy Sunflower—for one reason, that she lived in the lodge of the medicine man, who was having trouble and might become mean; for another reason, that she was too little to help much getting food and might be resented for that. And it was said that the shortage of food was hardest on the children. She hid a *yehp* cake as large as her hand inside the top of her dress and went to the lodge where her little sister lived. She found that Spitting Dog was alone in his medicine tipi, the grandfather and Burning Hand were away caring for the horses, and only one woman was there with Katy Sunflower. The woman was repairing clothes, and Katy Sunflower was sewing on a doll dress.

"Do you have food?" Helen Tehanita asked.

She had spoken to her sister, but the woman answered, "We have only enough for ourselves."

Katy Sunflower didn't even seem to be interested in food. She only wanted to talk about her doll and about the one she

called her brother, Burning Hand. Helen Tehanita was surprised as she looked carefully at her little sister, for Katy
Sunflower did not grow thin and hollow-eyed at all, as many
of the others did. It was clear that the lodge of Spitting Dog
might starve, but as long as they had any food at all, the first
portion would go to the daughter they had adopted.

She took the *yehp* cake back and gave it to Story Teller. He
grew weak but did not seem to worry about food. He ate what
was given him. Other children did not come much to ask for
stories, but he was as ready as ever to tell them. Sometimes
Helen Tehanita was the only listener on a long winter evening,
and she would lose for a time the gnawing hunger pangs in her
stomach as he carried her to another place and another time
where wonderful things happened.

The Moon of Howling Wind passed, and they entered the
Moon of Babies Crying for Food. Now snow covered the
prairies and did not melt. All was a blinding expanse of white,
with no trees for relief, and not even the course of Wild River
could be seen an hour's walk away from it. Lance Returner was
gone from camp a large part of the time as were the other men.
He hunted a day's ride away, afraid to go farther lest he be
caught out too far in a blizzard. He also took his turn following the main horse herd. Only one riding horse per lodge was
kept near camp; the large herd was allowed to roam a good
distance to find grass or browse. Usually when Lance Returner
came home, he would ask, "Have you got hold of any food?"
Come Home Early would say, "No. Did you bring anything?"
He would say, "No," then in a moment he would say, "Well,
let's get a good night's sleep." Sometimes he did bring something: once, a pouch of pemmican he had begged from the
Yamparika; another time, two rabbits; the best time of all,
half a deer he had killed while hunting with Wide Mouth. The
hungry neighbors visited for two days until the deer was gone.

They could not hunt roots with the snow on the ground.
Helen Tehanita worked with the women up and down the river

cutting cottonwood sprouts and hauling them to the small horse herd near camp.

When the snow had lasted a week, Lance Returner gave in, as many of the others had already done, and butchered an old pack horse. The muscle meat was stringy and dry; the liver and other soft parts were bitter, but it was food. They hated to eat horses. Some of the old people still called them god-dogs, not because they were holy, but because they were so much more valuable than dogs. They had an old saying: "He who eats his horses lays up famine for the future." But the men judged their animals, particularly the old geldings, and those that would not live till spring they butchered.

Some of the people, like the Cheyenne, ate dogs, which is a practice worse than eating horses. The dog is a cousin to the coyote, a tricky devil which has a bad medicine and delights in shrewd revenge against its enemies. Those who ate dog looked behind themselves often, waiting for and worrying about the bad luck that might come. Others ate things not much good for food, such as pounded and boiled rawhide. Still others ate things dirty and unfit for food: toads dug out of their holes in the banks, turtles caught in the shallow backwater of the river.

When time had passed to the beginning of the Moon of Leaves Come Back, the Mutsani had lost four of its number: two babies, still nursing, whose mothers had not given enough milk for them; an old woman who had refused to eat the dog the rest of her family ate; and an old man who had collapsed in the snow out on the prairie. Lance Returner had lost seven horses, two butchered and five dead for the buzzards. The members of his lodge were gaunt and hungry but still alive.

Then one day Buffalo Bones, who had been down south of Wild River, galloped an exhausted horse into camp and croaked, "The buffalo are back! They're back! I saw them! The buffalo are back!"

They kept the herd scouted while they carefully prepared the hunt. Then they rode south half a day, all who were strong enough. They stopped behind a ridge, where the men stripped down to breechclouts, strung their bows, mounted hunting horses, and moved out under close control of the best hunters.

The women tied their horses and moved cautiously up to the crest of the rise, staying low in the shinnery. Down ahead of them a herd of great humpy brown buffalo moved, grazing on the small spring grass. The women of Lance Returner's lodge crouched together, and Old Woman scolded at them, "Keep hidden. Lance Returner will whip you if you show yourself. I'll whip you. Stay down. Stay back. You don't need to see so much. You ruin the surround, too bad for you." She shook the big butcher knife at them.

Helen Tehanita hugged the ground but peered through the limbs of thin brush. She could not stay back even at the threat of a whipping. If things went right, they would have plenty of food. It seemed too good to be true. It seemed impossible that they might get that very day all anyone wanted to eat. The buffalo she could see were not the same as any other animal she had ever watched. They were food, that might escape or might be taken.

She could see the hunters going around. To the right a string of them rode hidden from the buffalo by a sandy ridge with sage growing on it. To the left a string of them rode in an arroyo with only their heads and shoulders showing even from her vantage point.

Blessed said, "I hope he gets a lot. I'd rather give meat than beg it."

Come Home Early said, "Lance Returner will get some. They won't get ahead of him."

Old Woman fussed at them. "Stay down and keep quiet. No one will get meat if you make so much noise."

Helen Tehanita could not see Lance Returner among the half-hidden braves, though she knew he was there. She was hoping that he was in a good place and that he would be lucky and that his arrows would go true. Some of the buffaloes had raised their heads and begun turning, looking. She held her body still and tense lest they run.

Some of the hunters were beyond them, upwind, and they went at a trot across the open to close the circle. The buffaloes whirled away from the riders. Then Ute Killer blew a shrill signal on his wing-bone whistle and all the hunters charged out of cover. The buffaloes turned back, dodged, milled. They were trying to stampede upwind but were constantly being scattered back.

The women of the lodge had risen now and were screaming, "Hold them! Kill them!" Old Woman was waving and slashing with her butcher knife. Helen Tehanita whispered violently, "Ride, Lance Returner, ride!"

They could see him charging and whirling in the dust on his hunting horse, turning back the frightened beasts, working for the whole band. "Go in!" they screamed. "Oh, Lance Returner!" Some had already fallen. Some of the women were already running. "Shoot, Lance Returner!" they screamed. "Why doesn't he shoot? Where is he now? Kill them! Kill them!" And Helen Tehanita pleaded with the others, "Go in, Lance Returner! Please shoot!"

Then they saw his unmistakable form above the dust that rose around the feet of his horse and the feet of his quarry. His shoulders were tensed with the pull of his bow for a long suspenseful time, then gave with the release of the arrow. He held his bow up by the end for a moment before he turned back toward the herd, giving the signal. They sprang forward with joy in their voices, which had held anxiety only a minute before, and raced toward the downed meat a half mile below them.

Blessed ran in the lead, laughing breathlessly, and Helen Tehanita came close behind her. She wanted to be even with Blessed, but it was hard to run on the sandy ground. She felt an eagerness mixed with the weakness of her body. She was shaky, nervous, hardly able to control where she placed her feet. She had no strength left to run, yet she flew as if something not part of her carried her on. It seemed as if Blessed were a girl her own age, and they played a game, yet there was something desperate in it that she could not have explained. They came upon the great beast lying on its side with only the feathers of the arrow sticking from its ribs. The yellow tip on the white feather marked it as belonging to Lance Returner. Blessed reached the buffalo two bounds ahead, struck it with her fist, and shouted *"Ah-heh!"*

Helen Tehanita struck the bulging, hairy side and shouted, *"Ah-heh!"* Only after she had done it did she think about it. Then, as they knelt, panting, waiting for the other women, she asked herself, What am I doing? Why did I run? Why did I strike the buffalo and cry out?

When Blessed said to the other two women, "I hit it first and Tehanita second," she wanted to protest, No, I didn't. I only ran to see. I didn't hit it. But she kept her thoughts to herself.

Old Woman said, "Never mind that. Here, someone hold the blood pot."

They cut the great animal's throat, split his hide down the back, and carefully separated out the long tendons that lie beside the backbone. Then they went into the cavity and took out the liver. Old Woman sliced it in broad brown slices on top of the rib cage. She dribbled green gall across it. They took pieces and ate.

Helen Tehanita took a small piece. She put her tongue against it, then took a small bite. It was the sweetest, richest thing she had ever eaten. She could feel the strength of it passing into her body. She took a large piece. When she went to work to help with the rest of the butchering, she could feel the blood drying on her face around her mouth.

4. INCIDENT AT MEDICINE MOUNDS

SHE WAS disturbed because she had lost count of the years. After not thinking of it for a long time, she had suddenly felt that it was important, but upon trying to separate them out and count them, she could not. All those times when the weather was not cold were full of travel and visit and hunting, time waiting in raid camps, time gathering seeds and roots and wild fruit in a hundred places. Only with the winter did one have a chance to keep straight the passage of long periods of time. Winters had to be spent in a permanent camp near water and good grass, in a place sheltered from north wind. It was a separate and distinct time that had to be prepared for with preserved meat and plenty of robes. But she had lost count even of winters. There had been a winter on a river where pecan trees grew, during which they moved, so that there had been two permanent camps that year. But the camps in the canyon with high walls—had that been two permanent camps in one winter or one permanent camp and one travel camp or had it been two different winters? She didn't know. She had been ten that first autumn. Now, by her uncertain counting she knew she must be either fifteen or sixteen. She had been with them either five or six winters.

It was early spring. They had come, the entire Mutsani band, to *Laguna Sabinas* as soon as the danger of severe cold was past, planning to wait for the New Mexico traders here in the land of the Kwahadi Comanches. First flowers were blooming on the nearly level prairies out away from the salt lake, and new grass was starting. Scattered wild onions had thrust their fine blades suddenly through the soil and had burst out in delicate white flowers. This day Tehanita had come out with a group of women on the prairie to dig the onions, whose hiding places were thus betrayed. It was not hard work, though they were widely scattered. She dug them, rubbed most of the dirt from them with her hands, and dropped them into her deep, narrow basket. Her mind was turning over her problem of years as she worked.

She believed that she was disturbed about losing count of the years because it might be part of a larger thing that was going on. She had learned to gather different wild plants for food and tea and medicine, to braid a rope from horsehair, to thin and tan hides, to cut out clothes and moccasins and tipi sections, to pack a horse. She had mastered the Comanche language and gained their trust. But she was forgetting things she wanted to keep. She could not see they were going away until she would one day realize they were gone. At times such as this, digging onions a distance away from the other women, she would whisper to herself in English, "Come Home Early is not my *pia* ... I mean, my mama. She's not my mama. Nor Blessed either. And Old Woman is not my *kaku* ... I mean my ... " She didn't know the word. She knew there was a word, but she thought she had never had a *kaku* among the whites. She believed she had known the word at one time, but couldn't even be sure of that. It was other things besides words. There had been a woman her mama had called Melinda when they lived in the place near all the other people, and she remembered it coming to her in a flash one day: That was Mama's sister when she was a little girl. Yet she and George had not called the woman Mama, though she was their mama's own sister. They had used a special word with her name; it had seemed to make sense then, but she could not now remember the special word nor why they had not just called her Mama. The forgetting went to many things. How had they kept meat in the winter? She could remember no meat racks with meat drying. She tried to remember all of the inside of the lodge of logs they had lived in, and she could not remember anywhere in it a rawhide parfleche box or a buffalo paunch packed with pemmican.

The two dresses that she had saved through the years, the brown one and the blue one, and which she sometimes took out to look at in secret, now seemed tiny and thin and strange. They were full of small crinkles from being tightly rolled. The stitches and the thread were fine beyond her understanding. The dresses were too small ever to be used, but she kept them as a precious reminder that could not change.

It was painful to know about the forgetting, and worse to be uncertain about the extent of it. Her hope lay in the sure belief that what she forgot she could learn again when she had the chance. As for her little sister, Sunflower, all she could do was hope that anyone who changed could also change back.

She had filled her basket by midafternoon and went back to camp with the others. A group of Kwahadi had arrived and were making camp at a spring of good water a short walk along the lake edge. The Kwahadi were a strong band, much admired by other Comanches. There would be days for visiting and feasting and games with them before the New Mexico traders came. Lance Returner had already gone to smoke and visit with them. His mother, long ago taken by the plague, had been of the Kwahadi.

Tehanita had not eaten since early morning. She cut a chunk of meat from the strip that hung before the burnt-out fire. The three other women of the lodge, who had been working together in camp all morning, came and gathered around her. Come Home Early said, "We've been thinking of something nice for you, Tehanita. You'll like it."

"What's that?"

"Tomorrow the girls-becoming-women will run with the horses. You remember seeing it. You must run this year. You'll like it."

Blessed said, "Two Kwahadi girls will run and also the granddaughter of Two Bulls. We'll fix you up nice. You'll be the prettiest one running."

"I'd rather not," she told them. "I'm not old enough." She had told them that the year before.

"Pish!" Old Woman said. "Not old enough? Another year, and you'll be too old."

"Oh, yes!" Blessed said. "I was smaller than you when I ran. I'll never forget it. It was when Lance Returner first noticed me. You'll see. It's really fun."

"I meant I'm too old," she told them. "I feel older than those girls like the granddaughter of Two Bulls. I'd rather not."

"It's an honor," Old Woman said. "Don't you know it's an honor? Besides, it makes you a fast runner and surefooted and strong. You want to be slow as an old terrapin all your life?"

She took the onions down to the edge of the lake to wash them, and all three of the women followed her. She went out on the stepping rocks, squatted down, and began to peel off the brown skin of the small onions and wash off the dirt. The water was good for washing but not for drinking. The three women stood back on dry ground and watched her.

"It's not dangerous, Tehanita," Come Home Early said. "You can go first with an old tame horse. You just get a good grip on his tail hair, and when he runs, be real careful to keep your balance. Let him do the work. If you fall, you turn loose quick. It's not dangerous."

"But it's fun, too," Blessed said. "We'll tie your hair with red cloth, and you can wear my silver necklace, and you can wear the sash that Story Teller painted for Come Home Early. You'll be pretty. Any girl is. I've never seen a young girl running that way that wasn't pretty. It shows you off, skimming along so fast and exciting. After that, the boys will choose you to dance." She giggled. "After you run, they'll notice you and flirt and wink at you."

Tehanita saw that they had been talking about it and had agreed to try to persuade her to do it. She wanted to put an end to it. "Thank you all for thinking about me, but I don't believe I will. Some of the girls never run, and I'd rather not."

"So you want to be slow as an old terrapin?" Old Woman said. "And weak, too, I guess? And ugly?"

"She's timid," Come Home Early said. "You'll forget people watching if you do it."

She didn't answer them again, and they didn't talk to her until late in the afternoon. Then Lance Returner came back from the Kwahadi camp, bringing some beads and arrows he had won at gambling. He sat down on a stiff deerhide in front of the tipi. As Come Home Early put food before him, she said, "I guess tomorrow a few of the girls-becoming-women will run behind the horses."

He thought about it a while as he ate, then said, "That's good. We've matched a few horse races too. It's good to do things with the Kwahadi. Next after us they are the greatest of all the People, and it's good to keep close ties with them. Next time the council sits I might make a speech about it."

"Well," Come Home Early said, "we've been talking about Tehanita running with them this year, but she's timid."

Blessed said, "We've been talking about helping her dress up pretty."

Lance Returner sat there chewing his food, and Tehanita hoped he wouldn't say anything about it. Then he said, "It's a good thing. She'll look better than any of those young Kwahadi girls. We'd better give a few gifts, too. What other girls will run?"

Come Home Early said, "Of the Mutsani, only the granddaughter of Two Bulls."

"Get together with them. I'll speak to Two Bulls. We ought to give a feast and give away a few gifts. Most of the men will be interested in the races and the target shooting, but if some will eat with us, we'll give gifts. If the Kwahadi chief comes, I might give him a horse."

She knew she had to speak now before the planning went any further. "I'd rather not run." All their eyes were on her. "Some girls never run, and I'd rather not."

He said, "Come here, Tehanita."

She had the tiny onions spread on a piece of cedarwood and was still pretending to pick at them in the dim light. She went toward him and stood across the fire from where he sat cross-legged on the deerhide. He was staring at her. Red light from the small fire came up and highlighted his features. The skin of his face looked dark. The great scar, which one became used to and usually did not notice, now stood out ugly and fearsome. He was studying her. It reminded her of that time, such long years ago, when he had stared at her fiercely, and she had been afraid, and he traded a barrel hoop for her.

He asked, "Are you a Comanche or a slave?"

She felt defiant toward him, and fearful. He had never touched her. She could not have said what she feared in him, but she knew he had the power to do anything he wished to her. "I'm a good worker," she said.

"I have two strong wives to do the work. If you are nothing but a slave, I'll sell you to the New Mexico traders. I could get a good price."

"She seems just like my daughter," Come Home Early said. "I don't think of her like a slave, but just like my daughter."

Story Teller came hobbling out of the small tipi. Evidently he had heard the conversation. He said, "Tehanita is my grand-daughter."

She was afraid the old man might get into trouble. He had not said that she seemed like his granddaughter, but that she was. She spoke up to draw Lance Returner's attention. "Some Comanche girls never run. I just thought . . . if I didn't want to . . ."

Lance Returner said, "Some girls are not the daughter of Lance Returner. I'm a war chief of this band. A hunt leader.

A speech maker in the council. I have the right to wear a horn bonnet or eagle feathers or to carry a lance if I wish. You are young, Tehanita, and don't understand. This is a strong lodge. We must set a good example. Some people of the band don't have good clothes as we have, and they don't have enough wealth to give feasts for others or to give gifts. Then some are not responsible. They would forget the old ways just because they don't want to go to the trouble.

"This seems like a small thing, but I think it's not. It's an old ceremony. It's our way from olden times. I may make a speech about these matters to the council later on. All of you should hear the way the leaders of the Kwahadi talk about the Penatuhka. And I don't blame them. Those Penatuhkas lose the old ways, flirting with the whites. We must hold to our old ways like these Kwahadi do, for, remember, it has been our old ways that gave us, the *Nuhmuhna,* the great power we have today and that make the savage peoples fear us and fear to encroach on our vast land. Well, I'll work up a speech about it some day. I want you to make a good showing, Tehanita, and I think you will."

"I'm going to let her wear my silver necklace," Blessed said. She was polishing it with ashes.

"That's good," he said. "She'll be the best-looking girl."

Tehanita said no more. That night she slept little, but vacillated between the impossible thought of defying them all and the impossible thought of running with the girls-becoming-women. When she told herself, "Why not just do it and satisfy them?" then came the long fear about her changing. It wasn't a thing like gathering food; it was a thing they did because they were Indians. She told herself several times, "I won't do it. They can't make me." Yet the alternative seemed to be that she would be sold to the New Mexico traders, for whatever the others might say, Lance Returner was the boss of the lodge and everyone in it. Or, he was within certain limits. She had sometimes entertained vague fears that he would make her be a wife to him or some other man. It did not seem possible most of the time, for he seemed too dignified and too important in the tribe, but at times when she felt most rebellious and yearned most for escape, it seemed that he might commit some insult to her person, not by physical force but by the force of his authority. The simple facts of sexual contact were not a mystery to her or to any of the young people, because they lived around animals and because little complete privacy existed in their camps; perhaps mostly because they did not avoid mention of such things, though the young people were expected to be chaste. What was uncertain was the question of who might be an object of love or lust to another person and under what conditions. Yet she did understand this limit on Lance Returner, imposed as much by himself as anyone else: that as long as the wives considered her a daughter and Story Teller and Old Woman considered her a granddaughter, he could not touch her. Whether he would in other circumstances was uncertain. If she were a slave, she didn't know. He had said he would sell her. She didn't know what it would mean to be sold. For one thing, she would be separated from Sunflower. Among the other vague things it might mean, she believed it would take her another step away from white people.

She lay in the small tipi with Old Woman and Come Home Early and Story Teller until the dawn light slipped under the uprolled edges of the tipi cover and she could see their dark forms lying around her. She rose quietly and went outside. No sound came from anywhere in camp. All was cool and still. She walked quietly down to the edge of the shallow lake and along the shore.

Bullbats and killdee birds swooped out over the water, catching insects on the wing, sometimes emitting thin cries. Their movements and sounds did not disturb the stillness.

The shore line was like a broad white road leading out around the lake. Minerals from the water had been deposited all around the edge. Some places the ground had a thin glaze that crackled under her moccasins. Other places the salt lay in beds like white sand. It was all smooth except for a few places where Indians had dug salt and those places where spring water seeped in, at which spots crawfish had erected their knobby mud piles. The surface of the murky water was dark, with glints of early light racing across it. It lapped patiently at the shore.

The swooping, thin-winged birds, for some reason of their own, rose away from the water and moved out across the lake. She watched them until they were only a group of mingling, weaving specks, then nothing.

Back toward camp only the tops of tipis were visible. She was at a location where some Indians had put stepping rocks in the past. She went out to the farthest rock, squatted down, dipped a single handful of water, and tasted it. It was bitter and nasty and strong with salt. She looked at the water a minute, gathering her determination, then deliberately began scooping it up in both hands, gulping it in large mouthfuls. She downed it fast, lest she gag. She ceased only when she was breathless and felt she could stand no more. Then she went back across the rocks and along the shore toward camp. She could feel the water like a large round stone in her stomach.

When she lay down in the tipi, Old Woman turned over and asked, "Is that you, Tehanita? What's wrong?"

"I just went to the toilet place. I feel sick."

Her stomach was cramping. By the time the others were up and puttering around to make ready some food, she had become so sick that she feared she had gone too far, that she must have poisoned herself. Her stomach was turning and grabbing in violent convulsions.

The three women came in and looked at her and shook their heads. When they went back out, she heard Come Home Early say, "I don't like the looks of her. She's white as a bone."

She finally started to vomit, pulling aside her bed robe to spill the vomit on the ground but not caring much what mess she made or what she soiled. She felt sick all over. She turned her head again and again to retch, then nothing would come up, and she felt as if the inside of her stomach would come up.

Old Woman brought in a horn of broomweed tea she had brewed. As soon as Tehanita had drunk a few swallows, she threw it up. Old Woman felt of her forehead. When Old Woman went back outside, she heard her tell the others, "She's cold on the head. I don't like it. It might be the plague."

She lay in misery all that morning, and about midday they brought Spitting Dog to make medicine over her. The skinny medicine man chanted and sprinkled sand over her from a pierced gourd. He said that it was not the plague but only a small sickness that had been put on her by the yelping of a coyote the night before. He made her take into her mouth a bit of gooey, spicy paste that he had concocted, and he painted on her forehead with the same paste the track of a coyote. He accepted a bag of clean onions and three iron arrowheads in payment, and left. He had to go make a spell on a racehorse, which belonged to Ute Killer and which was scheduled to run that afternoon.

They left her alone. Only Story Teller stayed near the lodge that afternoon; he was painting a bow case for someone. She lay there in the small breeze that was cool off the lake and felt the sickness easing. Away in the distance she could hear the shouts of games and the pounding of racing horses. Then came faintly the shrill laughter and screams of girls her own age and cheers of spectators. She felt relief when that part of it was over.

Later Old Woman and Come Home Early returned. They brought her a drink and felt of her forehead and asked how she felt and whether she wanted anything. When they went back outside, she heard Old Woman say, "But it's a shame. It helps a girl to be a fast runner and strong."

By the next morning she was well and took some food.

The New Mexico traders came with their heavy-wheeled oxcarts and stayed three days. The warriors of the two bands waited until the traders were gone, then made preparations for a raid west into Mescalero country. As usual, a clamor rose among the boys, all of whom wanted to go, but this time proved noteworthy, for Ute Killer judged that his own son, Little Wild Horse, was old enough to begin to learn what it means to be a warrior. He was almost grown, stockily built, a youngster of promise. He and two Kwahadi boys and Burning Hand, the slender son of the medicine man, made ready for their first visit outside Comanche territory. The four kept busy a day painting themselves and checking their shields and bows, then they danced the war dance with the full-fledged warriors, trying to keep from showing too much of either pride or nervousness. That night all the members of the raid party moved out in the darkness.

The camp settled into its period of waiting. Those men left behind watched the horse herd, leisurely hunted antelopes, worked on weapons, slept. The women did not worry much. They knew that the raid party had been strong in numbers and had gone for sport as much as for serious battle. Lance Returner had gone. The women of his lodge worked as they saw fit, going often to visit and gossip with neighbors or some distant kin over in the Kwahadi camp.

Tehanita helped the women. Sometimes she was sent to return a horse to the herd and catch another which belonged to the lodge, for they always kept one mount tied or hobbled near camp. At other times she went out on the prairie to dig roots. Sweet peas were beginning to put up their pale lavender flowers, and she dug their roots for food. Occasionally she went an hour's walk from camp to a ridge where yucca grew thickly and where the soil was easy to dig; the roots of this plant were good to use in bathing and washing things, also to put in a tanning mixture. Out by herself, she exulted in that she had not run with the other girls in their foolish ceremony. Next year she would certainly be too big. But one thing stuck in her mind: what they had said about her becoming slow and weak. Could it be true? She didn't feel weak. She knew that she could do as much work or carry as much load as the other young women or even the married women. But she had no way of knowing.

She did not want to be less able than a Comanche in any way. Out by herself she began to run for practice. She could run a long time on level, solid ground, but found that going uphill or in sandy soil, especially if she carried a load of roots, she would soon be short of breath and would pant. It troubled her. She practiced running each time she was out of sight of others, trying to run as fast as she might have run behind a horse as the other girls had done, trying to increase the distance she could run uphill. She would pause on a high place and look back at the distance she had run and wonder whether the other young people could run that far or farther. Since she did not run with them in their games, she did not know. The practice brought soreness to her in the nights, but by the time the raiding party returned, she could tell that she had already improved.

The braves brought home one scalp, of a Mexican who had herded sheep. They had fought a running fight against a group of Mescaleros, a battle which had not brought much grief to either side but had reminded that Apache band to fear Comanches and to stay in the mountains where they belonged. They had also attacked a village with one big stone house and several mud-brick houses, had caused the people to flee, and had got many ornaments and trinkets. Lance Returner brought back a silver pin with turquoise on it, a silver cross on a chain, a small cross carved of black wood, a wool blanket of red and yellow.

A week after the return from the raid, the Kwahadi moved south, and Ute Killer led the Mutsani east into the canyon country, then north across the rolling plains toward the next permanent camp they planned in the area of the River of Tongues. They traveled slowly, stopping when any shade was available in the heat of the day, camping here and there a day or more to hunt fresh meat or pick wild fruit.

The valley of the River of Tongues was excellent buffalo country, but gossip had it that the chief wanted especially to stay there a winter so that his son, Little Wild Horse, might have a chance of getting good medicine as he entered into manhood. Just north of the river was a holy place called Medicine

Mounds, where lived some of the most powerful and generous magic spirits known to the People. On the near side of the river they found Tanima and Nawkoni Comanches camped along a creek. They stayed one night near them to exchange news. Next morning they loaded up early and crossed the River of Tongues. Its bed had broad sand bars through which meandered the slow, muddy stream. Willows grew thick in patches, and cottonwood trees were scattered along the edge of the sand. The water was no deeper than the horses' knees. They rode up out of the valley, and when they could see the prairie ahead, Medicine Mounds lay in clear view. Some of the older men and women looked, then closed their eyes and mumbled prayers.

They passed by an hour's walk away from the mounds. The four hills rose abruptly out of the gently rolling plains. Their rough red and gray slopes were scattered with boulders and dark clumps of cedar. The one farthest from the river was the largest and tallest; they decreased in size toward the river, until the fourth was little more than a tit of rock jutting up out of the prairie. The Mutsani people looked at them over their shoulders as they rode by.

In the middle of the morning, still in view of the mounds, they came to Wanderers Creek, a stream bed that had damp gravel in it, and in places good pools of clear water. The men consulted and chose a camp site in a grove of trees by the creek.

Tehanita continued her practice running that fall, using as an excuse for going out alone that she wanted to dig roots or gather sunflower seeds or make up little bundles of broomweed, which when dry made good fire kindling. Sagebrush, tumbleweeds, and bunch grass grew out across the prairie, with some scattering of Spanish dagger, prickly pears, and scrub mesquites. It seemed a drab and desolate country in the fall. It was dominated by the Medicine Mounds, because of the way they thrust up so suddenly out of the level and because of the vague respect and reverence with which the Indians always spoke of them.

Often she went out toward the mounds. That way was uphill. When she was far enough away from camp that no one would notice her, she would begin to run, and she learned to run half the distance to the mounds without stopping.

One cool autumn afternoon she had run to a spot near the largest mound, which was called Warrior Mound, and noticed what she had not seen before: up toward it a pond of water that seemed to be fed by a small spring coming out of the hill. Near the pond sunflowers grew. After she had rested from her last running, she ran ahead toward the flowers.

She disturbed a flock of turkeys at the water hole. They scattered, flying low, running with wings outspread. Watching them, she did not notice at first how near she had come to the big mound; then she looked around at it, and it seemed to stand right over her, frowning. From nearby, its slopes seemed forbidding; the cedar trees were gnarled and twisted; they grew between and out of cracked and broken slabs of stone that tilted in every direction. As she looked, she was startled by a movement. The form of a man or a boy tumbled and slid down a clay slope that had small loose stones on it. The form disappeared behind a rough jutting portion of the mound.

She ran that way, crying, "Are you hurt?" At first it seemed right to go to the person, but as she climbed between the rocks, she remembered that it was visited by men as a holy place, and she went forward with misgivings. "Who is it?" she called. "Are you hurt?" Halfway up, she came around into a small hollow in the trees and rocks and saw him sitting there on the ground, holding his leg.

It was the son of the medicine man, the one who called Sunflower his sister. He looked at her angrily.

"Are you hurt, Burning Hand?"

He burst out, mocking her, "Are you hurt? Are you hurt? If I weren't so weak right now, I'd hurt you! I'd teach you a lesson. You've ruined my medicine, sticking your nose into something you've got no business in."

"I'm sorry. I didn't do it on purpose."

"You're sorry! You ought to have better sense than to come around here. I may get up in a minute and give you a good pounding. I would if I weren't so weak."

He looked rather wild and disheveled. His cheek was skinned, and his chest and his leg. From the way he sat, he did not look as if he were about to get up and hurt anyone.

"Why are you so weak?"

"I'm not weak! That just shows how dumb you are! I only meant I haven't eaten for three days and have been taking sweat baths and smoke baths in sage smoke. That's all I meant."

"Well, I didn't make you fall, Burning Hand. You did that yourself."

"I didn't fall! I slipped down a little way. But you messed me up. A mist had come before my eyes, and that's a good sign. It means one might see a vision. Then what happens? You come along and spoil it! But I didn't fall. I stepped forward and slipped, then I slid a little way. A thing like that doesn't hurt me; I'm not a girl!"

"Well, I'm sorry, anyway."

"A lot you know about it," he said. "You're just a girl and pretty young, too. I've been on a war party. But I need medicine bad. They kept on giving me and that Kwahadi boy the job of holding the horses instead of letting us go near the fighting. I want to be a warrior, not a horse holder. You wouldn't understand things like that, I guess."

She said, "I think you're as much a warrior as Little Wild Horse. You're a good rider. I've seen you ride and shoot arrows at a mark."

"You don't know anything about it," he said. He sat on the ground with his knees propped up and his arms resting on his knees. He looked back up at the crest of Warrior Mound, then looked down at the ground for a time without speaking. He raised his eyes and burst out, "Oh, Tehanita! what's wrong with me? Think of the spirits on the earth and in the air! But not one of them has come. What's wrong with me? I was sure I was clean inside and out, and I waited and waited and cried to them, but nothing came. Nothing ever comes. If I could have a strong medicine, I'd cherish it and honor it and take care of it. I'd be careful and obey every taboo. They should know how much I need medicine and want it, for my soul has been going around these magic mountains and searching in every bush and behind every rock. What could be wrong with me?"

She knew now that he would not hurt her. He had asked the question as if he thought she might really know the answer. She said, "I think some boys—maybe they don't get medicine either. They just come home and lie. They make it all up."

"What do you know about medicine?"

"I just guess that. I've heard the women talk about it and everything."

"Heard women talk! They don't know anything about it. You don't either. You better keep your place. It's not right for a woman to know things about medicine, especially a girl your age."

"You asked me."

"Well, I didn't mean to. What would you know about it?" He glared at her, looked back at the hillside, then his face slowly changed to a thoughtful frown. "I know some boys lie. I've thought of it myself. I don't want them feeling sorry for me and saying, 'He can't get medicine.' But it's bad to lie about it. Maybe a man lies, and later things go bad for him. I want to do great things. I want to fight like the best warriors and save the People and heal the sick and have a great name. I need strong medicine for those things. No telling what the trouble is. I can't even get a little bit of medicine. What could be wrong with me?"

She said, "Maybe you expect too much."

"How could I expect too much?"

"I think it could be that some young men fast for medicine, then they see a rabbit pass by, so they say, 'That's good. It's lucky for me. It's my medicine.' They don't lie. They just don't expect too much."

"So! A rabbit passed by! What good is that? What do you

know about it? Tehanita, you ought to be whipped for talking about medicine like that. You don't know a thing! Listen, my grandfather, whose name I cannot say because he is gone, was a young man, and he went out alone for medicine. A white buffalo came to him. He had passed out from weakness, and the white buffalo licked his face and woke him. Then the buffalo talked to him and told him all kinds of things, wise things. Everything that's worth knowing. He was a great man after that. It was long ago, but I want that kind of medicine for myself.

"Yesterday I saw a lizard, a plain skinny one, green with pink feet. I saw him nose under the grass and catch a bug with his tongue and eat it. Then he jerked his head up and curved his tail up and looked at me. I saw that he was delicate and quick. He waited as still as a stone. I kept thinking he would speak. Then I raised up and said, 'Here I am.' And, zip! he was gone. He was nothing but a lizard, like a hundred I killed when I was little, practicing with my bow. Just a lizard. That's no kind of medicine. I must have something with a spirit in it that will speak to me."

When he was silent, she said, "Maybe when you go back on the mound, you'll see a good vision."

"I've spent my three days. I'll go back to camp now."

"You want me to help you?"

"Help me do what?"

"Get back to camp."

He glared at her with disgust, then laughed. "You're sure dumb, Tehanita, in some ways. I'd rather die than go back to camp with a girl helping me. Thank you, anyway."

She started down, and he called, "Tehanita?" He had risen. At least his leg was not broken.

"Yes."

"Don't tell anyone you saw me fall, and I won't tell anyone you came near Medicine Mounds."

"I wouldn't tell at all."

She ran halfway back to camp, then went out on a branch of

Nawkoni Creek and picked sunflower seeds to take home. Later, after sundown, she saw him come into camp, looking slender and weak, and stumble into his father's lodge.

After that, when they passed, he spoke to her or smiled. Sometimes, even at a distance, she would see that his eyes were upon her. She was uncertain about the value of the medicine thing he sought, but hoped for his sake that he found it.

5. Mountains That Wander Away

During the Moon of Howling Wind, on a day when the sky was brown with blowing sand, the Nawkoni People, who had been camped south of the river and had been on a fall raid against the whites, broke camp and fled north. They were widely scattered, some on foot. Many of them had left behind all their possessions. Those who passed through the Mutsani camp told varying stories. All of them agreed that they had been attacked without warning by an army of bluecoats, Rangers, cattlemen, and Tonkawas. Some said the army had swept through their camp slaughtering babies, women, and many braves. Others said that they, the Nawkoni, had stood their ground, had fought bravely and defeated the invaders. Among the stragglers, many said that the whites had burned the village and then returned toward their own country.

The Nawkoni fled in the sandstorm as if they had been beaten. They were in panic and would not stop, though the weather was cold and might become worse. The Mutsani people gave them food and clothing. Tehanita gave a robe to a girl her own age who stopped long enough to eat but would not stay longer because she was trying to catch up to those of her family who were ahead of her.

Ute Killer and the council decided to move camp, not so much out of fear as out of a desire to choose their own time to fight, preferably not the wintertime. They thought it wise to move because the white army, which had been so near, might now know their location. They sent scouts to watch along the riverbank to prevent surprise while the Mutsani calmly packed everything, including their large winter supply of pemmican, and headed north. The band rode against a cold north wind to the valley of Prairie Dog Town River, thence upstream four days to a new winter camp ground protected by river bluffs.

Tehanita felt certain vague hopes in knowing that the whites had been so near. She did not know what direction they had come from nor where they had gone. Nor could she guess whether she would be safe if she should be taken by the whites when they were on the warpath. Finally, she decided that she must not hope for aid through what some other people might do, but must continue her own efforts to take Sunflower and return to those whites who lived near the West Fork River.

When they arrived at the new camp site, sleet was blowing in the wind, and she got no good view of the countryside. A few days later a spell of good weather came. She went with Come Home Early up on the prairie above the river bluff to find what the prospects were for gathering any mesquite beans, which would be on the ground but might still be good. As they came up where they could see some distance, she saw a flat-topped mountain straight before her. She felt her heart pounding and was afraid Come Home Early might be able to see that something was affecting her strongly. It rose straight out of the prairie, dark misty blue. It was the right shape. She turned her eyes and then began to see the others. A dozen of them rose out of the brown terrain on either side of the river. They were of different shapes, some with gentle slopes, some with sharp slopes; all looked blue in the winter light. It could not be the place she had thought at first.

She was not too much disappointed. She had come to accept during the long years that to learn the country and find the key to her deliverance would be hard. She and Come Home Early found that the deer had already eaten the last of the fallen beans in the area. They went back to camp.

After a successful hunt in early spring, they broke camp and prepared to move south. Tehanita assisted Story Teller to his travois and arranged his robe around him. She asked, "Story Teller, do you like flat-topped mountains? Mesas?"

"Yes, do you?"

"Yes. Do you know about one that stands by itself? The country is nearly flat around it, and there's more grass than here."

"I'd have to think about it. I see you're interested in things like that as I am. When you were smaller, you used to ask me about rivers. You'd make a good teller of stories."

She said, "I could never learn all the stories you know."

"We go south many days. Let's you and I watch for mesas on the way."

When they had crossed the river and were coming out of the valley south of it, she noticed the old man smiling at her. She dismounted and led her horse and walked beside the drag on which he perched. They were passing between two flat-topped mountains, part of those which flanked Prairie Dog Town River on either side.

"The mesas," he said, pointing; "maybe they gather in one place, so they can see each other for company."

"Do you think hills become lonely?"

He laughed. As the horse which drew him passed over a shallow gully, he thrust both skinny arms from under the robe to cling to the poles. She marveled how he bore the roughness of his ride and didn't even notice.

He answered, "Who knows about hills? You know what I think about flat-topped hills?"

"What?"

"Maybe a long time ago, many winters before our grand-fathers were born, or their grandfathers, all the little mesas belonged to the big mesa. The little ones broke away and wandered off, like children that leave their mother."

"But those aren't little, are they?"

"They are little beside the big one, *Llano Estacado*. If you go up that river back there, you'll see the big one. Maybe a long time ago these we see wandered away and went down the river and now they can't find the way back."

"I'd like to see the big one," she said. "Where is it?"

"Away out that way. You've been on top of it."

"I don't think so. I didn't see it."

"It's so big it's hard to see. You have to be at the right place to see it. It's many days of travel across the top."

"When was I on top of it?"

"Do you remember *Laguna Sabinas,* with bad water in it? One goes north from there, and the land is all flat. That's the top. Was it a winter ago we were there? We might have traveled north on that flat top all the way to Prairie Dog Town River or farther. One could, but there's not enough water up there in summer."

"Don't some small mesas stand by themselves with no others around at all?"

"I don't know," he said. "I lose some things from my mind these days. We'll study them as we move south."

The band moved generally southeast, changing their course this way and that to make night camps where they knew water would stand this time of year. For two days they followed a scattered group of white-tailed deer, until every lodge had killed at least one. Another time they altered course to avoid following a herd of buffalo, for the horses could not find enough grazing behind buffalo so early in the year.

The land was losing its dead brown winter appearance. Leaves were coming back on the mesquite brush, tender bright green, and its blooms hung like fuzzy caterpillar worms. Small spring flowers stood in patches of color, yellow and white and pink. Tehanita often walked beside the travois of Story Teller and listened to him relate some whimsical idea. One day he

talked about his painting and the colors he would like to have
in his paint case. He wanted different colors for hills, one for
those near, one for those far, for distance softens colors. He
wanted one color for a hill on a damp morning and another for
a hill in the heat of day, one for a hill in hot sun and one for
a hill when a cloud hangs over it and darkens it. He wanted
one sky color for spring when it is deep blue and contrasts with
white lumpy clouds and another for hot sky which is so bright
one cannot look into it. He said he needed a dozen green paints
and a dozen yellows. He wanted different reds for cactus fruit
or a brilliant sunset, or a cardinal's feathers, or ripe plums, or
the walls of a canyon, which is near to the color of dried blood.
Then he spoke of other things, as if they were paints he might
put on a picture, fine falling rain, blowing dust, sunlight, clear
air, approaching darkness. If they had all these, he said, and a
giant skin to paint on, they could paint a great picture. "Then
what would we do with it?" he asked her.

"It would be a wonderful picture."

"But what would we ever do with it?"

"Roll it up and take it with us," she said.

"And we'd unroll it sometimes and look at it, wouldn't we?"

"We sure would."

He stared back into the distance across the land they had
traveled. "Too bad," he said. "Too bad for us. Someone has
beaten us to it. There it is, already done."

She laughed.

"But we have the better part," he said. "We can look at it.
It's unrolled for us every day." He was silent for a while as
he looked at the countryside, then said, "Tehanita, I see better
now that I have only one eye and it a little weak. The land and
its things enter into me more. The whole picture and also the
parts, they seem kin to me.

"Look at those small clouds, Tehanita. They are so tender
and sudden and surprising. I'm always surprised. That's why
they are so far above our reach, I guess, because we might
touch them, and they are too tender. . . .

"But, no, that's not it. Flowers are within our reach. Clouds are like flowers that burst out from nothing. Flowers have that same thing. They are too tender and sudden, as if they didn't belong. How could they live, or even be there? How could they last? How could they dare to be so weak? And bright?" His good eye was not on the earth, nor the sky, but on her. "They insist that they belong, beyond all reason. And I insist, too."

They pushed through hilly country the next day, leaving Buzzard Peak off to their right and came down to a broad sandy river, with pecan trees along it. She knew it was not the river she was hunting at every opportunity, because of its width and the muddy water it carried. She heard them call its name. It was one she remembered seeing before at other places, the Arms of God River. Clouds had covered the sky, and while they were erecting temporary shelters, rain began to fall. The women ran about gathering fallen limbs for firewood. Before night they had built a snug camp, and the cool spring rain seemed good.

The next day light showers fell. She sat under a shelter with the old man, and they watched squirrels chase one another and hide from one another in the tall grass. One squirrel ran out on the ground away from the trees. He could be seen hopping around here and there in the wet grass.

"You know what he's doing?" Story Teller asked.

"What?"

"Hunting pecans he buried last fall."

"I didn't know they buried pecans."

"They do, usually in rainy weather. The rain reminds him of it. Do you think he'll find them again?"

"Maybe."

"He might find one or two. Squirrels are like people. He had good intentions. He ran around, excited and eager with so many nuts, putting one here and one there. But he has forgotten."

She said, "It's kind of sad, isn't it?"

"Well, he didn't really know what he was doing anyway. He

thought he was burying a nut to eat later, but sure enough he was doing something else. I see where he buried one right there. See? Dig around it."

Just outside the line where water dripped from the shelter two young pecan leaves sprouted out of the matted dead grass. She dug around them in the wet soil and found a rotten pecan, its shell split and out of it coming the sprouted leaves and a root that led downward. She packed the dirt back around it and washed her hands in the dripping water.

"That nut couldn't fall this far or roll over here," he said. "A squirrel hid it. He thought he would eat it later, but it may become a tree and maybe the grandchildren of his grandchildren will play in it. Squirrels are like people. Sometimes they don't even guess what they do."

"Do you think people do that way often?"

"Often enough. I'll tell you something funny, or sad, I guess. When that young man, Little Wild Horse, was six or seven, not long before you came to us, he used to like stories. He hung around me all the time. Well, one day Ute Killer came to me angry. He said, 'You've been telling my son stories about Comanches being defeated in battle. Why do you do that? Don't ever tell him that. If I ever hear of you telling him about anything but victories, I'll cause you plenty of trouble.' He was stirred up. He shook his fist at me. Well, he was the civil chief and the boy's father, so I obeyed. But think of this: Ute Killer himself knows about defeats. He made a mistake telling me that. He didn't know what he was doing. But if the chief makes mistakes, we may be sure that the rest of us do too.

"There's a wisdom for each age of life, Tehanita. Old men think they are wise, and they see much foolishness in others, but they put themselves above the passions of younger people in a way they could not do if they were young; yet they did not throw off those passions through wisdom. I think I return now toward the age of childhood, and I hope I find some of the wisdom of that age. I'll tell you a joke on myself, if you won't tell anyone."

"All right."

"Last winter, you remember, Lance Returner was gone for a time, and we didn't eat regularly but kept meat for anyone to take whenever he was hungry. I sat around looking at the river and the sky, sleeping, dreaming, talking to children. Well, one day I got up to go to the bushes or something, and I noticed that I could hardly stand. I said to myself, 'What's this?' and began to think about it. You know what? I had forgotten to eat for two days. There's an old man's wisdom for you."

The next day the men brought certain horses, which were not yet broken to ride or carry burdens, down to a broad section of the river, where one by one they were pulled out into knee-deep water and a rider helped to mount them. The horses pitched wildly, sometimes falling, sometimes dislodging the boys who rode them. There was much splashing of water. The men who were mounted on good riding horses laughed and shouted as they herded the wild ones. The women watched from a distance. She noted that young Burning Hand was one of those who rode the wild ones in the water. He seemed a good rider. On the following morning as they broke camp to move upriver the men loaded the newly broken horses with burdens or rode them.

They went south and southwest. In two days they crossed the river and headed west. At least once a day, Tehanita rode out among the pack animals, which moved in a scattered and laggard manner unless forced to move faster, dismounted, and walked beside Story Teller. They passed near a small flat-topped hill, no higher than a tall tree, standing alone on a grassy prairie. Remembering his fanciful story of wandering mesas, she said to the old man, "There's a small one to have come so far out by itself."

"Yes. He's small. Maybe he was large once and has been worn away by rain and wind. You know, Tehanita, this morning I got to thinking about these hills that are scattered out across the Earth Mother, and a strange comparison came to me."

She waited for him to go on.

"They seem to me like the People, scattered and wandering around in separate bands, some large, some small. The Kwahadi and the Penatuhka are large. Don't tell Ute Killer or even Lance Returner I said so, but we, the Mutsani, are small. Other bands are small, the Tenawa, for instance. But where is the Pohoi band, and the Nonaum band? I remember them from the time when I was young, but I haven't heard of either of them since—since Come Home Early was a baby. It makes me wonder whether they stand out alone some place, or whether they have shrunk to nothing from the wind and rain."

Far ahead of them to the left they could see the blue outline of Double Mountain, which was a well-known landmark. From here it appeared to be one flat-topped hill with two sharper peaks beside it. She remembered seeing it and hearing the name before, but it did not look the same. Story Teller explained, laughing, that mountains change shape as well as move.

They watched the Double Mountain change that day and the next as they moved west, until the shape seemed to be that of two flat-topped mountains sitting side by side. It was the shape she remembered. The idea that a mountain may appear to change shape as one moves around it seemed to mock her hope of finding the certain one which was the key to her escape. It seemed to her that the more she learned the more difficult she saw escape to be.

One day, when Double Mountain was behind them, he called to her, "Tehanita, come stop my horse."

She dismounted and stopped his horse. They were on the crest of a small rise. He pointed ahead. "Look. You can see from here what I told you. Straight ahead is the big mesa, *Llano Estacado*. The blue band on the horizon, see?" It was a narrow band, too solid and even to be a cloud bank. He pointed to the left. "But there, see. Flat-topped mountains break from it and start to wander away."

She saw that the misty blue band was broken at the edge where he pointed, and five distinct mesas stood separate, the same height, as if they had moved away from the big one. The old man seemed delighted to have shown it to her. She led his horse until they caught up with the others.

They turned south that day. The following day they passed a single flat-topped mountain, and Story Teller pointed out to her that here was one which stood alone, as she had asked about. But it was not the one at all. They continued south and saw others. None of them looked right. The band camped at Big Spring a week. The weather became hot. They moved southeast down toward the country of their enemies, the Tonkawas, and made permanent camp on the Concho River.

Excitement had run through the camp since early morning when the small raiding party led by Wide Mouth had returned. They had brought back a live *Nuhmtuhka,* a Tonkawa, one of those creatures for whom the Comanches held great hatred and disgust and fear. He was a thing, like the great cannibal owl, that mothers would sometimes scare stubborn children with, saying, "Hush! You want a Tonkawa to get you? And eat you up?"

They all went to see him where he was tied at the edge of camp in the place where they held dances. A spreading live oak grew there. His wrists were wrapped with rawhide thongs which led up to separate limbs of the tree, stretching his arms up like wings. His feet were spread a step apart, each bound to a stake pounded into the ground. He was naked. His skin was light brown.

Tehanita came with the others to look at him. She stood back with the children who were afraid to go near. The Tonkawa seemed like a captured animal. He had a thin face. He did not move except for his eyes, which constantly turned this way and that to view the men and women around him.

They taunted him: "Hey, Tonk, how you like it here?"

"You like feasts, don't you? We'll have a big feast tonight."

"How would you like a little human meat?"

"Look at him! What's he saying?"

"You'll stay for the feast, won't you, Tonk?"

He said something in a strange tongue. They made obscene gestures at him. Most of the time a deep frown creased his forehead, but once he smiled crookedly. The smile quickly went away, and his eyes darted among them, and he again said some words in a meaningless tongue.

A fat woman posed in front of him and drew her finger dramatically across her throat, making a foolish clucking noise. He frowned at her a moment, then looked away. Three women came with knives and began to slash the air around him as if to cut his naked body into chunks. He jerked back at first, dodging their thrusts as well as he could, then he stayed still and merely frowned at their threatening movements.

Wide Mouth strode up and pushed his way through the onlookers to say to the three women, "Here! What are you doing? Don't cut him!"

"We didn't cut him."

"We didn't cut him."

"Well, be sure you don't. You hear me? I want him held safe for tonight."

The Tonkawa said some fast sounds to him in his meaningless tongue. Wide Mouth paid no attention, but went back toward his tipi.

They continued to laugh and call out to the bound captive.

"Hey, you dirty cannibal, you'll catch it tonight."

"He likes meat, don't you, Tonk?"

"Sure he does. Hee! You'll stay for the feast, won't you?"

Tehanita went back to the lodge of Lance Returner, stretched up a hide half she had been working on, and began scraping on it. All that day a group was gathered around the captive out at the edge of camp. She could hear their laughter and loud voices. In the afternoon women began dragging up firewood and stacking it in the dance place in front of the spreading live oak.

Before dark, Wide Mouth and the three others to whom the Tonkawa belonged walked out to where he was tied. Most of the men, women, and children of the band followed. Tehanita again went out with the children. What would happen she didn't know, though she believed it would be a cruel thing.

Someone brought fire and others helped place firewood so that there would be good light as darkness came on. The three women again began to threaten the captive with their butcher knives, and now they were not restrained. At first the Tonkawa seemed to ignore them; then as they began to prick him and draw lines on his skin with the knife points, he dodged and lunged against the thongs that bound him. He called out a few strange-sounding words over and over, looking this way and that in the group of people around him as if to find the one who had stopped the women before. They took great delight in jumping around him and causing him to jerk by dragging the knife points across his skin. The sounds he kept repeating were like a demand or a question.

The four warriors who had been on the raid began to dance and chant a song about the evil of the Tonkawas and how that tribe eats human flesh. Others, men and women, elbowed through the crowd to join the three women who teased the man.

Tehanita watched in horror and fascination. She did not know well the men and women who were teasing and torturing the lunging Tonkawa, but she knew their positions in the band. One was a second wife, now cast aside without the honor of a first wife and without the love of a favorite. One was a widow who had been the wife of an important brave, but now lived alone and had to beg meat. These usually quiet women had lost their dignity. They screamed and jumped in a frenzy. The men who took part in the torture were braves who had acted like cowards or who had lost their strength and could find no satisfaction in painting or making things. As darkness came and the only light was that of the huge bonfire, Tehanita could not tell one from another of those who took part in it. They were ill-lighted figures who shouted hatred and laughed without merriment.

"Time for the feast," one yelled.

"Cut him up! Call the dogs!"

"Hey, Tonk, now you'll see!"

Those around him seized him so that he could not even make limited surges against his bonds. The fat woman handled her knife as if she were butchering and sliced straight into the live flash of his thigh. She brought out a bloody chunk larger than her hand and held it up.

"There's meat! Call the dogs!"

"Get a dog and see if he'll eat it."

"Now, Tonk, how you like it?"

The Tonkawa had sagged down to hang from his arms when they took their hands from him. He had made no sound since the knife bit into him. Now he half stood, half hung, and his face seemed frozen. Those around him whistled and called out the names of the camp dogs.

"There comes one. Let him in here!"

"Bring him in! He's hungry!"

One dragged the dirty gray dog forward by the scuff of his neck. The dog put his front feet out stiffly and held his tail between his legs. When he was released in the middle of them, he crouched low to the ground and looked around, seeking a way to escape.

"Go on, dog, eat!" one yelled.

"Look at him! He won't eat it!"

"That's all right, dog, eat it. Don't be afraid."

"Now, Mr. Tonk, you see. You're so filthy a dog won't even eat your meat."

By some petting and soft words the dog was induced to become interested in the bloody chunk held out to him. He gulped it down. Those around him cheered. The Tonkawa had closed his eyes tightly. His leg below the great wound was bathed in shiny blood.

"He's not looking! Hey, Tonk, look! Make him open his eyes."

They seized him again to hold his head still. He lunged

from them as well as he could in his bonds, then began laughing senselessly at one and another of them, in bursts of laughlike sound, as if desperate to find one who would respond to him. When they had gripped his head, the fat woman pinched up and pulled out on his upper eyelids, one, then the other, and sliced them off. After this he appeared ghastly, with unclosable eyes and tears of blood coming down his cheeks. He began to say only one senseless word over and over: "Migo. Migo?"

"Give that poor dog some more. He's hungry."

"Feed him. He's hungry."

"Migo. Migo. Migo?"

"Get more dogs. They're like Tonkawas. They like to eat that kind of meat."

The bloody bound creature pulled first at one arm, then the other, shaking the limbs of the tree above him. The firelight, rising and falling, made him appear even more grotesque. The moving group around him were like indistinct forms out of a dream. It called back to her a time long ago, that first night when she had crouched with her little sister and watched their movements and their shadows and the distortions as their shapes were cast by moving flames out onto the jumbled trees.

"Feed the Tonk some! He's hungry too!"

"Hee, yes! He likes that kind of meat!"

Their voices rose in falsettos, sometimes in meaningless sounds.

Those around him cut a chunk from one of his bloody legs and pushed it into his mouth. A man pounded and jabbed it into his mouth with the butt of a knife. "Eat it! It's good! Eat it, you fool! Don't spit it out! Eat it! You like that kind of meat! Go after it! Eat it whether you want it or not!"

The terrible creature could make no sound out of his stuffed, bloody mouth. A kind of moaning growl seemed to come from his chest. He moved, straining his arm muscles back and forth rhythmically, with no attention to what they did.

"Ho, look! He has something hard in his meat!"

"What's in his leg there? Listen to that!"

One of the forms before him slapped the flat of a butcher knife against his bared thigh bone. "What is that, Tonk? You got bones in your meat?"

Tehanita turned and fled into the darkness. She stumbled over some firewood beside a tipi, then rose and got her bearings and went back to the Lance Returner lodge. Only Story Teller was there. He said nothing. She lay down and pulled a robe over her head so that she could hear no sound from the edge of camp.

After some time she raised the robe and heard voices outside the tipi. Blessed said, "I wish Lance Returner would come on home. I'm afraid. I don't like that kind of thing."

Old Woman said, "They should be killed. They're cannibals. What do they do to our men they capture?"

"I wish they would do it quickly," Come Home Early said. "I don't like those people who do that way."

She covered up her head again, and her thoughts turned to her little sister, Sunflower. She hoped that she hadn't seen it but knew it was useless to hope. All the children from babies up had seen it. No more than a dozen of the Mutsani had done it, but nearly all had watched it.

Inside some of them, maybe deep in all of them, hid a dark thing, not clearly cruel, not anything certain at all. It seemed less a thing than a place in their souls, where ugly things played some unreasonable game. It was not just this night. She had felt in vague touch with it before. Not in Story Teller or the three women, but in Lance Returner she had. When he would sit brooding, she would sense it in his scarred, red face, as if he might suddenly, with no reason, announce some doom for her or one of the others, then take whatever horrible action he might need to bring it to pass.

It was not fear of danger she felt toward it as much as fear of its dim and repulsive nature. It might cause pain or death, as it had when it came out of the women with the butcher knives; but worse, almost unbearable, was that it lay in them waiting and silent and beyond understanding.

She had heard it in their voices sometimes as they danced, stamping the ground. It sounded as if they cursed and prayed together and as if the pounding of their feet had a meaning that she hated. It was not always so; only when they had danced too long and had come into a tired frenzy and into the middle of the excitement came a carelessness that could not be explained, as if something not human pushed them into sounds and motions. In the same way she had seen it in the thin face of Spitting Dog, when his chanting voice rose too shrill and his words became meaningless; while they were at their most wild pitch they might be blended with a sudden note of careless savagery that had no connection with what had gone before. Then his face would be contorted as in deep pain.

Even later, when the silence of night had been over the camp for hours, she could not sleep.

In the days that followed that awful night, she felt a new urge to leave her captors. She could not stay with them. She must take some action, even though it might be dangerous. She began to cast about in her mind for a definite plan. It might be no more than taking some food she could carry, leaving at night, going downriver in the hope of somewhere finding white people who would know how to help her come back and rescue Sunflower. But as her mind was agitated with these thoughts, she heard news that upset the confidence she had in white people and made her doubtful about what help she might ever expect from them.

Most of the men were asleep or sprawled out under the shade trees, gambling, when four Penatuhka Comanches rode into camp. A few of the men stirred themselves and went to greet the visitors, then they began to shout to others. A crowd started to gather about the visitors. A man hurried by the Lance Returner lodge and said to Tehanita and Blessed, "Is

Lance Returner in there? Tell him to come on and hear the good news."

Blessed asked, "Is it a council? I don't know whether I should wake him."

"Wake him! It's great news! The whites all fight a big war against each other."

Blessed woke him. In a few minutes the entire band had gathered around the Penatuhkas, the important men in the center asking questions, then the others, the women, the children. Tehanita followed and stood at the edge of the crowd, tiptoeing to see.

"All the whites in the world," one of them said. "All of them. They kill each other off."

"The Texans, are they in it?"

"Sure. All of them are in it."

"But why do you say they'll kill each other off just because they fight a little among themselves?"

"They don't fight a little. Those whites, when they fight among themselves, they go after it. They gather in great bunches on the hills and in the valleys like herds of buffalo, and they slice each other down with wagon guns. When a battle is finished, so many lie on the ground it looks like all the Mutsani and the Penatuhka bands and more besides lie there killed.

"The madness in them has risen to the surface and taken charge of their acts. Blood soaks into the ground like rainwater, but still they are not satisfied."

Gasps and whistles of astonishment rose in the crowd. Someone brought water for the visitors and forked sticks with chunks of cooked meat. One of the four who seemed their leader answered most of the questions, except when his mouth was full of food, at which time one of the others would take the opportunity to speak.

Ute Killer said, "If they kill each other so fast, it looks like they would soon be all gone."

"No, not soon. You Mutsani have never understood the numbers of the whites as we have. They're thick as ants. We've seen more of them than you. Ask the Cherokees about it; they'll tell you. But now their numbers won't be so great. I doubt that any will live through it."

"Where do they fight?"

"Up on Trouble River and everywhere out east. All over their country."

"What's it about? Why do they fight each other?"

"Because they're angry. Each side wants to have its own way. And the more they fight, the more angry they become."

The leader busied himself at picking off pieces of the meat and stuffing them into his mouth while one of the other Penatuhkas went on: "Remember that Captain Marcy who came out on Wolf River quite a few winters ago with wagons and soldiers? He had another captain named McClellan with him, and they wandered around lost a long time, and we told the Wichitas we had killed them. Would you believe it? They say McClellan is a big war chief now with thousands of soldiers. And Marcy is a little chief."

Another one of them put in, "And that Lee, the one who was at Camp Cooper and Fort Phantom Hill, he's a big war chief too. They say he has a hundred times as many soldiers as he had out here. But they won't last long; they fall like bugs that fly into a fire."

Ute Killer asked the one who seemed their leader, "How do you know all this? How much is rumor and how much have you seen with your own eyes?"

"It's all true, believe me. As for what we've seen, we were living at peace on the reservation, sometimes making a few small raids; then they come to us and give us lots of presents and swear they are our friends, and we shouldn't help the other side because they are evil. Then the others come and give us lots of presents and swear they are our friends, and we shouldn't help the first side because they are evil. They keep doing this, but when their paths cross, *wham!* They fight like the *pukutsi*. It's all wonderful for us. We can raid all we want to and get plenty of presents besides."

"Have they left their forts? Who holds the forts of the whites?"

"Some are held by one side, some by the other. Many are left alone to the rats and owls."

To Tehanita, it was not all true merely because they said it. She knew there were ways in which they exaggerated or fooled themselves, as in the case of Ute Killer not allowing his son to be told about Comanche defeats. However, she could see no reason why the visitors would have made it all up. She decided it must be partly true.

In early spring they set out toward a place called Springs of the People. It was a place, so Tehanita learned from their talk, that had been held by the whites and had been abandoned. The Mutsani, especially the warriors, were jubilant at the thought that it was open to them once more, and the purpose of the trip seemed to be no more than to see the place they had once called their own, that had been usurped by the whites, and that was now their own again. Though it was in Apache country, they had claimed it for the People, the southernmost such place that they claimed, and the warriors thought of it as the best of their camping spots on the war trail to Mexico.

The direction they were going made no sense to her. She had developed the ability to tell directions from the sun and moon and stars. She believed from many observations that most rivers run a little to the right of east. She knew if she found the one flat-topped mountain whose image she treasured in her mind and went east a day and a half ride she would come to the country of white people. She believed that country to be somewhere east of the big mesa Story Teller had shown her. She believed if she ever found the West Fork River and went downstream, which would be east, she would find the country of white people; further, that the West Fork River must lie east of the big mesa. But now they were going to a place where the whites had lived, and they were traveling slightly to the left of west. It puzzled her and cast doubt on all she thought she had learned of such things.

The country into which they moved was more desert-like than any she had traveled. Bunches of grass grew far apart. Yucca and agave and many kinds of cactus could be seen, as well as scattered, stunted salt cedar and mesquite. As they neared their destination, large mesas stood up in the terrain as if to mock her. Then they saw the cluster of houses the whites had left.

At the Springs of the People, out of the flat dry land, great quantities of clear water rolled up and made a running stream. It was the water which attracted the Mutsani and caused them to wonder. But for Tehanita the place was dominated by the vacant houses of white stone and adobe bricks and by the roads and paths worn by the feet and horses and wagons of white people. The Indians did not care for the houses, even felt uncomfortable inside them. They tore off the wooden doors and brought out any tables and chairs and other wood to use for firewood.

Sometimes she went into one of the empty houses alone, stood on the strange wooden floors, looked at the walls, tried to imagine how it had been when they were here. She tried to feel how it had been when they sat here and walked here and talked here in their place. Dust had blown in and settled on the floors and window sills; mud daubers had made their nests up in the corners; birds had scattered their droppings. These things came between her and those who had made this their home.

Once, in a house with two rooms, she stood in the middle doorway and softly tried the sound of her own voice against the walls, using the difficult English language. "Hello ... my name Helen Morrison ... *Pabvi* Katy Morrison ... hello ... hello ... I make many years *Komantcia*. ... Hello?" She could imagine no answer from the vacant room. She could feel them a little, but what they had looked like and done and said was a mystery.

From the Springs of the People, two of the double trails of the white man led away, one eastward, one westward. She could not imagine which direction they must have gone, nor even whether they were still alive at all.

The band remained in the place half a moon. The men planned a raid, but they could not leave the women and children and old ones alone so near the Apaches. They moved north to safer territory.

6. One Spring in Blanco Canyon

SOMETIMES she worked at a job that demanded all her attention and engaged even the deep parts of her mind so that she forgot to nurse her hatred and her secret designs. She would forget her reason for wanting to be a good worker and to be known as a good worker. She would lose herself in the satisfaction of the work, saying silently, "It's going well. Yes, I must do this in this way so that it will match the rest. Then when I finish this part, I'll go on with that. It's looking nice. It's going to turn out well." It would be that way when she was thinning and tanning skins for clothing or when she was making a bead design. It was that way when she worked with the three women on the new tipi covers, so much so that she hummed one of their songs with them while she worked and was caught up in the process of making a good new thing and felt satisfaction at the accomplishment. But after these times of forgetfulness, she would suddenly see herself clearly, and a feeling of guilt would flood over her. How could she have forgotten? She would feel as if she had been unfaithful to those who had loved her and were dead and to those who might have loved her because they were white people as she was. They, the white people, who lived away at some uncertain place on the earth—whose very location became more of a mystery the more she learned the land of her captors—were fighting, so rumors continued to affirm, a great war among themselves; and she had no idea what it meant or where her loyalty might lie, as between the white factions, but that it should lie somewhere with them she had no doubt. She believed that any small chance she might have ever to be a good person or a decent person or a happy person lay with them. She felt that she must remember always what she was and what, in some way at some vague time in the future, she must do. It was difficult.

One of the main anxieties had been the welfare of her sister. It had been an uncertainty, sometimes causing her to feel guilty, sometimes causing her to assert to herself that she could do nothing, sometimes making her wonder what, even if she could have her way, she would have her sister do.

Sunflower was a favorite with the other youngsters and with the older ones who noticed and loved children. Wherever the children were playing kick ball or shinny or call-over-the-hill or playing house or playing in the water, yelling and laughing, her yellow head could be seen bobbing among the black heads. She loved joking and good-humored teasing and horseplay and was usually in the center of it. Her hair, sunburned so that it was lighter than her skin, did not set her apart; rather it called attention to her as a part of what is gay and frivolous and innocent in children. She was spoiled by her adopted mothers and her adopted father and her adopted brother, Burning Hand. She always owned her own pony and had become, as many of the older girls were, a daring and reckless rider.

Tehanita had given up long ago trying to speak English with her and had almost given up trying to influence her. Partly it was because they were separated so much. Sunflower had always been with the children; she had always been alone or working with the women. Then she had thought it might be just as well if Sunflower were satisfied and happy with her lot until the time came when they could escape. Finally, she had lately become almost afraid to test her influence over her little sister, lest she cause a rebellion against herself which might ruin her influence at some crucial later time.

The band had lived through the winter in Blanco Canyon with one of the small Kwahadi bands. That spring, the buffalo were nearby and plentiful. There was an informal dance the night before the hunters and butcher women would go on the spring meat hunt. Tehanita was astonished to see that one of those among the young unmarried women who danced was her sister, and equally astonished to see that Sunflower suddenly no longer even looked so much like a child.

When she had returned from the meat hunt, Tehanita learned that the two bands, before they split up and went their separate ways, would hold races and games. The girls-becoming-women would run behind the horses in the old ceremonial way. Immediately, she asked questions and discovered that what she feared was true: Sunflower meant to run with the girls-becoming-women. It was ridiculous. She was just a baby.

The day before the races she went to the lodge of Spitting Dog and called her little sister out. She didn't want to talk there among the lodges where others might overhear. "Will you come with me out among the rocks? I want to talk to you."

"No, you come with us, Tehanita. I'm going with some girls to get a bunch of flowers."

"No, please. I have to talk to you. Just out where the grinding holes are. Please."

"Is it a secret?"

"Yes."

"I'll come in a minute. I'll tell the girls to wait for me."

She went out among the boulders, far enough beyond the last tipi to be out of the hearing of anyone. When her little sister came, she realized that she hardly knew how to start, except to come directly to the point. For some reason, it seemed embarrassing to say what she had to say.

"It's about running tomorrow," she said. "Don't do it, Katy. Just tell them you don't want to. I'm sure they won't make you."

"Make me! Of course they won't make me. What are you talking about? What's the secret?"

"Don't run with them, Katy. It's a thing you shouldn't do."

"Don't call me Katy. I'm not a baby anymore. What's the secret?"

"Don't you see? To run with the girls-becoming-women— It's not like just having fun with them. It's not just playing. You'll become a Comanche woman."

"But I want to be a woman. I begged my mothers and my father, and that's why we get to have the ceremony. It's fun. You'll see. Why don't you come with us to get flowers? We're going to hang them all over us in the morning when we run; then we'll throw them at the boys."

"Katy, don't you see what I mean? You can't do this thing. We're here alone; we can talk. I'm your sister, and I only want to help you and you must listen. Can't you talk seriously a minute to your own sister?"

"You're my sister as much as the other girls, I guess. Anyway, I love you as much as the other girls, Tehanita, even if you do act like an old woman."

"Don't joke, Katy. Don't tease. Please don't."

"Why do you call me Katy? I'm not a baby anymore."

"I can see you're not a baby, but what does that have to do with it? Why did I ever call you Katy?"

"It was your pet name for me. But I'm not a child anymore. I want to be called Sunflower."

Her little sister stood there, no longer little, her breasts swelling the blouse of her fringed doeskin dress, her face seemingly innocent of any kind of lie or joke. How could it possibly be? Either that she did not know or that she knew and could brazenly deny it? How could it possibly be? She tried to think of a way to stop this impossible and frustrating denial. "No,

Katy! No! Do you remember calling me Helen? Why did you call me Helen?"

"I guess it was my pet name for you. What's the matter, Tehanita?"

"No, Katy! Please! Don't you really remember? Don't do me this way. Don't you remember the day we started to carry water to *Papa?* And they came . . . and took us and . . ."

Her little sister's face did not change at all. "What's *Papa?* You're like Talking Woman, always saying foreign words. I don't know what you're talking about."

"But, Katy! No! How can it be? Don't you really know? Don't you? If you're trying to forget it— If you've decided to give up, why don't you say so? Why lie to me? This is me, the only sister you have. This is Helen. Oh, little Katy!"

Her little sister's face was puzzled, but as innocent as ever. "You have a bad spirit inside you, Tehanita, and it's troubling you. Ask your father to get my father to help you. He can make a spell and drive out the bad spirit, and you'll be happy again."

She started to scream the question, then held herself in enough so that she would not be overheard. "Why do you have yellow hair?"

"I don't understand you, Tehanita. Some people just have yellow hair. It's like a white buffalo or an all-black skunk, I guess. I like it, myself."

She turned and sat down on a rock and buried her face in her hands, overcome by the frustration of it and the sadness of it. Her little sister patted her on the shoulder. It was the pat of a sympathetic friend, not that of a real sister. "Have your father pay my father a fee, Tehanita, and he'll make a spell to help you. I have to go now. They're waiting for me."

She couldn't decide what was the truth of it. She couldn't remember ever having said, any time during the long years, "Katy, you're a white person; we are captives." Whether it were possible she did not know, but rather than believe Katy was lying, she believed that somehow her little sister had managed to drive, on purpose, from her mind everything that she had known before she was five and a half winters old; and had done it so successfully that everything now, all her life now, fitted together as if that other had not existed at all.

Since the first light of dawn she had been helping to roast a deer which would be a part of the feast of that day of games. Fog had lain along the canyon floor earlier, but the spring sun had burnt it away, leaving a clear morning. It was during the Moon of Thunder, that time when rainstorms come across the land and make the leaves and flowers full and rich. She went out several times to the edge of camp among the rocks, from which vantage point she could see the grassy playing fields where the people from the two bands were gathering, near enough to hear their gay voices without understanding their words.

In the middle of the morning she saw that the young girls were starting to run. She climbed on top of a flat rock and stood watching. It was a daring, even dangerous, ceremony, only semiformal in nature. To an ignorant watcher it might have seemed an unscheduled prank played by playful girls, but to some members of the Comanche bands it seemed the most important event of the day. The girls who were the center of it, flowers in their hair and hanging in every fashion from their clothes, one by one would seize the tail of a horse and go bounding across the playing fields. The horses were urged by shouts and thrown clods to run their fastest. Yells of encouragement rose from the scattered spectators. Among the girls, six of them on this occasion, a great amount of giggling and screaming was mixed in with the breathless running as each of them tried until she was satisfied she had performed a satisfactory spectacle. It was as much a last rite of childhood as it was a rite of entering womanhood. As in childhood games for years among the Mutsani, the yellow hair of Sunflower stood out in the center of the action and laughter.

She heard the sound of a hoof against a stone and turned to see a rider coming from the opposite direction, from a branch of the canyon where some of the horses were kept. When she realized the rider had stopped beside the rock on which she stood, she glanced at him. It was young Burning Hand. Astride his horse he was about on a level with her and could see the scene she saw.

He said, "She's a wonderful young woman, isn't she?"

"She's a child."

"I wish that too," he said.

"What?"

"That she would stay a child."

She turned to face him. "Why? What do you care?"

"Well...you know...a person can't be sad around her; she's that way. But now she must stay away from me, and I must stay away from her. It's not right for a brother and sister to hang around together as they become older."

When he said "brother and sister," she turned away and pretended to watch the game area.

He went on, as if he needed to explain, "No one could guess the difference she made in our lodge. My first little sister—she was just out of the cradleboard and talking and running around. Then the plague took her. We mourned all the time. I guess... we wished the plague had taken us too. But then Sunflower came to us. It..."

"Did she come to you? Or was she taken and brought to you?"

"Well, I can't argue about that, but I remember the difference she made. She was like spring coming after a bad winter. My father—sometimes his medicine would go wrong. It's very hard to be a medicine man. Sometimes he wouldn't speak to us for a long time. But Sunflower—she won't let you be sad, no matter what. She's like a bird."

She said nothing in answer to him but was strongly aware that he stayed there beside her, holding in his nervous prancing horse. Finally he said, "Why don't you come on over there? I'm going to be in a race pretty soon, and I expect to win."

"I'm cooking. I guess the others expect to win too."

He laughed. "Maybe they do. If you watch, you'll see what happens. I'm getting the name of a good rider."

"I suppose your father makes a medicine for your horse, so you think he'll win."

"Well, no, I've kept him on the best grass all winter, and I've been running him a lot. And then I think I'm the best rider."

"I suppose when you go on a raid with the warriors, you still have to hold the horses."

"You ought to smile when you tease, Tehanita. You're hard-hearted."

"Well, it's nice to hear what you think of me."

"I didn't mean it. I hope you watch me in the race. I expect to win."

As he rode on, holding in his eager horse, she had the impulse to wish him good luck. The words were on her tongue, but something in her checked them. She went back to her cooking and did not watch his race. Later, she found that he had won as he had predicted.

They were beginning to strike the tipis before sunrise, making ready to move south. Tehanita had gone to the stream to scour with sand the cooking pots. When she returned, she saw that Story Teller had risen from his bed, by himself, and was clinging to the end of the old meat rack. He had been sick a great deal during the past winter. His legs were as skinny as shafts of cane, except for his knobby knees. He wore only a thin breechclout and his walking stick was in his hand. He was motioning to her to come near.

"Get Lance Returner," he said.

"You must lie down," she said. "We'll bring the travois up here and help you get on."

"Get Lance Returner and Old Woman."

She wanted to protest but could see something in his sagging face to make her believe he would keep on saying the same thing, no matter what she said. She ran down to Old Woman, who was packing a horse with water bags, and told her.

Old Woman came with her, and Story Teller said to them, "Get Lance Returner."

"He's busy," Old Woman said. "I thought you knew. We move today. You lie down till we get ready."

"I don't move. Get Lance Returner."

Old Woman stared at him a while, then said to Tehanita in a low, dry voice, "Bring Come Home Early and Blessed. I'll get Lance Returner."

When they had all come together, they went up to the old man, hesitantly. Lance Returner frowned in silence. Tehanita thought some kind of argument might start. Something strange was happening, a bad thing. Somehow, whatever it was, it gave Story Teller more power for the moment, in spite of his weakness—enough to make all of them come and listen to his thin voice.

He looked from one to the other with his good eye, as if seeing that they were all there. "I have no medicine secret to give. But my name is Story Teller, and I give that name to Tehanita. She can have it to use however she wants to.

"My paints I give to Old Woman. She can keep them or give them away. I don't remember if I have a horse or what. If I have anything else, Old Woman may keep it or give it to anybody." He looked slowly at each of them again.

"Is that all?" Lance Returner asked.

"That's all."

He turned loose of the old meat rack, balanced himself on his two legs and his walking stick, and began to shuffle away.

Blessed said, "We enjoy taking care of you."

Come Home Early said, "Down south we can pick those curly beans and make sweet soup for you."

He seemed not to hear them, but hobbled on through the camp and into the trees, going away from the rising sun. He moved away until all that could be seen of him was his wispy white hair with the sun on it. High ground that he could never climb lay ahead of him.

Tehanita said, "I'll get him," but Old Woman put out her hand and shook her head.

"Get this lodge on the horses," Lance Returner said. "Ute Killer means to make a long distance today."

Old Woman gave her two daughters their tasks and said to Tehanita, "You help me."

"But who will get Story Teller?"

"Don't call him that anymore. Didn't you hear?"

"But where's he going? We're moving. Who will take care of him?"

"He throws himself away."

"But who will get him food and water? He has no robe to lie on."

"Pull stakes. Get to work. Pull stakes. All men die. Some are killed. Some die of sickness. Some grow old and wear out and become of no use to themselves or anybody else. They are more trouble than they are worth. Yes, they become like old leggins that are worn full of holes."

Slowly the meaning of it sank into her. When they were loaded and starting to join the trek of those moving, and she saw the usual travois of the old man scratching along almost empty, she burst out at Old Woman, "How can you do it? How can you leave him this way?"

"Did we throw him away? No. He did it himself."

"You said he was like old leggins worn full of holes."

"Did we say he is a nasty old man, and we don't like him? Did we say he is a heavy burden, and we don't want to carry him around anymore?"

"Well, I don't see how you can do it. You could get him and make him go with us. I don't see—"

"No, you don't see. That's right. It's him, not us. He doesn't want to go with us anymore; it's too hard for him. But you say we ought to make him."

"I just don't see how you can leave him this way."

"Talk, talk, talk. Tehanita, you talk too much for a young woman your age. If you are going to talk, talk, talk all the time, go ride near someone else."

All that day it never left her mind. She had come to allow herself to believe that not all Comanches are animals, that some of them could be understood and would be found to have affection and tenderness for one another. But this! They seemed to think Story Teller was like an old mangy dog or an old horse that is too feeble and crippled to keep up with the herd anymore.

She watched Old Woman and Come Home Early and Blessed as they rode, and she thought that she was now seeing them for what they truly were. How could they ride on and on this way, knowing he would die? How could they ride and talk and eat and drink and look ahead, knowing what was behind them?

Could it be that she somehow had the wrong idea about Story Teller's place in that family? Hadn't he been the husband of Old Woman and the father of Come Home Early and Blessed? Comanche families were not always what they seemed. A girl child called her mother's sister "mother." Sometimes a child even called the friend of his father "father." Somehow the old man must not have belonged in the family, else Old Woman would remember a happy marriage day long ago and many winters of lying side by side at night. Come Home Early and Blessed would remember long winters of childhood when he was their father, the kind strength in their lodge, the one who killed the meat. It would explain it if the old man had really not been in the family. But that wasn't it. He had certainly been in the family. There was no way around it. He had been the husband of Old Woman and the father of Come Home Early and Blessed. They just didn't care. The answer was that they were like animals who have no feelings. She wouldn't speak to any of them about it again.

That night they made dry camp where only mesquite trees grew, and those small. She helped them build two shelters for the Lance Returner lodge, of hastily cut and trimmed and tied branches, covered with extra skins. One would be, as usual, for Lance Returner and Blessed, the other, for the rest. But as she was banking the small fire in the cook hole, she heard Blessed ask her husband, "Maybe I could sleep by my mother tonight?"

"If you want to. We get up early tomorrow and travel to reach water for the stock before the heat of afternoon."

Tehanita waited until Old Woman and her two daughters had lain down under the shelter, then picked her place, wanting to be as far away from them as possible. She was out from under the edge of the shelter and didn't care. She hated them.

She lay on her back listening to the night sounds. A mare's bell rang faintly from the other side of camp, and farther away a dove or an owl patiently called. Listening more carefully, she could hear the wind breathing in the lacy leaves of the mesquite brush. Then she could hear tiny sounds in the grass, the snap of leaves and stems as they arranged themselves, the footfalls of insect feet as they rustled their way. She was turned from the sounds by the sight of a falling star that drew its white line in the sky and faded. It seemed strange that she could pay attention to the small sounds and, though her eyes had been wide open at the sky, not see the stars. She forgot the sounds and looked at the star patterns that seemed so distant and beyond understanding and so familiar. It made her think of Story Teller.

Was he already gone? She thought that he was. Something of his last look made her believe he could do what he had decided to do whenever he was ready. He had not been able to walk for more than two moons, yet he walked. She believed that he had gone only a little way, that he had laid down his tired body and said to himself, as to Lance Returner, "That's all."

And had he found that place where the dead go? White people had a name for it, but she couldn't remember it. It was said to be a good place, no war and no pain. It was not too hot or too cold, and there was always enough food, and water for drinking and bathing. One's friends were there. There was feasting and dancing and games: horse racing and ball and shinny and the plum-stone game. But if there was such a place and he had found it, who would take care of him? She had heard them speak a little about a warrior, a son, who had died in a raid against the Jicarillas. He had been between the girls in age, the little brother of Come Home Early and the big brother of Blessed. He would be powerful in that land, because he had died bravely in battle, and he would welcome Story Teller and take care of him. It might even be that children lived there, some who had died young from fever or the plague, and surely they would want to hear stories. That would make him happy.

She was brought back to the night sounds by a new one that she couldn't identify. The wind still breathed in the leaves; the grass still made tiny shiftings. The new sound might be a small animal sniffing. It was a soft-drawn breath with quick little jerks in it. It seemed to come from one of the women, a strange sound for one to make in her sleep. She turned her head toward them to help in hearing. They were three dim, still forms. She could not tell which was which. The breath repeated again and again, and after she had listened for a time, it was clear that it came from different distances. It was not one sound, but three. They were awake and crying as softly as wind in lacy leaves or the footfall of an insect in grass.

She turned her head up. The stars were blurred, and she heard herself making the sound. She cried through the night with them. For Story Teller first. But also for what Old Woman had said, that all men must die—some killed, some of sickness, some of growing old and wearing out. For her papa and her mama. For George. For the son who had died bravely in battle fighting the Jicarillas. She cried with all three of them, but with Blessed more than the others, because she could see a vision of the old man telling a story and Blessed squatting alongside her, listening.

7. Winter in the Sand Hills

THE LODGE of Lance Returner was a peculiarly lonely place. It was as if a hole were torn in each of their lives. The four women would come to a silent place in their talk, and after a moment their eyes would glance at the place where he might have lain or sat had he been there, and each of them would know that all their minds dwelt on the skinny old man who was gone. They would speak no more until one of them found something to say about some new subject. It affected the master of the lodge too. He would come in, and the sense of the missing thing would seem to slap him in the face, and whatever had been in his mind would desert it; in a moment he would say something in an attempt to be cheerful: "Well, the horses are doing well this year," or "They say the antelope are thick south of here."

They could not publicly mourn the old man's passing, for he had lived out his life to its end. It was also true that there was no taboo against speaking his name, for he had freely given it away; yet they did not speak it; the silence spoke it enough. Perhaps through some vague feeling of guilt or perhaps through an understanding that all felt the loss, the five in the lodge, the master, the two wives, the mother, the adopted daughter, all were more kind to one another because he was gone.

These were times during which Tehanita lived in uncertainty, not able to settle on any clear relationship with those she lived with, suddenly seen in a new and kinder light; not able to accept or alter the new role Sunflower was taking as a young belle eligible to marry; not able to understand the war that took place in the vague world of white people or guess what effect it might have on her future. She drew on her patience and waited.

The pressure of white settlement and military activity against the People had eased. The Mutsani, as the other bands, took advantage of the fact to live a freer, less apprehensive life and to raid the whites more boldly, sometimes in groups of only three or four braves. Tehanita knew that many of the raids were against the whites, but which direction they went and exactly what they amounted to she could not discover. The warriors seemed to have contempt for any opposition they were meeting. They seldom brought back scalps, but brought spoils of all kinds: horses, bridles, saddles, guns, powder, lead, cooking pots, knives, axes, an occasional bag of flour or sugar. Sometimes they drove back a herd of cattle, which then had to be driven a long distance and sold to the New Mexico traders.

In the year following that spring when Sunflower ran with the girls-becoming-women, she was courted by several of the foremost young men of the band. At any social dance she was always present, and young men crowded around to dance as near her as possible. They gave gifts of fresh meat or trinkets or skins to her father, Spitting Dog, and her brother, Burning Hand. But one day the chief's son, Little Wild Horse, who had recently led his first raid and had successfully stolen a rifle and three horses, called Burning Hand "my brother." After that the other suitors ceased their attentions, and the chief's son was given a clear field. Sunflower seemed to welcome his suit. The match was the talk of the camp.

Tehanita thought she had resigned herself to some such development, but as it became clear from gossip that the marriage was being planned, she felt herself strongly against it and had to restrain herself lest she say something that would reveal her feelings.

The matter was arranged between the two families. Spitting Dog's family, of which he was the most important member, had long been a powerful one, but he had not added much to the luster of his name by his many failures at making medicine. He made, as they said, good "camp medicine"; which is to say that his pretensions were high, and he put on a good show, but on the warpath and the hunting path, where it counted seriously, his medicine was often weak. Only in recent years his medicine to promote the success of raids against the whites had seemed more effective, but some said the difference was not caused by him.

On the other hand Ute Killer's position was unimpeachable. His position as civil chief and the most important war chief had gone unchallenged for years and was not likely to be lost any time soon. He had won the right to wear in his hair a fistful of eagle feathers, and he carried on the warpath a lance, which imposes on the bearer the responsibility for conspicuous bravery. Whatever mistakes he had made in leading the Mutsani were wiped out by the scars he carried on his body, won fighting for the defense and the glory of the band.

These ideas about the two families were expressed in various ways in the women's talk. The consensus was that Ute Killer's son might offer any dowry he chose, and Spitting Dog would do well to accept it; but that Little Wild Horse should offer enough to show that Sunflower was valuable to him. The women of the camp were satisfied when they learned that the offer, accepted before it was made, was four high-quality horses. None of them seemed to consider important that Sunflower was not born a Comanche; she was merely a friendly girl, well liked by the young people, the daughter of the medicine man.

The marriage day was one of feasting and fun. Its high point came with the bringing of the four good horses to the lodge of Spitting Dog. He and his family came out, dressed in their best finery, and acted surprised. The horses were taken to the medicine man's herd, and Little Wild Horse led his bride to the new lodge that had been prepared for them. Gifts were given out by both of the families involved, and Ute Killer sent a man around to announce the event, about which everyone already knew.

They had been up on Arrowpoint River that summer, the braves taking part, along with warriors from two other Comanche bands and one Kiowa band, in a powerful strike against the Utes. After the men returned from their successful raid, Ute Killer began to move the Mutsani south, for he wanted to spend the winter in a place where the weather was less harsh. They traveled with a party of Penatuhka Comanches who had been with them. Down on Wolf River they came to the main camp of the Penatuhkas and, since winter was not yet pressing, camped beside them for visiting.

The Penatuhkas had news. The whites had ended their great war. That first night Tehanita went with Old Woman, Come Home Early, and Blessed to the fire where Lance Returner smoked with Buffalo Bones and two men of the other band. She squatted back in the shadows with the women, quiet, waiting as they did, to hear what the men had to say.

Buffalo Bones talked at length about the adventures in Ute land. Then Lance Returner asked, "What's this about the whites? They've stopped fighting, have they?"

One of the strange men said, "Yes, it's finished, I guess."

"Then I guess they didn't kill each other off?"

"No, not everyone. At least one side is left."

"Which side won?"

"I'm not sure. But one side did. They had some chief named Grant who was the main chief on the winning side."

"But that side lost many warriors?"

"Yes."

"What I'm trying to make out," Lance Returner said, "is how strong the whites remain now. Those we have raided are weak. They run off and leave their lodges. If they try to fight, they don't have much powder for their guns, and sometimes it won't fire off. It seems to me that the whites have come to the end of their road. I don't think they'll ever give us any more trouble, and we can get anything we want from them; if they won't give it, we can take it. We must keep them down like we do the Utes and the Apaches."

The two strangers were shaking their heads. The firelight that came up onto their faces showed both of them to be frowning. They wore curious clothing, shirts and trousers of cloth and moccasins without tops. One of them said, "You've got the wrong idea. They can lose many warriors and still have many left. You haven't been around whites enough to understand them, Lance Returner. Right now some of our chiefs have gone to meet them and work out new treaties."

"What?"

"Sure. They met with eastern Indians in the spring, and now they meet with the whites."

"What's the matter with you Penatuhkas?"

"Oh, but it's not only us. Some of the Nawkoni go too, and even some Kiowas."

Buffalo Bones put in, "What's this treaty business? What is a treaty?"

"We don't know exactly," one of them said. "You just make peace and mark on a paper; that's about all."

The other one said, "Also, they give you gifts."

Lance Returner said, "That's not all, and you know it. They tell you where to make your camps. They tell you not to go to this place and that place. They tell you they can make forts and send their stagecoaches anywhere they want to. They tell you not to raid. I don't understand you Penatuhkas and never will. I've been making speeches about this matter in our councils. When the panther makes friends with the deer, when the wolf makes friends with the rabbit, when the eagle makes friends with the ground squirrel—that's the time we should make friends with the white man."

She could see the women nodding at one another and at her. There was no accusation or embarrassment in their manner. They had forgotten that she was a white person, or believed somehow that she had lost any shreds of loyalty to her real people.

The band moved south, leisurely at first, then with some concern. Ute Killer and the council, as usual at this time of year, were thinking about a location for a winter camp, not yet decided upon, and a meat hunt. In addition, they had agreed, up on the Arrowpoint, to move far enough south to miss the worst of the coming blizzards. Ordinarily they would have made winter camp before the meat hunt. Now, as they moved south and did not in the first few days find more than enough scattered buffalo for fresh meat, they began to recall the cold, hungry winter which had followed their raid on the Utes several years before. The problems of moving south, settling on a camp site, and making winter meat became entangled in their minds, and they determined that if the buffalo were going to hide, they would not be caught in a cold place where even roots and grass might be covered with snow. They would travel southward and not be stopped except by a buffalo herd. Their steady travel made locating a herd harder than usual.

They traveled half a moon and came upon a party of Kwahadi Comanches making salt at a salt spring. The party gave them salt, but no pemmican or jerky. They said they had up in the canyon where their band was camped enough meat for themselves, but no more.

The Mutsani moved on. They were not desperate or short of fresh meat, only determined not to be caught by cold and hunger at once. They had traveled another half moon when they reached both their goals at the same time: an area far enough south, next the country of the Lipans, where only the tail end of a blizzard could come; and a herd of two hundred buffalo, which would supply most of their meat needs. Further, it was a land where the small red deer could be killed the year around if a hunter knew where to find them.

They camped around a pool of water in the edge of a broad band of sand hills. Near camp the sand was held in its mounds by a mat of bunch grass and sprawling dwarf oaks. Farther away the sand lay in bare dunes, some three or four times as high as a tipi, free to be blown and patterned by the wind. Back east from camp, in the direction where they had discovered the buffalo, the sand hills diminished and thinned, and the prairie opened out. In that direction, their horse herd could find pasture through the winter.

The hunting party, with which Tehanita went as a butcher, hounded the buffalo for days. They got the larger portion of the herd, turning back only when the remnants scattered. Suddenly the band realized they were in a safe position in regard to winter food, and they laughed about their recent fears.

After the meat was taken care of, the women turned their attention to the acorns growing in the sand hills. The stunted oaks which sprawled on the dunes, a dark mass topping the light sand, bore long, fat acorns. They were bitter but rich. As the women realized what a fine crop existed nearby, they set out in parties daily to gather them. They cleaned the nearest bushes first, then pushed farther out, the women of each lodge wanting to get their share while some remained. The nights were cold, but the days were pleasant.

Tehanita, Old Woman, Come Home Early, and Blessed foraged with the others. One afternoon they went an hour's walk out into the sand hills to a place that had not been picked over. They gathered into two leather bags, Tehanita and Old Woman with one, the two wives with one. Tehanita and Old Woman had their bag half full as they came up a dune where the nuts looked promising. Ahead they could see Come Home Early on a similar dune and out to one side three other women working together. One of the three suddenly burst out with a piercing scream of fright.

The three huddled together. The one who was screaming

pointed ahead. Her scream turned into the words, "Lipans! Lipans!"

Come Home Early and Blessed stood up and looked, then turned and started back. Blessed jumped with long strides down the sand slopes, speedily. Come Home Early scrambled heavily, bringing the bag of acorns, bogging and sliding, losing the bag, pulling herself back through the sand after it.

Old Woman said to Tehanita, "Help her. Don't leave the bag." Then to the younger wife, "Blessed, come this way!"

Tehanita scrambled down the slope in front of her, across the blown-out hardpan between the dunes, and half way up the next to take the bag from Come Home Early. They headed back toward camp as fast as they could go. Running was difficult in the sand, especially uphill. One's feet sank out of sight. The sand would not give a good foothold. They caught up with Old Woman and Blessed, and the four labored as fast as possible toward home, looking back over their shoulders often.

As they came hurrying across a low place where the footing was good, Old Woman asked Come Home Early, panting for breath as she spoke, "Are you sure . . . they were Lipans? Did you see them?"

Her heavy daughter had sweat running down her round cheeks. "Yes, I saw two. They were Lipans."

Old Woman seemed as well able to run as either of her daughters. She thrust the bag she carried into Blessed's arms and took the one from Tehanita. "Run on ahead, Tehanita. Tell the men."

She ran ahead and found it easier to go fast without the load of acorns. She went on all fours up the dunes and jumped in long strides down them, her feet sending up sprays of sand. She ran around some of the high points of sand, but needed to climb some of them in order to see the direction toward camp. Not long after leaving the other three women, she came to where the sand hills thinned and were covered with grass, and shortly afterward to the camp. She yelled the news to some men who sprawled on the ground talking, then went on to the center of camp and found Lance Returner and told him.

Some men began to paint themselves for war; some ran for their horses; others grabbed their weapons and set out into the sand hills on foot. Soon all the women were safe in camp. It developed that only four Lipans had been seen, those picking acorns rather than threatening attack.

The men returned at dark. They had found the Lipans' sign, had found where they had cooked a rabbit and two snakes. The enemy Indians seemed to be two men and two women, going on foot. The following morning a party of Mutsani set out to track them down, but a wind during the night had erased all tracks.

As the moons of winter progressed, the location proved to be good for a camp. No bad blizzards threatened. Frequently small parties of warriors went out on short searching raids to try to find any enemy Apaches who might have pushed this far north. They found nothing, but could not forget that the Lipans had shown brazen audacity by coming into Comanche territory and could not but suspect that they might do it again.

The mothers of Sunflower from Spitting Dog's lodge and the mothers from Ute Killer's lodge began to show great concern for Sunflower. They did the heavy work of her small lodge and followed around watching her. It was obvious that Sunflower was going to produce a grandchild for these two important families. The mothers would not let her go out into the sand hills, where the children played sliding down the slopes, and they would not let her ride horseback. Sunflower took it good-naturedly, teasing them by pretending that she wanted to run in the sand and carry heavy loads.

Tehanita watched with mixed emotions. Sunflower still seemed a child to her, and she felt that she, as the only one in the band who knew or remembered the truth, had a partial claim on the coming baby.

The winter passed easily. The pool of water around which

the camp was centered froze a thin sheet of ice sometimes at
night, but it never failed to melt the next day. The pool, like
the others scattered among the sand hills, did not go dry. It
seemed to be fed by some covered spring somewhere in the
expanse of sand so that water seeped into it as fast as it was
taken out. At some of the water holes a distance from camp,
small red deer came to drink, and the men would lie in hiding
to kill them. They provided fresh meat regularly. Javelinas
also could be found in the area. Sometimes the young men made
sport by riding them down and spearing them from horseback,
but they were not needed for food.

In early spring it rained several days and turned off warm.
New grass began to sprout. Along with these signs of a new
growing season, Sunflower's time came. She had not dropped
her baby prematurely as many of the women did, in spite of
her teasing. She had Talking Woman, the first wife of Ute
Killer, for a midwife, and around her little birth lodge, just
calling distance outside of camp, her other mothers clustered
for a night and a day. They were all pleased when the baby
came, but no celebration was held, for the child was a girl,
looked upon as a thing to be cherished but not like one who
would someday be a warrior.

It was several days before Tehanita got to see it. She went
with Old Woman to visit and take a gift of some raven
feathers, which are a good luck decoration for the clothing or
cradleboard of a baby. The baby was a tiny thing, well formed,
its fine hair as black as its father's. Its skin was red. The delicate eyes, when they opened upon the approving women who
clustered around, were dark.

Some talk of moving camp was going around, but before any
decision could be made the men found something to hold them
in the area longer. To the east they discovered a band of wild
horses, made up of the variety usually seen in such a band,
mostly scrubs, but led by a superb stallion. The animal, the un-
doubted master of the other males in the band, was a dark

brown paint, and the dark spots were small and sharp against a clean white.

They went out to chase the stallion, hoping to wear him out and get ropes on him. Instead they wore out their own mounts. Party after party went after him, saw him at a distance, used one strategy or another to effect his capture, but returned to camp exhausted with increased admiration for the animal. No timber for a trap of any kind grew in the area.

It was clear that they could not get the stallion himself, but they decided to try to get the next best thing—some offspring from him. Before the wild band had been disturbed, they had passed regularly, so many tracks indicated, across a broad flat about an hour's ride from camp. The Mutsani had several mares ready for breeding. The men took them one morning, five good mares, and hobbled them and staked them in what they hoped might be the path of the stallion. They brought them home for water that night and returned them to the flat the next morning. From the highest sand hill near camp, the staked mares could be seen far out on the flat. One of the mares' owners sat on the hill all day as a lookout.

On the third day, in the middle of the morning, the lookout set up a furious yelling. At first he shouted for the other owners to come look, then he began to curse and shout, "Lipans! Lipans!"

Several men scrambled up to see. They stared, shading their eyes and squinting, watching helplessly while three strange Indians rode up to the mares, cut their hobbles, and led them away toward the south.

The camp became a busy confusion of preparation for pursuit and battle. As usual, some horses were tied near camp, but many grazed at a distance, and several warriors set out hurriedly to catch their best war-horses. In the hustle some of the older council men stopped Ute Killer and began to consult with him. In a short time his voice rang out through the camp: "Stop! Everybody stop! Those devil Lipans! They might fool us!"

He ordered that only five men were to pursue the horse-thieving Lipans, those five who owned the mares. The rest were to prepare for an attack. He sent lookouts to take up vantage points in the near sand hills. Wide Mouth was one of the five owners. He rode out at their head.

The wisdom of their tactics was soon apparent. Strange battle cries rose out in the sand, and the lookouts shouted for help. The Mutsani warriors, by now armed and ready, poured out of camp and up into the sand. The two rifles owned by the Mutsani, the only ones they owned which could be used, began to crack. They were answered by one farther away in the hands of an enemy. Some of the braves moved out of sight beyond the nearest hills; others could be seen on the near slopes, stringing their bows or fitting arrows to them. They yelled, beating their hands against their mouths, to scare the enemy.

Old Woman said, "I don't like it with Lance Returner gone. I wish we had our horses here close."

"I can get them," Tehanita said.

"No, we stay together. You have nothing to ride out there."

"But I can catch my horse or a packhorse, then catch one for each of us."

"No, you stay here. If they break through, we'll run on foot. I don't believe they'll come after us with horses."

Come Home Early said, "They wouldn't bring horses through the sand hills."

Old Woman agreed. "No, those crazy Lipans are always going around on foot like the Pawnee. But listen, you girls, if I say run, you run! Don't get caught by the Lipans. They're worse than Utes. You run! But don't run off and leave me."

The fight near camp continued. The guns cracked at irregular intervals. The spring wind was blowing the sand, and it came up in spurts where an arrow hit or in a stream where some fighter ran. Suddenly the women saw a development that caused some of them to scream in panic. From a draw south of camp, about the distance of a long arrow flight, six Lipans came running with bows at the ready to come up behind the Mutsani warriors and cut them off from camp.

Some of the women fled immediately. Some ran about gathering children or began packing bundles to carry. The lodge beside Lance Returner's belonged to Horse Roper. It was made of two tipis, and with the approach of spring, the wives had taken down one tipi to repair the seams. The long dry lodgepoles were stacked against the other tipi and tied. In trying to get a rope to tie up a bundle, Horse Roper's first wife upset the stack of eighteen long poles, sending them clattering and rolling over one another. Such noise seemed to belong in the running, scattering melee of women and children and dogs.

Old Woman said to Come Home Early, "Bring the iron pot." To Blessed, "Bring three robes. Hurry! We run! Tehanita, get the small box of pemmican. Come on! Hurry."

Tehanita brought the box out to the door of the tipi, then stopped. The women were streaming north out of camp. Instead of following, she ran back toward the lodge of Little Wild Horse and Sunflower. She was not thinking so much of her sister as of the baby, which would be a heavy load if the new mother had to carry anything else. The lodge was empty. She ran back to the Ute Killer and the Spitting Dog lodges, calling, "Sunflower. Sunflower." Her sister was gone, undoubtedly with the aid and care of her anxious mothers. By this time the last of the women and children were fleeing out of camp toward the north. She was alone.

The six newly arrived Lipans had established themselves in clear view of the camp on a near slope, shouting and firing arrows quickly, trying to give the impression of a strong force to the Mutsani warriors, who could not see them. At the same time that Tehanita satisfied herself that Sunflower and her baby were safely gone, one of the Lipans turned and bounded down the slope into the unprotected camp. He was armed only with a large knife, which he brandished as he came. She was not greatly afraid as long as the path the women had taken remained open, since she had developed confidence in her ability to run. She moved back toward the Lance Returner lodge, keeping somewhat hidden from him, toward the box of pemmican Old Woman had told her to bring.

He was showing off. The first tipi in his path, he slashed wildly; then he kicked over the cooking pot full of stewed meat which sat in front of it. He came on, running like a squat bear, shouting, "Aye-hee! Aye-ho!" He was ugly. His hair was cut short like a woman's, and he wore a sweatband around his forehead. She watched him and waited for him to turn aside so that she could go around in front of the tipi and get the box before she ran. If he gave her time, she wanted to go inside and also bring her little bundle of treasures, the two little tightly rolled and faded dresses, her glass beads, her sewing materials.

The Lipan bounded from tipi to tipi, arrogantly shouting, brandishing the knife, slashing with it. He ripped open an *awyawt* of mesquite-bean meal and kicked it, scattering the contents. She thought of the work that had gone into gathering that food. He found a bag of salt in a doorway, broke it, and flung it into the air. He slashed into a large box of acorn meal and spread it wildly on the ground so that it could not be recovered. She was incensed at his spiteful waste of food, that he should do it so arrogantly, gleefully, as if food were nothing, easy to obtain. He came on and kicked over another pot, still shouting, "Aye-hee! Aye-ho!" Her fear rose as he came nearer, but her anger rose with it. It was maddening to see him thus sporting with precious food. Her years of food gathering, the tedious hours of root digging, nut hunting, seed gathering, fruit picking, the hours of preserving food and caring for it, knowing its value—the teachings of these years converged to a single feeling, hatred. She could not bear what the Lipan was doing.

In front of the Lance Returner lodge was a woodpile, made partly of mesquite limbs, but mostly of root wood from the small oaks. The oaks had long roots like grapevine runners, which could be pulled up from the sand and hacked into lengths for firewood. The woodpile was waist-high. On top of it she and the other women had spread to dry the meat of a deer Lance Returner had killed three days before. Straight to it the frenzied Lipan came. He began to toss away the strips of meat with the point of his knife.

She hardly knew what she did. As she started around toward him, the scattered lodgepoles Horse Roper's wife had dropped lay before her. She took the first one that came to her hand. It was cured cedar, three times as long as a man is tall, as big as a man's thumb at the small end, as big as a man's arm at the large end. She grasped it nearer the small end and was raising it to strike as she came to the front of the Lance Returner lodge. She swung with all the angry force at her command.

She had begun to cry out to him, and the Lipan, hearing, had barely begun to turn his head; but in that instant before he could see and move, the butt of the pole caught him in the back. The sound and feel was not that of wood striking flesh, but of wood striking bone. His back folded in a way that a man's back will not bend. The force of the blow carried him into the woodpile. He went down in a clutter with the wood and rolled off.

She had shouted at him, "You stinking, wasteful devil!" Before she had finished the words, he was on the ground. His knife fell to one side. His two hands clutched briefly at the dirt. He made a little sound, blowing air between his teeth; then his mouth stayed open, and his eyes stayed open, and he lay still.

She had seen nothing of the battle for a minute. The Mutsani warriors had broken back through the weak forces behind them and sent the five Lipans scurrying toward the cover of the draw they had come out of. A dozen Mutsani men had been on the high ground and had seen the event that had taken place in the almost deserted camp. Now they came running. Buffalo Bones was in the lead. He struck the downed Lipan with his bow and shouted something. She didn't understand at the moment what he said. They swarmed around her, mixing war cries and praise. They gathered around the strange Indian on the ground, poking him; those who wished shot arrows into his still body.

She dropped the lodgepole and moved a little away from them. Then it came to her clearly what the shout had said and meant. Buffalo Bones had shouted, "Second coup!"

The remainder of the day the band spent coming back together again and reestablishing order. The attacking Lipans had been not more than thirty in number, and when their attempts at surprise failed, they had quickly pulled back. Mounted pursuit discovered that the Lipans themselves had horses, which they had left on the other side of the band of sand hills, and they had enough head start to escape. The five breeding mares were lost. A little food was lost. Three Mutsani braves had wounds that would heal without trouble. The Lipans had carried off several of their warriors, one of whom had seemed dead with two arrows in him. Then one Lipan lay dead in the middle of camp. The Mutsani considered it a victory.

The following day a dance was planned. In the afternoon, the women of the Lance Returner lodge began to tell Tehanita to dress up and get ready.

"But I don't know anything about it," she said.

"What do you need to know about it?" Old Woman said.

"Come on, Tehanita," Blessed said. "It's mostly for you."

"We'll help you get ready," Come Home Early said. "The dance is mostly for you. You're the main thing."

Her protests accomplished nothing. They insisted and fussed around her, helping her get ready. She could not muster enough indignation to make them stop because they were good-natured and praised her and told her she was pretty. By this means she was moved, halfway against her will, at dusk to a place near the bonfire, beside the pole on which the scalp hung stretched on a small wooden hoop. She was the center of all their eyes.

She feared, from having watched such celebrations, that they would expect her to speak. She had nothing to say. It was a relief to hear from the crowd: "Let Lance Returner tell it.

He saw it all." "He's good at speaking." "Yeah, let Lance Returner make a speech about it." He seemed not hard to persuade. She felt thankful to him, even though she knew he enjoyed it, perhaps had even been practicing it to himself.

He stood beside her in the firelight under the scalp and spoke grandly:

"Now, listen to this and remember it. Be quiet and hear it so that you can tell it to children in the future. Let the youngsters hear it and the strong warriors as well. Let the wind hear it and carry it to the ears of our enemies and give them fear.

"My daughter Tehanita has done a great thing today. Many of us are witness to it, and it's true. The stinking Lipan Apaches came against us here in the edge of the sand hills. They hoped to sneak around and steal our horses and surprise us and kill some of us and spoil our camp. They attacked us from three ways, hoping to fool us. While the men were out of camp, the last bunch came to cut us off from camp, and one of those came down among our tipis, where he would have no men to fight but only helpless women and children.

"The women fled, as they should, for they ought to save the children and themselves. So the Lipan ran through our camp, dishonoring it, doing as he pleased, passing along our paths as if they were his own. He was a full-grown man, healthy, not wounded. He was armed, traveling the warpath.

"But one woman did not flee. That was my daughter Tehanita. That she is a woman and a woman is weak did not stop her. It made her very angry to see that hateful Lipan warrior acting like he owned this camp of the People. She chose her weapon and came out against him. The weapon she brought was a lodgepole belonging to Horse Roper, the nephew of Wide Mouth, who is the cousin of Ute Killer.

"So she came out to the enemy warrior, and in the moment that she came to him she stood as tall and strong as *Kahwus*. Then she struck him! She rebuked him and struck him. Never was such a blow struck! It would have been a great blow for the strongest man to strike. They don't get up when Tehanita hits them. That's all, except in closing let me add this: May this story be known by the Lipans. I hope they saw it, and it makes them tremble and makes fear run down their backs. Let them sneak back to the mountains where they belong and stay away from us. I may turn my daughter Tehanita loose on them.

"That's all, and it's true. If anyone doesn't agree, let him speak up, for I think this story will be repeated a long time."

When he stopped, some of the younger braves yipped to cheer her, and the drummer beat a tattoo. Various men and women called out: "She did it!" "It's all true!" "I saw it; it's true!"

Then, and sometimes later when she remembered the event, she said to herself: If he was our enemy, if there is war between the Apache and the People—I don't understand why it must be so, but if it is—maybe it is right for him to fight us. But why should he destroy our food? If he had stolen it for himself or his friends— But why should he destroy food?

8. The Wide Mouth Raid to Mexico

She found it both easier and harder after her deed during the Lipan attack. Every member of the band now accepted her in the way that the members of the Lance Returner lodge had accepted her before. They spoke freely to her. If, at her work, she started to lift something heavy, any of the women might come forward to help. Sometimes the women alluded to her deed in an easy, joking manner. They would say, "I hope you never lose your temper with me, Tehanita," or, "It's all right. Tehanita is going with us; we'll be safe." Sometimes the young unmarried men would speak to her, trying to engage her in conversation, but she would answer quickly and pass on.

Their attitude said to her: You belong with us, and we like you; if you are different in some way, it doesn't matter.

But all that could change nothing. They did not know the depth of her long determination.

She had gained some of the things which through the years had seemed necessary for escape: strength, the ability to find food, the ability to travel a long distance on horse or foot, a considerable knowledge of the land, without the knowledge of the definite direction to go to find white people. She still had the puzzle of the white people, of what they had done to themselves with the war they had fought; though the rumors that passed among the Kiowa and Comanche bands were beginning to suggest that the whites had changed little in numbers or otherwise as a result of the war they had fought. Then she had the puzzle of Sunflower, for her duty to escape included the duty to take her sister, and she found it difficult to think of it in any other way. Also she had the puzzle of the baby girl, as yet unnamed, who was half white even though she did not appear to be.

Early in that autumn when the baby was growing out of her cradleboard and could stand alone and was learning to toddle around, a raid to Mexico was planned. It was Wide Mouth's idea. He had been one of the leaders of a summer raid against white settlements. The raiders had split into three groups, and the other groups had been successful, but his group had brought back no loot at all. He was dissatisfied, and so a few days before the beginning of the Mexican Moon, he carried the pipe to certain other braves of the Mutsani. Nineteen of them accepted his plan and agreed to follow him. One of these was Little Wild Horse. Most of the other young men his age, including Burning Hand, had gone to deliver to the New Mexico traders some cattle they had taken during the summer.

Ute Killer became interested in the raid plan after his son had joined it, but since its leadership was already settled, he declined to be a member of the party. Gossip had it that his son was hoping to prove his mettle out from under the domination of his father.

It would be a long raid. Some of the raiders wanted to take their women. Wide Mouth thought about it and discussed it and decided that any wife might go if she were young and strong and a first-class rider. As a result, four women became members of the party. One of these was Sunflower. She was as eager and excited about the prospects of the trip as was her young husband.

It came as a shock to Tehanita. Her first thought was to talk her sister out of it or to prevent her in some way. It was not like a closer raid, on which a woman might go and wait in a raid camp for the men to return; the trail into Mexico was deep into enemy territory, and a woman who traveled it was a part of the raid itself. The trail went through that sand-hill country in the south, over Horsehead Crossing, past the Springs of the People; but in those familiar places the war trail to Mexico was only beginning, and beyond them all of it was held by various enemies who hated Comanches and permitted them to pass only because of fear. She had seen them map the war trail on the ground, putting sticks to mark the camp spots, talking about the mountains, canyon, deserts. It was no leisurely ride. At many points the safety of a party depended on the speed with which they traveled.

The nature of Mexico and its people were vague ideas to her, defined by much hearsay. Some of the people down there were white people or in some way kin to white people, as they were to New Mexico people. The whole idea of white people was confusing. There were Texans and bluecoats and Rangers. There were black white people. There were dark white people such as the Cherokees and Chickasaws. There were New Mexico traders who spoke Comanche and Spanish and cursed white people in both languages, yet wore the clothes of white people. They were the ones who sometimes paid money for white captives. She had heard of it. She had seen them read the names of white people from a piece of paper and inquire about them. She believed that such captives, if paid for, might find their way back to their own homes, but how such a thing might come about seemed vague. The one thing certain about Mexicans of the far south was that they were agelong enemies of the *Nuhmuhna,* once aggressive fighters, now put down by fear, so the Comanches believed. They sometimes joked arrogantly about Mexico: "... down there in the land where they raise horses for us ... where they make silver trinkets for us ..."

It seemed extremely improper for Sunflower to go on the raid. But as she watched her little sister making ready, she doubted that anything she might say would have any effect. It might be that the raid would change Sunflower, who was a good rider but had never before endured such a long ride, who had never patiently suffered the hardships some of the less fortunate of the band had suffered. And surely Sunflower had never realized what it really meant to raid. She might come back changed. In any case, Tehanita determined that when her little sister had returned, she would take her aside and speak clearly to her. She had more confidence now, since the deed with the Lipan. She would take her aside and say definitely and clearly to her, "Sunflower, you know now that you didn't belong on the war trail to Mexico, and the reason is this: You are white. You are my true sister. We are not kin to any of these. We are captives. It is our duty to try and find a way to escape and take your baby and go back where we belong."

It was customary that after the war dance, on a raid about the size of this with twenty braves and four women, the raiders would leave camp quietly in the dark to rendezvous with their leader. This night after the painted braves had danced and all the band had joined in singing war songs and songs of separation, Wide Mouth disappeared, and one by one the others. But the crowd would not allow the handsome young chief's son and his popular wife to disappear without notice. When the two turned to go, some of the singers picked up firebrands to light the way and followed them. Tehanita followed silently with the others, first to the lodge of Sunflower's adopted father, where Sunflower picked up her baby and hugged it; then to the couple's own lodge, where their war-horses and travel horses and weapons waited. They mounted, he with the saddlebags of food and she with his shield and the bow cases. The watchers cheered. The young couple, in response to their well-wishers, yelled and kicked their horses and thundered out of camp, out of the dim light into the darkness. The hoofbeats could be heard going up a rise south of camp, then fading.

As the crowd dispersed, she overheard two old men commenting. One said, "I wish I were his age again."

"Yes. To be his age and to be heading down to Mexico with that wife at his side."

"If he does well, we'll see him leading his own big raids next year."

"I think so. I think something else too. She'll be the wife of a chief, and the mother of chiefs."

The sounds of locusts in the late summer nights were a thing one did not hear without listening for them. They were there for a lonely person: high and keen, low and buzzy, many of them. Some of them came in broken chirps, even and patient and never-ending. Others were a constant, steady background from all directions. Behind the clear sounds were others, more distant. Behind those, still others so far away and faint that they seemed not so much insect sounds as a sigh of the living earth itself. Sounding of locusts was like standing of grass, or spreading of sunlight, or moving of leaves, or blowing of wind, a thing that went everywhere far out across the boundless land and lay ready before the People for them to feel wherever they went; or before such a one who was lonely, for her to feel whenever a quiet time came. It was a help, a familiar thing, a source of wonder. For her thoughts could not follow them to their end; they spread on forever, to strange people, as far as the endless earth herself.

She recognized the sounding of locusts as a part of the unrolled painting Story Teller had bequeathed to her. Some of his paints, he had said, were things like distance or fine rain or coming darkness. Some of them, she recognized, were stranger still, not even known by the eyes: They were things smelled, the damp among the tules at the edge of the water, the old odor of stirred leaves, the many smokes of different woods; they were things felt, the unyielding roughness of a tree trunk, the silent texture of a stone under the hands; they were things heard, like the locusts. The secret of their entreaty lay in their surprise and their familiarity, like the feel of one's own hands on one's own body; it lay too in the suggestion of abundance, in the feel of never-ending extension, so that one's thoughts were led away to unknown distant places where the familiar thing also lived and then returned to surround and penetrate the familiar thing close at hand.

These understandings eased her loneliness, made it bearable.

While most of the band were gone on the fall meat and robe hunt, the young men who had taken cattle to the New Mexico traders returned. They brought back a supply of knives and iron arrowpoints. Lance Returner had owned no interest in the cattle which had been traded, so had no claim on any of the trade goods; however, Burning Hand brought him as a present a fine new knife with a hardwood handle.

During these days the women of the Lance Returner lodge had plenty of work. They worked on the new skins and watched over their meat which was spread to dry, making sure that none of the tied dogs got loose and into the jerky. When some of the meat seemed dry enough for pounding, they went one morning to the rock outcrop where the grinding holes were, going early to be ahead of any other women. The grinding places were upstream beside the creek, just out of sight of camp, at an old camp site no longer used. When they were satisfied that the meat would pound all right, Tehanita and Come Home Early returned to the lodge to bring more.

They found a strange horse tied in front of the large Lance Returner tipi. Come Home Early said, "That's not one of our horses."

"Maybe Lance Returner has come back," Tehanita said. He had left early with some other men to train colts.

"Why would he ride someone else's horse home?"

They did not find Lance Returner in the lodge, nor any evidence that he had come back. Everything was as they had left it except for the horse.

"I know that horse," Tehanita said. "I remember it, but I can't remember who it belongs to. Why would anyone tie it here?"

It was a dun gelding with black mane and tail. He seemed gentle, but alert. He was well formed and of good appearance, except that his skin was black and every small scar or scratch on him showed black through the light hair, giving him a flea-bitten look.

"It's a mistake of some kind," Come Home Early said.

They took two armloads of meat strips and a rawhide box and started back. Then Come Home Early stopped and said, "That's that horse of Burning Hand's, isn't it? Sure, that race-horse, don't you remember?"

She remembered it. The young man had won a big race with it back in the spring, a race against a Kiowa. He had won a wool blanket and other things. "Yes, it's his. I remember it. But why is it tied there?"

Over Come Home Early's simple, round face a smile was growing. "Did he ever make love to you?"

"What do you mean? Of course he didn't."

"It's a marriage proposal, Tehanita."

"No, it's not anything like that," she said. "It must be a mistake of some kind."

Old Woman and Blessed were too much interested in the situation to go on immediately with the work. They went down into camp far enough to sneak a look at the horse, then returned. Blessed was the most intrigued by it. She asked Tehanita, "Did he ever make love to you?"

"No, he certainly didn't."

"Not even a little bit? Didn't he ever talk to you?"

"No."

"Mother, did he speak to Lance Returner? Or did his father?"

"They don't have to talk about it," Old Woman said. "This is the old way. No haggling and trading. Just yes or no."

Blessed hugged Tehanita. "What do you say? Are you pleased?"

"It's just a mistake of some kind, but if it's not, I'm sorry."

"But why, Tehanita?"

"I don't know. It's not much of a horse."

Come Home Early said, "Oh, it may not look like a beautiful horse to a woman, but a man would consider it a great horse. Remember, it's a racehorse. It's fast, too."

"He's a nice young man," Blessed said. "He's really a nice young man, Tehanita."

Old Woman said, "Shush! You girls stop trying to tell her what to do. You think we should talk to Lance Returner about it, Tehanita?"

"No, I think it's a mistake of some kind. I don't want anyone else to know about it. They might laugh at me . . . or him . . . or something."

After a while she gave the excuse of going after some drinking water and returned to camp alone. The horse was still there. Some other horses were tied around at different places in the camp. It was probable that no one had noted the strange horse at Lance Returner's lodge. But she realized that he must be watching from somewhere. He had a small tipi of his own near his father's. She was careful not to look in that direction.

The horse looked at her with his large dark eyes. It was actually a beautiful horse. He blew softly through his nose, then lowered his head and stretched it out toward her as if he were used to being petted. She unknotted the hair rope from the stake, looped it loosely around his neck so that he wouldn't step on it, and tied it there. "Go on," she whispered. "Go on." He stood still. She took him by the mane and led him a little away from the lodge and left him.

Back with the three women, she said, "Someone came and got him. I think he must have belonged to one of the old men, and he made a mistake where he tied him."

She wasn't bothered that only one horse had been offered. Burning Hand and his kinfolk were not rich. One horse from him was equal to three or four from someone else. It was a beautiful horse, too, a fast one, plenty good for a hunting horse or a war-horse.

As for Burning Hand, she thought him by far the best of all the young men. He wasn't handsome, but neither was he fat and sloppy like some of them. She liked the way he held his shoulders, the way he sat on a horse, the look of his face. The sins and cruelty of some of the People were not in him. He could be thoughtful, and probably tender, too. Knowing about his long wait for medicine—still unsuccessful, so the gossip said—made her feel that she understood him, and it made her respect him too. Altogether, he was the finest person of them all, not just of the young men, but the finest of all the People. If she were forced to marry an Indian, she would be lucky if it were him. Or if things had been different, if all her life had not happened as it had, if she had been born of the People, she would have chosen him or would have been full of joy that he chose her.

The offer brought her reason for pride. It was an honorable offer, according to the old ways, though only one horse. It proved that she was not ugly, that a man could still want her for a wife, even if she were as many as twenty-three winters old. And not just any man; he was spoken well of; some said he would turn out to be one of the leaders of the tribe. The offer had its bad side; it made her realize that when she escaped and went back, he would be one that she would hate to leave and never see again. Then, too, there were three or four giggling young girls of the band who thought they were pretty, any one of whom would accept Burning Hand at the blink of an eye. Now that he was once refused he might take one of them. Who could tell what foolishness a man might do when he was ready to marry?

Later that afternoon she went out of camp by herself and stood in the dusk. She could see lingering pink streaks in the sky from the sunset. She could see the trees turning mysterious and dark with the coming of night. She could hear the singing of locusts. These things lay before her, but they were not good and satisfying. A kind of rebellion had come into her. The things did not carry her thoughts away from herself or give her comfort as they had before.

The talk of all the band turned to the south, for Wide Mouth did not come home at the time he had planned. Winter struck, wet and cold. The north wind blew. Talk among the men who had been down that long trail in past years was about the things that might have held up the party: They might be bringing a great drove of horses, might have found a river high out of its banks, might have decided to detour around certain enemy territory. The talk of the women echoed that of the men, and they told each other anxiously, "We shouldn't worry. Wide Mouth's a good war chief. They could be even later than this and still all come back all right. We shouldn't worry."

When the wind had eased and the sky had cleared, the early-winter weather became more bearable. The sunshine made it warm in the middle of the day. Early one morning some of the men began to speak for a council; they thought a party should go south some distance to see if the raiders might be helped. It was a serious decision. The council met at noon.

As some of them had started to gather in Ute Killer's big tipi, two young hunters galloped their horses into camp. The two went to the mother of one of them, and she headed for the council place. They had already lighted the council pipe, but the old woman cried out to her husband, who came out, followed by other council men, all angry at the interruption. The old woman was crying. As her husband started scolding, she said, "They're coming. They come back." It was clear that she must be talking about the Wide Mouth party, since she surely would not have done such a stupid thing as call out to a man in council for only a small matter; but they did not understand at first how she knew anything about it or what had caused her tears. She would say no more. The scolding and loud talk brought the entire camp out to see. Some of the council men pushed their way through the crowd toward the edge of camp.

Then they saw. From the south through the low brush, a small procession came single file, a man leading a horse, another leading a horse, five other men. They looked like strangers. Some of the watching men might have run for their weapons but for the harmless look of the procession. It came slowly and deliberately with all seven men looking at the ground. Not many of the waiting people knew it was Wide Mouth till he was in the edge of camp.

The horses' tails and manes were shorn off short. Each man had one pigtail of hair cut off. They had ashes on their heads and on their shoulders and falling down their clothes. Their clothes were rags. Their faces had been painted with paint made of water and charcoal.

These signs had an unmistakable meaning, which caused the people to stare in horror as they parted to let them pass. A woman began to moan. Then men and women began to pelt them with questions.

"Where are the others?"

"Is it you, Wide Mouth?"

"Where's my son? Where's my son? Do you hear? I want to know where you left my son?"

"Where are the others, Wide Mouth? When are they coming?"

"Where's my daughter? When will she come home?"

The questions came too fast to answer, but Wide Mouth was making no effort anyway. He dropped the bridle reins of his horse and plodded on to the center of camp. There in the loose dirt of the path in front of the council tipi he sat down, his knees up, his arms on his knees, his head on his arms. Several of the women had begun to moan. As he sat, making no effort to explain, the useless questions became desperate and demanding.

"Speak up!"

"Say it, Wide Mouth!"

"Where are the others? When will they come home?"

One of the seven returning raiders who had been at the rear of the procession was speaking. Perhaps he felt more free to speak because he felt less subject to blame than the raid leader. The crowd quieted enough to hear him repeat the thing they already knew was true. "The others—they don't come back from Mexico."

The women began crying in greater earnest. Near Tehanita two women fell upon the necks of one another, sobbing. One of them was Talking Woman, the real mother of Little Wild Horse, who would not come back from Mexico. The other was a wife of Spitting Dog, who kept crooning, "Sunflower! Oh, Sunflower! Little Sunflower!" As Tehanita saw the woman's twisted face, she knew that the emotion was deep, and she understood that some of them probably had loved her sister more than she herself had. The truth was that hers had been a feeling of duty more than love—that and sympathy for a child five years old who had long since ceased to exist.

The families of the seven who returned, particularly the women, persuaded the men to get up from the dirt and go to the lodges where they belonged. Then began a period of mourning, during the first few days of which all the members of the band learned the facts of the unsuccessful raid, through visiting and sorrowful talk. Past the broad Salt River they had gone southwest deep into desert country, then into a land of high mountains. In a valley past the highest mountains they had raided three *rancherías* and taken many horses and much other loot. But as they returned to their nearby temporary camp, just as they came in from the third swift foray, short of arrows, on tired mounts, a great band of Yaquis had hit them. The strange Indians had swarmed down without warning and overrun them, and they had fought desperately for their lives as they fled. Little Wild Horse and Sunflower had tried to escape the losing fight on a single horse, her behind him, and they had been pierced through by a single Yaqui spear. Eight of them had come out of the fight, but one had died of a wound two days later. They had started the long trek north with four horses and had eaten two on the journey.

It was the most severe blow the Mutsani band had suffered in many years. It had lost thirteen first-class warriors and four young women of the age to bear children. The band had left no more than fifty warriors now. The loss also had touched every family group with personal grief.

Ute Killer cut off the small finger on his left hand for his son. He threw away his favorite pipe, his silver medal, his beaver-fur hair wraps. For his daughter, Spitting Dog, who years ago had chopped off a finger in grief for another daughter, cut off the small finger of his right hand. Many women in the camp cut off fingers, slashed themselves on breasts and arms. They sat around in the cold, unwilling to feel the comfort of a fire. In the warm afternoons they came out to sit in the dusty paths and jerked the scabs from their self-inflicted wounds, causing them to bleed again, searching for relief from sorrow in the pain.

Wide Mouth had been a jolly fellow, liked by most of the men. He had a broad face, round shoulders, and long arms. He was one who loved to be in a crowd of people, to slap other men on the back, to call out jests and greetings. He was dumpy and ungraceful, but strong as a bear and willing. But after he came back from the raid, he was a different man, morose, gloomy. He threw away every personal possession except what clothes he needed on his back to keep from freezing; his womenfolk retrieved his things and hid them, with the hope that he would sometime take pleasure in them again.

After a full moon time of mourning, the council decided to move camp, hoping by a change of scenery to brighten their spirits. It was a difficult move in wintertime, though only half a day's ride upstream. The work of moving and establishing camp eased their minds for a time. But sorrow would not be so easily escaped; it followed them and sneaked under the flaps of their doorways. The moaning started over again, and red eyes were seen among the women as they went about the second camp.

For Tehanita it was a moody time. She did not feel the wild grief that some of them felt. They did not seem to expect her to. It was as if they had all forgotten that she had been the sister of Sunflower. Her final reaction to the ill-fated raid consisted of the feeling that a duty had been taken out of her hands. The remaining duty lay to herself; perhaps also, though she couldn't make up her mind about it, to the baby who was half white. Her problem, sadly enough, was eased by the tragedy. She had no doubt of her ability to escape the Mutsani when she had made up her mind just how and when it should be done, nor did she doubt her ability to travel through the wilderness alone, nor did she doubt that the opportunity would come for her to contact white people. There had been times when, had she possessed her present strength and ability and the trust of the Indians she now had, she could have escaped. There was the time she had run after the bluecoats. There was the time the whites had struck the Nawkonis on the River of Tongues; she could have gone after them and trailed them. It was even possible that she could now go back to the Springs of the People, from where a white men's double trail led both east and west; she could go west on it, and if she found no white people, come back and go east. When she found a party of whites, she could spy on them from cover until she had determined whether they were peaceful and could be trusted. Finally, there was always the chance that she would someday come upon that one flat-topped mountain whose appearance was burned into her memory, or upon the Fork River, down which she could travel and find friendly whites.

As for the half-white child, she had time to make up her mind about it, for it was still too young to suffer the hardships of long, fast travel. If she decided it was her duty to take it, it would be better if the child were four or five or six, old enough to ride well. By that time, she was determined that she would find her opportunity or make it.

Grief hung over that winter camp until it was eased by springtime; it was blown away by *yuane,* the warm wind. Ute Killer had sworn at first that he would take a revenge raid to Mexico, but as the winter had progressed, he had changed his vow to say that when he next went to Mexico he would strike hard at the Yaquis. With the spring, they picked up camp and moved north.

9. THE OFFER OF NINE HORSES

SOMETIMES a piercing loneliness came through her from viewing the skies in the summer nights. The other women of the lodge wanted skins over their beds, or a thick leaf roof, but she would move away a little distance to be under open sky, seeking some nameless comfort. If sleep did not come, or any thoughts to occupy her, and if the moon lay up in her place, distant and silent, then she might be taken in by the sad solitude. The companionship of the women during the day would be forgotten and her hoped-for reunion with something called whites would become tenuous and unreal. What were they, the whites? Did they exist at all? She would feel that she was the only living person on an earth that stretched away for mute distances, that the sky and earth were one thing held together by moonlight, that she had no one to turn to, but must face all the emptiness by herself. Sometimes it was almost too much to bear. Then she might rise and pull her robe over nearer the other women, where she could hear their breathing. If, then, Old Woman started to snore, it seemed a comfort and a good thing.

For several winters the band had been out of direct touch with northern Comanches. They had heard rumors of new white forts, of a strange new thing called a fire wagon or *train,* of fighting and treaties, of white buffalo hunters. The rumors were vague, not worthy of belief. But into their camp on the headwaters of Lodgepole River came a delegation of three Indians who claimed to know the truth of these matters.

The visitors were two Comanches, one so fat that he had difficulty dismounting from his horse, and one Kiowa. They wore strange trousers and shirts made of cloth. After they had been recognized, they took the feathers out of their hair and put on black hats such as the white man wears. They wanted a council. Ute Killer sent word around, but when the men gathered, there were too many of them to sit in the chief's big tipi. As they moved out into the midday sunlight, some angry voices rose, from words already spoken by the visitors. In a short time the entire band had gathered, because of the commotion, crowding and tiptoeing to see what was going on.

"Let's be quiet," Ute Killer said. "What do you fellows expect? What can we believe when you come around saying crazy things, especially dressed like that? What is your band?"

"I'm of the great Nawkoni," the skinny Comanche said.

"I'm of the great Yamparika," the fat one said.

"Are you a Kiowa?" Ute Killer asked the other.

He answered in the tongue of the People without accent, "I certainly am. And I expect my brothers to treat me with respect when I come into their village."

"You have respect. You have respect. I'm not criticizing your clothes either, even if I don't understand them. We just want to know whom we're talking to. For a minute we thought you sounded like Penatuhkas. Also, please talk straight so we can understand you."

Some warrior called out, "Have them start over, Ute Killer."

"Start from the first," Ute Killer said.

The three looked at one another. Finally the skinny one said, "We're not looking for trouble. You seem to think we're looking for trouble."

"Well, just start from the first and see if you can explain it."

"It starts with the Treaty of Timber Hill. Can you understand that much?"

"I don't know," Ute Killer said. "What does it have to do with us?"

"It's the last treaty. They say it's the very last treaty for all time. There will be no more."

"Well, I can understand that much. If you want to know the truth, it makes me happy to know that all the treaty nonsense is finished."

"But it's not finished. They say the Treaty of Timber Hill will stand. That's the point. It's the last one. No more breaking treaties on either side, then going to war, then making more treaties."

"We've never made a treaty with the whites nor broken one. Why do you come around here saying it's peace with the white man, telling us our enemies are good people? What has all this to do with us?"

The fat one said, "We didn't come looking for trouble. It seems like you would offer a smoke instead of treating us this way."

Ute Killer said, "There's plenty of time for smoking when we learn who you are and what you have to say. You come in here talking like a bunch of Penatuhkas and acting smart."

The skinny one said softly, "Did you ever think perhaps the Penatuhkas have been right all along?"

"What?"

"I say, could it be that the Penatuhkas have been right from the first?"

Everyone was quiet for a minute. Ute Killer stood stiffly and his black eyes studied the three. He said, "You are messengers from the white people. That's it, is it?"

"No," the skinny one said. "I speak for Chief Horseback. You know him. He made his mark on the Treaty of Timber Hill. This one, he speaks for Chief He Bear. Our Kiowa brother speaks the words of Chief Kicking Bird." He seemed defiant.

"Those are powerful names. Explain what they would do. Tell it plainly, if you can."

"They believe we all come under the treaty. We don't go south of the Prairie Dog Town River or north of this stream here, without permission. We listen to the white agent. He gives us teachers and carpenters to build wooden houses and a white medicine man, also seeds and coffee and sugar and clothes and cloth. He teaches us to plant corn and watermelons and raise sheep, so that when the buffalo are gone, we'll have food like the Wichitas have."

A buzz of angry talk came from the circle of men. Ute Killer said, "I hate to hear that kind of talk from a Comanche. It makes my ears hurt."

Someone shouted, "Let's strip them off naked and send them back where they came from."

Another shouted, "Let's cut off their hair and show them what we think of their words."

The three seemed to edge closer together. The skinny one said, "Well, I'll never bring another message to the Mutsani. You don't offer to smoke. You don't offer a robe to sit down on. You treat us like dogs."

"We're only trying to understand," Ute Killer said. "Who all are in this treaty? We're certainly not."

"Many Comanches, Kiowas, Kiowa-Apaches, Cheyennes, Arapahoes."

Several men around in the crowd shouted: "Who cares about the Cheyenne and Arapahoe? I never liked our peace with them anyway." "Me neither. With their soldier societies and fancy ceremonies and superstition." "That's what I say. Give me a Comanche with his strong right arm and his personal medicine." "A Comanche can fight circles around a fancy Cheyenne."

The Kiowa looked furtively at his two companions, then blurted out, "If that talk is meant as an insult to me, I spit on you!"

"No one insults the Kiowas," Ute Killer said.

"Then what's this talk against warrior societies and ceremonies? I didn't come here to be insulted. I only say what Kicking Bird says, and Chief Cat. You know them. And what many Comanche chiefs say."

"No one insults the Kiowas," Ute Killer repeated. "I just find it hard to believe that those chiefs take the road you say they do. I see no reason for it. Have all those chiefs decided the white man's things are good, or what?"

The skinny one said, "That's part of it. Then also they believe that buffalo are becoming fewer. But most of all it's what they've seen in the land of the whites. Chief Shaking Hand got inside a *train* and went to that land. Chief He Bear did too. He went clear to Washington. They saw things, and it made them say that we must all come under the Treaty of Timber Hill."

"What things?"

"Just things. Many things."

"What things?"

"Strange things. Things of all kinds."

"Don't play games with me," Ute Killer said. "What did they see?"

"Well, the great numbers of the whites and . . . other things."

"What else?"

The skinny man seemed to search for words. "If we told you some of the things, you wouldn't believe them, and it would make you angry again. We didn't come looking for trouble but for your own benefit; yet you hold it against us. Why don't you go east down toward the Wichita Mountains and find some of those great chiefs and ask them?"

One of the men in the crowd pointed at the fat visitor and said, "You claim to be a Yamparika. What about Chief Voice of the Sunrise? What does he say?"

He answered, "I'm not telling any more news. You won't even offer us a robe to sit on."

The skinny one said, "I won't hold it back. We're not trying to fool you. Chief Voice of the Sunrise disagrees with those others. He sends messages to the agent and the white soldiers

to stop piddling around with treaties and come out and fight
like men."

"Ho!" Ute Killer exclaimed. "That sounds like him! Now
we learn something! But tell me; what about the great Kwahadi? What about Black Horse? Wild Horse, and those? Do
you know what they say?"

The skinny one shrugged. "I'm not trying to hold back any
secrets. All those Kwahadi chiefs keep on sending taunts in to
the whites. They all say the same thing: Come out and fight."

"That's the Kwahadi!" Ute Killer said. "I knew it! So now
we begin to see the truth, and all it amounts to is this: Among
the Comanches, a few Nawkoni and Yamparika have changed
their loyalty to follow the ways the Penatuhkas have long followed. Isn't that about it?"

"It's more than a few," the skinny one said, shrugging again.
"But you can judge it for yourself. We've told you what we
know. Are we welcome here?"

"We'll feed you, I guess. Listen, I have a message. If anyone asks you what Ute Killer and the great Mutsani warriors
say, tell them this: We not only invite the white soldiers out
to fight; if they don't come out, we'll come in after them! And
when we come swooping down, let all the poor Indians around
there put on their old-time clothes, lest we take them for white
men."

Much laughter followed these words. The three visitors
grinned a little, then looked at each other and frowned.

When Tehanita had heard the suggestion that the three
men were messengers from the whites, the idea interested her
intensely; but she had decided during the course of the talk
that they were not. One idea, however, stuck in her mind:
Some chiefs had gone into white men's land and found strange
things too powerful to talk about. What could those things
be? It would seem that she ought to know. She tried to remember her home and her life that she had been taken from by
force. What things back there had been strange enough and
important enough that a chief, seeing it, would fall out with

other chiefs? She could not remember her white home as well as she could the empty houses at the Springs of the People and even those were fading. It was a hopeless puzzle.

She was coming into camp with a load of mesquite beans, a bushel or more in a buckskin net bag. The carrying rope was cutting into her hands. She rearranged her fingers and swung the bag to the other shoulder. As she paused, she heard the laughing and squealing of women. She saw someone duck behind a tipi. A girl thrust her head out of a door and called in a teasing voice, "Tehanita! Burning Hand is back." The girl was jerked down inside.

There was much laughter, and a voice from somewhere else said, "Here she comes now."

She could see eyes peeping at her from under the raised sides of tipis all over the village. It was some kind of joke at her expense. Another voice said, "There she goes to her lodge."

She turned the corner and the lodge of Lance Returner was fifty steps straight in front of her. Some horses were there. It was impolite for a bunch of silly women to be making a joke when Lance Returner had important visitors.

Quite a few horses were there. A lariat was tied from a tree at one side of the door across to a heavy stake on the other side, and nine horses were tied along it. They had no saddles or halters, only ropes around their necks. They seemed well-trained horses, accustomed to being tied, but spirited. They carried their heads high on arched necks and kept moving, prancing, occasionally nipping at one another. The tree swayed with their movements. A fantastic idea came to her in explanation, and she put it away; no man ever offered so many horses of that quality for a wife.

They were all different. A deep red pinto, *ehkasunaco,* was on the end, then a yellow roan, *ohaesi,* a clean white, *tawsa,* a yellow with flowing black tail and mane, *dunnia,* a *dupsikuma* with three white feet and a white blaze in his face, a black pinto, *duuhtsunaro.* All of their shiny coats were brushed. They were the most magnificent nine horses she had ever seen together, any one of them worthy of being used for a hunting horse or a racehorse or a war-horse.

It couldn't be what she thought. It was some kind of practice or ceremony that she had never heard of, even though she had been certain that she knew every public practice of the People. It must be some kind of thing done by the Kiowas or another tribe. That was why some of the silly females thought she wouldn't understand and would get excited and get the wrong idea and make a fool of herself in some way. She would pretend she didn't even see the horses.

They were tied so close before the door that one could hardly get through. She swung the carrying bag to her other shoulder and walked, as if that were her usual route, down around the tree and up between the picket rope and the tipi. She ducked down and entered. It was dim inside after the sunlight. Lance Returner sat cross-legged on his robe with a smile on his face, looking at her. Old Woman and Come Home Early and Blessed squatted, also smiling.

She set down her load and said, "The beans are good this year. They seem sweet."

"They're good, are they?" Lance Returner said.

"Yes. And they are not eaten up so badly by the small worms."

"Did you notice anything in front of this tipi?" Come Home Early asked.

"I saw a few horses out there."

Their big grins and the fantastic thought that she couldn't put away were almost unbearable. She cried out to Lance Returner, "What is it? Is it a joke? What is it?"

"What could it be, daughter? It's the biggest marriage proposal I've ever seen. That's what it is."

She sat down on the sack of mesquite beans and glanced toward them, still not sure. She asked him, "Is it for me?"

Old Woman cackled, "No, it's for me. My lover is mad with desire, and he's trying to get me away from Lance Returner."

"Is it Burning Hand? How could he get such horses?"

Lance Returner said, "That young man turns out to be a great raider. He led his braves against a big herd of horses some foolish white men and Mexicans were trying to drive up north. They split the herd to pieces. Then they just took their pick and drove them away. Their families will throw a big feast tomorrow, and the braves will brag about how it was done. They say Burning Hand was a good leader, and daring.

"I tell you, daughter, I thought that young man would never stop bringing horses to our tipi door. I saw him stringing his rope, and I didn't show myself, because I guessed what he was up to. He brought three, and I said to myself, 'Oh, boy! those are fine horses.' I got the women inside so he wouldn't be embarrassed. Next thing I know here he comes with two more. 'Five!' I say. 'He must think my daughter is valuable.' But what? Here he comes with two more. All the camp is watching! And he comes with still two more!

"Tehanita, there are horses, and then there are horses. A few years ago among the Kwahadis, a brave gave nine good horses for a wife, but he got her sister thrown in extra, and they say only three of the horses were really first class. But this! This is like old times when Comanches were rich and generous. They paid high to show the world what they thought of their girl and to compliment her father and to show that they were not afraid of ever becoming poor themselves. Yes, daughter, this is a great day in our lodge."

His words added to the confusion she felt. She was happy that Burning Hand had come back safely, fiercely proud and thrilled about the offer, even forgiving toward all those silly females—they were good-hearted—but how was it all to end? To turn the horses loose was going to break her own heart, she knew, and be a deep insult to the finest young man among the People; and it was clear that it would also hurt her foster father and others.

"It's a big surprise to me," she said.

"It's a big surprise to us all," Come Home Early said. "Such

an offer for a woman your age! You'd better hurry out there
and get those horses and put them with Lance Returner's herd
down the creek, before that young man changes his mind."

"I . . . need time to think. It's such a new idea . . . to be his
wife."

"Ho! It's a new idea," Old Woman said. "She needs time
to think. Listen, I know what a young woman thinks about.
Young lady, you'd better get out there and grab those horses
quick, before he cuts down on the offer. Do you want your
father to lose some of those good horses? Someone may be
talking to Burning Hand right now to bring him to his senses."

She sat on the mesquite beans and stared at her hands. It
was only partly true that she had thought of it before. She
had only thought that he would be the one if it were possible
for her to marry. Perhaps she had even thought that it would
be nice if some way it were possible, as long as it were Burning
Hand.

Lance Returner said, "Tehanita, there was a time when I
would ask myself: 'Is she a Comanche or is she a slave?' Since
you broke the back of the Lipan, I don't ask that question anymore. You are a true Comanche as much as any woman that
ever lived. It is only for me to say a few words as your father.
I don't believe a father should say you marry this one or you
marry that one. It causes girls to elope, and it causes divorces
and bad feelings between families, or even causes bands to
split up. It has happened. So I give up my privilege of ordering
you to marry a certain one. But I want to give you plenty of
good advice.

"I've had my eye on that young man a long time. His grandfather was one of the best and had strong medicine, I tell you
for sure. He was my hero when I was young. Now, his father,
Spitting Dog, well . . . he tries. Listen, maybe you've heard
some gossip. I'll tell you the truth about it. You've got a right
to know. Burning Hand could have got medicine freely from
his father, but he's very serious about it, and they're both too
proud. The youngster wanted to seek it on his own; that's nat-

ural for some boys. Then some men began to make jokes about
Spitting Dog and laugh behind his back; he keeps trying but
his failures hurt him. So now the father is too proud to offer
medicine, and the son is too proud to ask. But don't worry.
The young man is a good raider and a good hunter. He'll get
medicine. Another criticism you may have heard of him: He
doesn't boast enough about his abilities and his accomplish-
ments, as a warrior should. I admit it's not good. Speaking
about one's self gives spirit and confidence and instructs the
young, as well as making a warrior feel good. On the other
hand, we shouldn't forget this: Sometimes, when evil days
come and the way to turn is dim, then, sometimes the People
turn to a quiet one. Who can say? In the years ahead, I believe you'll never be sorry you accepted Burning Hand.

"And think of the horses out there! I know you want your
father to have this fine gift. Those two pintos are stallions.
Already I've been planning what mares to breed them to. I'll
be rich with those horses.

"One more thing: It is proper for a girl to think about food
for her father's lodge in his old age. The best way to do such
a thing is to marry a man who can get meat. Burning Hand is
a good shot and one of the best of hunters in every way. He
knows hunting. Now, I don't want any gossip about what I
am about to say next. I may take a quirt to some wives. But
I've seen a good many winters. I used to be as strong as a
he-bear. I've been a great warrior in this band. I could go on
about that, but I'll stop by saying that I'd have a good chance
to be civil chief if I were ten winters less in age at this time.
Now my arm is not as strong as it once was, and my bones
hurt me on a long ride. At this age I deserve to have a son-
in-law who is good at hunting.

"So that is about all, Tehanita. I would remind you that you
are not getting any younger. Then, in closing, I would have to
say that I'll be sorry to have you leave my lodge, for it's
true. I'll miss you. That's all, unless you want to ask me any
questions."

She knew all at once that she would miss him too as well as the women when she finally escaped. It was true. But that could be faced when she came to it. This offer of marriage had to be faced now, and any answer seemed impossible. "Would it be all right for me to go down to the creek a little while?" she asked him. "I got sweaty picking beans. I want to wash off a little."

"Nine horses tied outside," Old Woman said, "and she wants to wash off a little!"

"Grab the horses," Blessed said. "You can wash any time."

"Wife, stop telling Tehanita what to do. I gave up my right to tell her she must marry Burning Hand. It's up to her. If she wants to make him wait a while, it's up to her. You go wash yourself, daughter, but don't take too long. I think this whole camp is holding its breath, waiting for you."

She went out the door, edged along in front of the horses, and walked with eyes averted down between the tipis toward the women's bathing place. She heard no laughter now but could hear many voices without being able to understand the words. She felt many eyes on her back. Somewhere his eyes must be among those watching her. What was he thinking? She had to discover some kind of answer that would not be an insult to him in front of the People.

She could never give up her duty to escape, to go back. It was a constant duty to herself, perhaps also to Sunflower's child, to work for the day and plan for it. When she went, a winter from now or two winters, she would say to the white people ... she couldn't remember the words; she might need an interpreter to help her tell them. But she would say, "I'm Helen. This is my sister's child. We have come back." They would understand and welcome her. Among them surely must be many good people.

There would never be a Burning Hand among them—many good people, but not a Burning Hand. If.... Except for the half-white child, she would be almost willing to give up her duty to herself and marry him and put the escape away forever. Yes, willing, or even more. The fact was, she wished she could forget the duty.

What was he thinking? He couldn't guess how she was about to insult him. She could imagine the form of his face before her, and it seemed a bitter thing to decide against his wishes. There was no answer to it, and time to think seemed only to make it more sad. Her mind was like a butterfly that has fallen helpless into a flowing stream.

As she splashed water over herself, she thought for a moment that she had found the answer: She would tell her adopted father that she couldn't decide, and he must decide and order her to marry or not marry. She thought about it for a brief, sweet moment, then knew it was a false answer. She knew already what Lance Returner would say. It became clear that she could put neither act away, the marriage or the escape. For herself, she would be willing to be his wife for the winter or two that she stayed—happy to do it that way, even if she lived in sorrow from then on among the whites. But would it be fair to him? What was he thinking?

But the answer to that was clear. For unlike her, he had put his thoughts before the world in the clearest manner, so that no one could doubt what he thought. He might have made an offer of four horses, then added one more to show how beautiful and desirable he thought her; but he had done this reckless, mad thing. Suppose he knew it would be for only one or two winters . . . ? Suppose she said to him, "All right, but in one or two winters, I must leave you and go back. I can't marry you any other way." What would his answer be? She tried to answer for him, and it came out "Yes," but she knew it was her own word instead of his. She had no way to find out what he might say. It would be wrong. Unless she could in some way make it up to him.

She stepped up on the rocks, pushed the water drops from her skin with her hands, and put on her clothes. While doing this, she began to make a solemn vow that was an answer to it.

She would take on a debt that no one else would know, that maybe was foolish, but that would free her from wronging him. She would owe him nine horses. When she went back, some way she would get them and send them by a New Mexico trader to him, along with a message that she was sorry and would have stayed with him except for her duty. White people have strong medicine; somehow, she could get the horses, when she went back in one or two winters. But now she could put that sad time from her mind; it was one or two winters away. Now she must forget it, for this was the most important day in her life.

She walked back to camp. The paths were still empty, the voices still hummed, the nine horses still pranced with heads high in front of her lodge. She stuck her head in the door and said, "Blessed, please come help me lead these horses out and put them with Lance Returner's band."

The three women sprang up and came out. They chattered like a flock of blackbirds. The two younger helped Tehanita. Old Woman hobbled along behind the horses, calling out orders and advice. As they came back, they could see a flock of Burning Hand's relatives out at the edge of camp among the trees, erecting a new large tipi.

She began to gather her things: butcher knife, hide scraper, sewing case, the doeskin dress with the long fringe, the new moccasins she was beading. Old Woman began to cry and say, "My little girl! My little girl!" Blessed said, "We will visit you, Tehanita, and you can visit us." They told her she must find out what cooking things Burning Hand's kinfolk had furnished, and if she needed it, she could come back and get the small cooking pot. Old Woman said, "Oh, my little girl!"

She folded her things into her two sleeping robes and tied it into a big bundle. She took it out in front of Lance Returner's lodge, where the horses had been tied, and stood waiting with her head down, modestly. The camp was alive again with movement, people passing, but none spoke to her. Though they were exclaiming about it all over camp and would gossip about it for months, they pretended not to see her waiting.

It was about sundown when he came. Three women were peeping out of the lodge. Old Woman was sobbing.

"Take up your bundle, wife," he whispered. "Let's get away from here."

10. Message of a Metal Horn

The occupation of her life had been simple hard work, keeping the lodge tidy, mending, gathering and preparing food, tending the fire, tanning skins. Without realizing it she had been the best worker in the Lance Returner lodge, and the reason had been that she wanted to earn a place so secure that she would have their trust and so secure that she could afford to refuse any of their demands to which she did not agree. Now she worked hard for different reasons, out of pride and a keen desire to have everything right for him.

Her life was made out of two kinds of time: when he was with her and when he was gone. When he was with her, she had no worries, hardly knew what was going on in camp or that anything existed except the two of them. When he was away, she worked hard and took great care in the work so that it would engulf her, trying to keep her thoughts from going beyond the time when he would be home again.

If she ground mesquite beans, she always took care to clean out the grinding holes first. She broke the beans and threw away the parts that had been penetrated by small insects. Sometimes, if they were not brittle enough, she would pound all of them to break the skins, then heat them a while over a fire. In taking the meal out of the grinding hole, she would lift it and let it sift back through her fingers, over and over, so that the grit from the stone would go to the bottom. The stringy pieces she threw away; the large pieces she put back to be ground over. Then she would consider how she might cook some cakes of the meal for her husband, whether to pick a few seeds of the pepperweed or try to borrow a little salt. But sometimes in the midst of such occupation, whether she was alone or surrounded by chatting women, this thought would penetrate her busyness: Time is going by, and in a winter or two I must leave him. She would push the thought away and plunge back into the work, but it would hang there, waiting, like some skulking coyote spying on the butchering of a buffalo.

As for Burning Hand, she believed that he was happy and that she had a great part in it. He had started going sometimes to sit with the council, and when he returned from a meeting, he might be fussy, not toward her, but toward the leaders of the band for the way they handled the common business. He and some other braves, on a trip to trade robes to the New Mexico traders, had met some other Comanches they trusted, who had said that all Indians were expected to go out east to a place called *reservation*. After that trip Burning Hand had believed that the camp should post guards at night, should send out scouts at all times, and should have plans for defense against attack or plans for coming together if they were scattered. Evidently he did not argue his views strongly in council, for the reason that the other men understood that he had no personal medicine, though they had respect for him as a hunter and raider. He would come back to the lodge after council and complain about their shortsightedness. She did not object to it, but, to the contrary, was proud that he would explain his ideas to her. She was uncertain as to the exact nature of his concern; it seemed to be mostly about differences between different tribes and bands of Indians. But she had come to realize that he knew more about these matters than she did because he had traveled more.

It was just over a year from the time they were married till she became pregnant. When she was certain that she carried a child in her belly, the disturbing thought that kept trying to enter her mind moved farther away. Her sister's child, now called Bird Wing by her fond grandmothers, was three winters old, nearly old enough to begin learning to ride. But if she, herself, had a baby, she could put off the escape to some uncertain future time, and in good conscience.

Burning Hand was pleased. He had heard somewhere that the reason why so many women lost their babies was that they rode horseback too much. He suggested that she ask his mothers and her mothers about it. When she had asked them all and listened to their experiences, she came back and told him. He then forbade her to ride horseback at all. He would take care of anything that needed doing on a horse.

The permanent camp that winter was at the head of a small stream they called Milkweed Creek. It lay in a valley flanked by low hills upon which grew scrub cedar and mesquite and from which jutted sandstone boulders. A dozen large trees grew along the creek. The camp was beside a pool an arrow-flight distance below a spring, which trickled from layers of a sandstone bluff. The pool had green moss in it, and the rocks in the stream all the way to the water source were damp and green covered. Just upstream of camp, between it and the spring, were the lodges of a dozen Kiowa men who had separated from their own people through some argument.

In early winter a small incident occurred which was an annoyance at the time but was to prove important and may have saved many Comanche lives. A skunk waddled into the center of camp, and a foolish boy shot it, making a stench that would not blow away. They picked up camp and moved it the short distance up to the spring, upstream of the friendly Kiowas.

The weather had been alternately cold and warm. It had rained a rain that turned into sleet, then back into drizzle. The sky had cleared one day, and the ground had dried somewhat but remained damp. On that morning, half an hour before sunrise, a thin fog drifted slowly along the ground, wisping out into the low places. The camp lay quiet and still. The campfires were still banked deep beneath their ashes.

Then the strange sound cut through the dim morning like a blade slashing the air.

The Mutsani people were half awake, half asleep. At the time the sound came, some lay awake in their blankets and robes, languidly recognizing the new day; others slept easily, about to awaken. The sudden, piercing sound had in it the cawing of a crow, the broken howling of a wolf, the scream of a panther; but it had a peculiar metal quality that cannot be made in an animal throat. It was urgent, demanding, sharp. Of the Mutsani people, three fourths, mostly women and children, had never heard a metal horn before. They said to themselves or to those awakening nearby, "What could that be?" Many of the men, having fought the whites or spied on the white forts, knew the sound and guessed its meaning. It rang out once as if stating a harsh message, then repeated, then repeated, but after the first, the sound was mixed into the rumble of approaching horses.

Tehanita moved toward the flap door. Burning Hand was already there, framed in the dim angle of the doorway. He was stringing his bow. He said quickly, "Bluecoats! Run! Right now!"

"I'll get a cooking pot and—"

"Obey me, Tehanita! Take that blanket, nothing else. Go up the hill that way. When you get on top, go west."

When she ran out, he was already going, fitting an arrow to his bowstring, moving toward the crack of guns. She crossed the stream in front of the spring, taking care of her footing on the slick rocks, then ran up through the low cedars. Behind her rose the screams of fleeing women, the shouts of men, the tardy barking of dogs, the noise of horses and guns. Inside her belly she felt a tiny foot kicking, and she slowed to a walk. She looked frequently back over her shoulder as she climbed.

The Kiowas, located half an arrow flight downstream from the Mutsani camp, had taken the first brunt of the charge, had stopped it for the moment. The Kiowa men, having had more contact with whites, all owned guns, and perhaps because they were more suspicious, had some of them slept with their guns loaded. It might have been, too, that they realized more quickly the meaning of the bluecoats' bugle when they blew the charge. The front horsemen had paused in a milling throng, still fed by those oncoming from the rear, held back by those in front, who were slashing with their long knives at the tipis and firing their carbines from plunging horses; held back, too, by their downed horses, for the Kiowas were falling, but were taking their toll. The milling glut of bluecoats had spread around the pool. On the side where the pool bank was steep and undercut, she saw one of them break the bank off and plunge, horse and all, into the water. Somewhere one wounded, frightened horse cried shrilly.

She saw them break the thin barrier of the Kiowa lodges and spill through it into the Mutsani camp, from which women were still running. The old uncle of Bull Heart, who was blind, came out of the tipi where he lived and turned in confusion straight into the first of the horsemen; he went down with one stroke of a blade. She saw a woman trying to carry away a heavy *awyawt,* saw her fall, evidently from a bullet, in the little stream.

She tried to search into the confusion and pick out the familiar form of Burning Hand. The Comanche warriors had moved toward the invaders at first, then had retreated, using whatever cover they could find, had split up and moved up away from the stream on both sides, giving ground slowly. From her vantage point she could see some of them crouching behind boulders and brush. Daylight had come quickly, but now the smoke of the guns was spreading over the floor of the little valley, hanging with the thin fog, drifting gently in the still air. She could not see Burning Hand.

At the top, where the ground became more nearly level, she

paused a minute, reluctant to go on and leave him. But she knew that he, as the other men, was fighting and risking his life to cover the retreat of the women and children. She turned her back on the pop of guns and the faint shouts and moved away from the rising run. Scattered across the winter terrain some hundred and fifty Mutsani people moved, escaping the fight. Most of them walked. She could see four horses, each loaded from withers to rump with women and children. They moved in every direction away from the fight, but many went the same direction she did.

From nearly a mile away she saw the familiar form and walk of three women and ran to catch up with them. It was Old Woman, Come Home Early, and Blessed. Come Home Early was carrying a heavy bundle. The other two carried nothing. Blessed had been crying and her mother was still shaming her for it. They were worried about Lance Returner, for he had recently started wearing a buffalo-horn headdress and might do something rash to show that he deserved it. They were also concerned for their possessions. They had just finished the long, tedious work of preparing hides for new tipi covers and feared that their work might be wasted. They found further reason for their fear when, in the middle of the morning, they looked back and saw smoke rising from the area of Milkweed Creek.

Tehanita did not think of the bluecoats as white people. She actually was not sure what they were nor why they had come out of nowhere with such ferocity. She knew at one time she had thought of them as white people, but now it seemed that her earlier belief must have come from childish ignorance and a lack of some older person to explain such things to her. By her own harsh knowledge, they were like the Lipans. By what she had heard, they were also somewhat like the hated Tonkawas and Yaquis and Utes. Somehow, too, they were like the Mexicans, who might be friends at one place and enemies at another; for the bluecoats had a kind of connection with whites, and certain Comanches evidently had made peace with them. It was confused. The only sure thing was that her loyalty lay with her husband.

About noon Lance Returner came galloping up to them on his best war-horse, leading one of Burning Hand's horses which had been tied near camp. Her heart stopped, waiting for his dreadful news, but he said, "Your husband sends you this horse, daughter."

"He's all right?"

"A little cut. Nothing to worry about."

"Why didn't he come?"

"Because we still have plenty to do. The enemy's pulling back. We watch him. He's cut us off from the main horse herd."

Old Woman asked, "Are our things all right?"

"We'll see. Don't expect too much. The enemy has tried to burn the camp. He's thrown ropes over the tops of the tipis and pulled them down. We'll see. But that's enough questions."

He said that they were to travel straight ahead toward a rounded hill on the horizon. In a low place on this side of it they would find water. They could make it before night. All the women were to gather there, and they must not build any fires. Any fools who would make war in the wintertime might also go prowling around at night and see a fire.

"All the women must obey orders and help each other," he said. "No nonsense. It's a time of trouble. I think we'll come out of it if the weather holds clear."

He was starting to ride away. Old Woman asked, "Are many of the People killed?"

"Too many. But those devils have paid. The Kiowas have suffered more than we. I'll never criticize another Kiowa as long as I live."

He kicked his horse, but reined up and called, "Daughter?"

"Yes?"

"Remember I told you Burning Hand is a good man? He has pulled a bluecoat out of the saddle with his hands and killed him and taken his gun." He kicked his horse again and galloped toward a small group of women and children some distance away.

They tried to get her to mount the horse, but she would not. Finally they put Come Home Early's bundle and Tehanita's woolen blanket on the horse. Then the women of the Lance Returner lodge took turns riding, one at a time, while the other two walked with her. It was not a hard journey, cool enough to make walking easy. They went on without stopping and converged with the others before nightfall at the low place where water stood from the recent rains.

Inside Come Home Early's bundle was an antelope's stomach bag stuffed with pemmican. They ate a little, then it became clear that some of the women had no food for their children. Come Home Early portioned the pemmican out into small cupped hands until it was gone.

When the sun went down, it became cold. The order against building any fire seemed harsh, but they were all afraid to disobey. The women began to pull dry grass to sleep on. Tehanita found the women of the Ute Killer lodge, who were caring for Bird Wing. She thought briefly of bedding with them, but knew she would not feel at ease. She went back to the women of the Lance Returner lodge. The four of them lay on a pile of grass, huddled together, and covered themselves with Tehanita's blanket and Come Home Early's robe. Because of the lack of any kind of shelter or fire, the area did not seem a proper place to sleep. The robe and blanket were too small to cover them well. They could feel the damp cold earth through the crushed grass. When it became dark and they had given their bed a good trial, Blessed said through chattering teeth, "Mother, I'm cold."

"I can't help it. Stop pulling cover."

"I'm cold."

"Get up and run around a minute."

"It's too cold."

"Then shut up. And don't pull cover."

Tehanita slept fitfully with her back to the cold and her belly against the broad form of Come Home Early. She lay cramped and stiff; any little movement seemed to let the cold in faster. The night dragged as if it would never end. Some few of the women could be heard crying for kin they knew had been struck down in the surprise attack or for kin who were missing. She could not sleep deeply enough to forget the cold. At last, feeling that she must do something, she rolled out from under the cover and rose. Her legs were wobbly and did not want to support her. Dawn was coming faintly. She began to walk around among the sleepers, briskly beating her arms against her sides.

Daylight brought no comfort to them. Because there was no food and no fire, the place seemed not at all like home. It seemed a ridiculous place to stay. The proximity of the water hole, now iced over, did not help; they did not need icy water. The children were silent and clung to their mothers. When the sun rose, it helped. They turned their faces toward it and felt its warmth at once. Shortly thereafter some of the children began to play, running and jumping into the piles of grass which had been used for beds. Then some of the women began to chatter and look hopefully back in the direction from which they came.

It turned out to be an agonizing day, with a continuing uncertainty, a hope that something would happen and a fear that something terrible would happen or had already. They wanted something to do. Here and there one said, "This is no place to stay. We can't stay in this place another night." The fact that the sun brought enough warmth to allow them to stop shivering did not help; the order against any fire seemed a severe restriction. They milled about, proposing to one another that they go back, that they move on farther, that they try to build a fire, that they take the four horses and go hunting for food, that someone go back to find what had happened to the camp and the warriors. It was perhaps hardest of all on the half-dozen old men among them and the half-dozen boys who were nearly grown. Here in a time of trouble they found themselves classified by circumstances among the women and children. They stood around frowning, saying little.

When the sun had risen to the middle of the sky, a messenger from Ute Killer rode in. They swarmed around him. He remained mounted and waited for the questioning to die down.

"You are to wait here," he said. He had to wait again for the complaining to die down.

"You are to wait here, and if no one comes, start back at sunset."

"Come back at night?"

"Yes."

"Do they still fight? Are any men killed?"

"No more killed. They set the camp afire, but we forced them back. They went back and met another bluecoat army, and now they camp together. They have our main horse herd, but we burned a wagon that was coming to them yesterday. Also, yesterday the bluecoats dug deep holes and put their dead in them. That's all I know."

There were more questions, but he shouted, "Unless Ute Killer sends orders, start back at sunset," then wheeled his horse and left.

They waited through the long afternoon. Some of them slept. As the sun touched the western horizon, they had already packed their few burdens and were waiting as for the start of a race. They moved out. Tehanita wrapped her blanket around her and went along with the three women, who took turns riding her horse as they had the day before. As darkness came, the stars appeared. They set their course through the winter night on the rising stars.

The walking was not hard, and with the blanket and the exercise she kept warm. Some time past midnight her legs began to feel weary, but about the same time she felt the tiny foot kick inside her; it seemed to give her added strength.

At daylight they came straggling up to the high ground overlooking Milkweed Creek. A young brave rode up the slope to them and shouted, "Gather here! Gather here! Ute Killer is coming!" Shortly thereafter Ute Killer rode out of the valley, followed by Wide Mouth and another young brave. The chief did not have on his war paint, but he sat straight and proud, carrying his bow and his rifle across the saddle in front of him. His voice was fierce when he spoke.

"No grieving! No mourning! Be Comanches! Go down and wrap the dead and put them in the trees. Don't waste time!

"Then pull apart the piles the devil bluecoats made. Save everything that's good and make it ready to move. We move soon."

Talking Woman yelled at him, "What about horses? Will we have horses to move?"

"If my name is Ute Killer, we'll have horses!"

"Can we have a fire?"

"Small fires. Don't make smoke." He turned and rode away, followed by the three other warriors, going downstream toward the northeast.

As the women descended the long slope toward where their camp had been, they were shocked by the appearance of it. The first thing they saw was that all the lodges and every kind of property had been piled in two great piles, now blackened by fire. They could see some good lodgepoles protruding. The wet weather of recent days had left it all damp enough so that the fires had gone out. Then they saw dead horses, bloated, stiff-legged. All the area of camp was trampled by horses' hoofs so that not a blade of grass stood up. As they came down through the scrub cedars and the boulders, they began to see the bodies of the People, scattered and still, lying where they had fallen. They seemed to be proving their deaths by lying so unconcerned in the torn and barren camp.

When they were down to the tiny stream, they saw spots of dried blood on the ground, of horses and people. The count of the Comanche dead would total ten—four women, three children, and three men, but only two of the men were warriors. The Kiowa dead would total twenty-three; they were all gone except for some few who might be riding with the Comanche warriors.

The older women began to say, "Don't waste time!"

They gathered up the bodies gently, and some of the women began to sob and break down. The older ones said, "No grieving! No mourning! You hear? Be Comanches! Don't you hear? Be Comanche women; don't be a crybaby!"

They pulled precious blankets and robes out of the blackened piles and wrapped the still forms in them and tied them. Of the trees strung along the small creek, only a dozen were large, one a spreading live oak, the others cottonwoods, With great labor they hoisted the bodies as high into the tree limbs as they could. They wedged them into crotches and bound them. The work was exhausting. They sat on the ground awhile and did not look up at the burdens carried stark against the sky by the leafless branches.

Some of them began to say, "Let's don't waste time." Their hunger served also to move them. They clawed into the great cluttered piles and found their rawhide boxes of food, some slashed open and spilled, others whole. They ate handfuls of pemmican and raw meal and drank cold water from the stream.

Mixed up in the piles were forty-six lodges, made of some seventy separate tipis. These made up the greater bulk, but in the piles also were bedding, extra clothes, tools and implements, cooking gear, possessions of every kind. Crisscrossed through the rest was the supply of firewood. All of it was black and dirty, much of the wood charred, much of the leather and rawhide stiff and bubbly at the burned edges. All of it was laden with the strong smell of burned hair and hide. It appeared a hopeless mess from the outside, but as they began to pull it apart, more than half of it turned out to be only dirty and otherwise undamaged.

They worked together, pulling out whole tipis at a time, dragging everything far enough so that it could all be spread out. Some of them became sick from losing sleep and too much walking, the hard work, being hungry and eating too fast, and now the smell. They went aside to sit alone until their sickness passed.

Clouds came over the sky as they worked. Over them in the bare trees the bodies appeared dark against the sky. The possibility of bad weather and the inescapable presence of death made them cooperative and generous with one another. One of them would say, "That's my pole, isn't it? I think I recognize it."

"No, I think it's mine. It's one of my smoke flap poles. I trimmed it down thin. See?"

"All right."

If a difference of opinion about ownership arose, the one who had already found the greater amount of her property gave in quickly. To those unlucky ones who had lost nearly everything they all gave equipment.

Tehanita found fourteen of her twenty-two lodgepoles; the others were burned beyond use. Her tipi cover was partly burnt. She trimmed the bottom, took out one hide, and altered the whole thing so that it would cover a smaller tipi. The painting and horse-tail streamers had burned off Burning Hand's shield so that she hardly recognized it, but it could be repaired. One of her iron cooking pots was broken. She had owned a small cedar box in which she kept certain treasures—beads, a silver chain given her by her husband, a tiny flint arrowhead, two tightly rolled dresses (small, one blue, one brown, now faded, so old that they could not be straightened out without tearing). She found a piece of the broken box but nothing that had been inside it.

By the middle of the afternoon the wind had turned so that it came from the north. It grew stronger. They hurried their work, getting everything ready to move. Some of the women began trying to strike a fire, sparking flintstones into touchwood or into a powder made of broomweeds mixed with gunpowder. Finally one of them succeeded. They fed the fire with dry twigs and took firebrands to start other fires in the lee of boulders where the slope of the hill began. Fine snow began to whip in the raw wind. It melted on the ground at first, then began to draw thin white contours at the whim of the wind currents. The People gathered in huddling groups, wrapped with covers over their heads, with the wind-whipped fires for company.

In this manner they waited. One woman had a sister among the dead, and that sister's baby son. Her eyes dwelt on the small bundle high in the wind in the leafless tree, and she began to talk to herself. When she began to talk loudly enough that they could understand her, the woman was saying, "He's too little. It's too cold. He's so little, it's too cold for him. He's too little." She came out of her covering robe and moved toward the tree, and they had to catch her and bring her back to the fire and make her turn her head away from the trees.

Darkness closed in. The night was dominated by the wind sound. They could see nothing but their small fires, blown to intensity by the coursing wind. Late in the night the warriors came, shouting to identify themselves. They were tired and cold but jubilant with the news they brought. They had taken back the horses, which now were herded together in the shelter of the banks just down the valley.

Tehanita searched among the men, calling his name until she found him. She huddled together with him under all the robes they now possessed. He said it was the first time he had been warm in three days. The next morning she saw that his jacket was cut over the shoulder and that he had bled. He said it was only a little stiff.

That morning they quickly loaded the blackened remnants of camp onto the shivering horses and went south. The north wind blew unabated, but the snow had stopped falling. It lay in a streaky film over the bleak land. They moved southward solemnly, all walking to avoid the brunt of the wind, shoulders hunched, seeking a new winter home.

11. Story Teller

THE REMAINDER of that winter was difficult because of their inadequate shelters, but the trouble which they feared most, shortage of food, did not develop. Buffaloes were plentiful. The men could go out any day and kill one within a few hours' ride from camp. The beasts acted strangely. Some of them were skittish, so wary that they stampeded at any slight noise or unusual smell; others seemed unnaturally tame, blind to danger, stubborn. Some stood a half day at a time and bellowed. Others wandered listlessly. Sometimes from no more threat than the shadow of a hawk moving on the ground a group of them would gather, cows on the inside, bulls forming a protective circle with horns outward, and they would stand, ready and nervous, long after the harmless shadow had passed. Altogether, they acted somewhat as a herd may act after it has been depleted by a hunting party; yet this was no single herd; all the buffaloes which the Mutsani hunters encountered acted in a strange, disturbed manner. Rumor had it that white hunters had been thick the past year in the country around Arrowpoint and Wild River, but the Mutsani men did not understand how the influence of white hunters could be so widespread.

As soon as the danger of sudden severe weather had passed, when the prairies were faintly tinged with new green, they planned a skin hunt. The hair on the hides would be loose, and they would be unfit for robes, but would make good tipi covers to replace those lost and damaged by fire. The men discovered a concentration of buffaloes a half-day's ride from camp. Every member of the band capable of working would take part in it.

Tehanita was heavy and clumsy with child. She walked and led a pack horse. In the pack, in addition to the things necessary for a temporary camp, she carried a little blanket of rabbit skins, powder made of the soft rot of cottonwood, and a cradle-board made for her by the women of the Lance Returner lodge. She knew that her time was near.

They made a crude camp that afternoon. Some of the band danced in anticipation of a good hunt; others proceeded to get a full night's rest. Tehanita slept well after the long walk, but when she rose in the morning, the first pangs of labor began. She went and spoke privately with Old Woman, asking her, "Would you not follow the hunters today, but stay here with me?"

"I guess I could. Why?"

"I've had some pains. It might be my time."

"Why, that's good! Why are you whispering? What's the secret about it?"

"I want Burning Hand to go ahead and get some skins and not worry about me."

"Oh, pish! It does them good to worry. Well, he wouldn't be any help anyway. Men are useless in some things. As soon as I get Lance Returner and the girls off, I'll help you."

She went back and prepared food for her husband and helped him get ready to go. Because he had his mind on the hunt, she was able to conceal her pains from him. As soon as the men rode off, Old Woman came to her and asked, "How many pains since daylight?"

"Six times, I think."

"Fine. We have time. Get your hatchet. We'll make a birth lodge."

They moved a little distance from the temporary camp and began to construct a shelter of mesquite brush. When she felt a pain beginning, she lay down and allowed Old Woman to work alone; when it passed, she rose and went back to work. One of the wives of Spitting Dog saw them and realized what was going on; she came hastily to help. So the adopted great-grandmother and one of the paternal grandmothers of the coming child competed with each other in preparing for its arrival. The brush had no leaves so early in the year. They covered the shelter with two robes. The dirt floor they chopped up to soften, then covered with sage and a robe for a bed. To Tehanita, it seemed that it was done none too soon, for the pains were leaving her too weak to work.

In the birth process she lost track of time. It was not so painful as it was tiring. They put warm rocks against her back and made her drink hot water and squeezed on her stomach and continuously spoke words of encouragement and ordered her to push. When at last it was down, she was exhausted and fell into a kind of patient half sleep with a drowsy awareness that there was news to be heard, good or bad, but that it would wait and be the same whenever she was ready to open her eyes and inquire.

Some time later she became aware that the two old women in the birth lodge with her were giggling like two girls. She heard the voices of her husband and Lance Returner and Spitting Dog calling anxiously from some distance away.

"Let them call one more time," Old Woman said.

It was Lance Returner calling: "Has anything happened in there?"

She opened her eyes and saw the two women make themselves serious and dignified in manner. Old Woman lifted the edge of the lodge cover slightly and shouted, "A new Mutsani warrior has come!"

She held out her arms toward Spitting Dog's wife, who was

holding the small bundle in the rabbit-skin blanket, and they put the new child on her breast. It was afternoon. Spitting Dog came to burn a bit of sage in the birth lodge and make a bit of medicine, but she thought his first reason for coming was to see his new grandson. She rested all the remainder of that day and that night. The next morning she got up and made food ready for her husband. That day she worked, hanging meat to dry and staking out skins, while the baby in his cradleboard was propped against a tree.

After four days they packed everything and started back toward the permanent camp. She rode horseback with the cradleboard on her back, guiding her pony near behind her husband. He said to her, "I guess it's good to be riding again?"

"Yes."

"It would kill me not to ride for nine moons."

"Why did you give away a horse yesterday?"

"Why did my father and Lance Returner each give away a horse? It's not their son."

After a while he asked, "Is he heavy?"

"No, he's light as a feather."

"What do you think we should name him?"

"He's too little for a name. We have plenty of time."

After a while she asked, "Why do you keep looking around at us and grinning?"

"I can't help it," he said.

That summer Ute Killer thought of revenge. He declared that he was ready to make a great raid and wipe all the white forts off the face of the earth. Other leaders of the band thought they had taught the bluecoats a lesson, for the bluecoats had lost several killed and wounded warriors at the Milkweed Creek fight and had lost a wagonload of supplies. Perhaps they had learned better than to make war in wintertime. It might be as well to leave the forts alone and make only small occasional raids against the whites as they had done in the past. The issue was decided by their shortage of lodgepoles. Every tipi was small and cramped, and some families which had lived in two or three tipis now had only one. Altogether several hundred poles were needed, and they did not want to go through another winter without them.

They moved west into a canyon called Cedar Draw along whose red clay slopes grew cedar trees. They strung their lodges out in a long string in the center near the stream, for the trees which were tall and straight enough for lodgepoles were widely scattered and each family wanted to be near some suitable timber. When they were settled in this camp, the men would go up into the rough ground to cut and trim trees. The women tumbled and dragged the logs down near their lodges to work on them. Each had to be peeled and thinned down so that the butt end was as little as half of its original size. Then, during the dry, hot days of summer the poles needed to be turned in the sunshine and sometimes needed to have water put on them so that they would become seasoned without cracking and splitting. Tehanita went about the work with the child on her back, singing to him.

Buffaloes were still present in the country in numbers greater than usual. The men rode west and met the New Mexico traders and promised to bring a great many robes for trading when the buffalo hair would become good at the start of winter. They wanted no trinkets or ornaments, only guns and cartridges and powder and lead. They wished to arm every man of the band with a gun.

As the weather cooled, the band kept scouts out to watch the condition of the buffaloes and keep up with the location of the larger bunches. The scouts brought in favorable reports. The entire band began to prepare for the winter meat hunt and for a large harvest of hides. But on the day before the hunters would depart, a scout brought in bad news: Bluecoats had come and made camp in the center of the proposed hunting area.

Ute Killer was furious. He raved at first against the council men who had argued against his raid on the white forts. Then he ranted against the bluecoats themselves, because of their lack of any sense of propriety; the big fools seemed not to realize that there is a time for hunting and another time for war; they seemed not to realize that horses cannot carry men on the warpath when they have nothing to eat but winter grass. Buffalo Bones, the eldest active warrior, pointed out that the bluecoats brought wagonloads of corn for their horses to eat. At this Ute Killer lost his anger and began to seek a way to hunt without being detected by the enemy.

Scouts watched the bluecoats; others went out to the north and south to seek concentrations of buffaloes a long day's ride or more away. For several days riders went in and out of camp. News came. A wagon train had brought supplies to the bluecoats. Another group of bluecoats had Tonkawa scouts who were painted for war and who daily ranged farther from their camp. The Mutsani camp was in danger of being discovered. Ute Killer met with the council, and they reluctantly gave up the hunting plans and ordered that the entire camp pack up and prepare to move.

They moved west, over ground ever rougher and higher until they came out on the top of the broad *Llano Estacado*. To Tehanita the move seemed right, even though in early winter they were moving away from the buffaloes. To go with her baby and her husband and her new lodge, made with long labor, away from potential danger seemed the only thing to do. The treeless tableland was barren and empty this time of year. It was so flat that they seemed traveling always in a shallow dish, and one could imagine that the same monotonous land extended on forever.

They came into the broken valley called the Yellow Houses and made winter camp.

The New Mexico traders were there with guns ready to trade for robes. For several days argument arose. The warriors who had no guns wanted to take the guns and bring robes

later. The traders refused. At first they nervously asserted
that, though they trusted all Comanches completely, the Mutsani might never again have the opportunity to make robes and
deliver them. Challenged to explain, they could not, but would
only insist that trading was bad and confusing and bad feeling
rose from it unless both sides presented their property at the
same time. Some of the warriors threatened to take the guns
by force, and the traders asserted that, if such a thing were
done, they would never again bring anything to trade, not even
cooking pots or arrowpoints or knives. The trouble was finally
settled by an agreement that the traders would bring the guns
back the next summer; they would trade for flint hides, taken
in the spring and untanned. The traders then departed hastily
toward the west, prodding the oxen which pulled their heavy-
wheeled carts.

The winter camp lay below a cliff six or eight times as tall
as a tipi. From the base of the cliff gushed a stream of good
water. In the white and yellow rock outcrops on either side of
the valley were many caves. By digging into the floors of these
caves, a person could uncover pieces of matting and pieces of
pottery, but the Comanches believed it was proper to stay away
from such places rather than risk offending the spirits of people
who had lived there.

Prospects for the winter seemed bad. There was little wood,
only the trunks and knotty roots of scattered brush. The
women gathered bags of antelope chips for fuel; they made
small, hot fires that glowed rather than blazed. The men were
surprised to find a few buffaloes up and down the valley. They
had believed that the heavy animals never came this far west;
it was another example of the strange behavior they had noted.
They also found and killed an occasional bear, usually around
the caves. Their primary game was the pronghorn antelope.
At first they went out on the flat plains to find these fleet animals around the shallow lakes. As the lakes dried up and winter became more severe, the antelope were driven into the

valley. The hunting of them was difficult because of their speed and the lack of cover for concealment. It required fast horses and cooperation between hunters, but by going out every day except the coldest, the men were able to keep meat in their lodges.

Tehanita carried the child on her back whenever she left the tipi. She did not go up onto the plateau country with the other women to dig roots, but kept the children of other women and in return received small portions of what they gathered. This practice started her on another activity: she started telling stories. After she had told a few, the children began to ask for them; then, whenever Burning Hand was away, they would come to visit even when their mothers were at home, little Bird Wing and three or four younger than she and three or four older than she.

Tehanita told them stories about the Little People and about wonderful animals of long ago such as the bird so heavy that he left tracks in stone. She told about battles, such as the one when it rained and the enemies' bowstrings became wet, but the warriors of the People removed their bowstrings and protected them in their armpits and won; about the great victory on the Wichita River when the Apaches were forced to leave the country. She told about the strange enemy warriors long ago who wore iron clothing, which could not be penetrated by an arrow, but who, if they were thrown from their horses, were too heavy to run or defend themselves. She told about a long trip by Comanche raiders to a land where the birds had brilliant feathers and little men danced in the trees and would not answer questions even in sign language.

As she spoke to the children and saw their small round faces all turned to her and their brown shining eyes intent upon her, her heart seemed to become large toward them, and she felt it important that she tell the stories vividly so that they would always remember. She told the meanings of the stories with expressions on her face and aided her words with movements of her hands. She told them about how the first buffalo came. She told them how the Great Spirit looked down on the People and saw them using dogs to carry their burdens, so he sent them strong, fast god-dogs, which they came to call horses. She told them stories about the great *Kahwus*.

Seeing how the children hung on her words and movements, finding herself inspired by her listeners as well as her stories, and perhaps remembering the old man who had been her teacher, she sometimes became carried away. When she told the story about the women who cried so much they started a river, she felt tears in her own eyes. As she was feeling them come down her cheeks, she looked at her son, propped there in his cradleboard, and his little eyes were wide and round, staring at her. His mouth was screwing up to cry, though he was too young to have understood a word of the story. She laughed along with the children, at the baby and at themselves.

In the spring the band moved east down into the vast buffalo range on the rolling prairies. They moved slowly and sent out scouts to search for any enemy and for concentrations of buffalo. They had no trouble finding enough buffaloes to supply fresh meat, though the animals still acted strangely disturbed. Then they began to find wagon tracks and the places where white hunters had taken buffalo hides.

One afternoon they moved toward the crest of a ridge. The light spring wind bore a strong odor of rotten meat. They could see buzzards circling high ahead of them and ravens rising. On the crest Ute Killer signaled for a halt. The procession moved ahead to the high ground so that all could see what those in the lead saw.

Straight down ahead of them were the carcasses of a hundred skinned buffaloes, dead half a moon. Clumsy buzzards scurried away from their meals, wings outstretched, puking to lighten themselves so they could fly. Ravens rose, cawing. Some of the carcasses were greatly swelled so that the legs stuck out like short spikes. Other bodies, torn by the carrion eaters, seemed skinny and small in comparison with the woolly unskinned heads of the dead beasts. All of these remains lay in a space no larger than a camp site of the band.

Out to their left some distance a similar bunch of killed and skinned buffaloes lay. Out to their right, another. Farther away, other bunches. Over each, the ravens flapped, quarreling. The land ahead fell away in rolling prairie; it was gray in color from old grass, with a fresh green tint from new grass. Against this light background the still, dark buffalo heads lay in scattered patches. Where they were hidden by the swells of the land in the distance, their location was revealed by ravens, which were like black flecks of dust in the air. As far as the Mutsani band could see, dead buffaloes lay on the ground, altogether enough to have fed the entire Comanche People five winters. Their nostrils were accustomed to the smell of bad meat, but the light wind was so saturated with putrid odor that they were sickened.

Ute Killer was angry, but not loud as he sometimes became. He gazed on the scene a long time, then turned the procession crosswind toward the place where they would make night camp. He called a council, but every man came to listen whether or not he usually sat in council, and all the women and children gathered. Ute Killer stalked back and forth in front of them. His face was dark.

He blurted out, "Now, they have pushed me too much! Tomorrow we move west to a good camp for the women. Then ... war!

"I'm going to wipe these white hunters off the face of the earth. I'm not going to raid them a little; I'm going to destroy them. They've gone too far!

"No man in this band is forced to smoke with me when I plan a raid. We're Comanches. But I make this a point of honor. We've allowed our brothers, the Kiowas, to hunt here, and the Wacoes and Wichitas and Cheyennes and Arapahoes. But we didn't invite the white man; he means to take his hunting ground wherever he pleases. Besides being wasteful, he means to insult us. So, I say let every brave of the Mutsani think about war and prepare to follow me."

Lance Returner and several others spoke. They agreed with all the civil chief had said. They asked only that a good camp be found for the women and that a few braves be left with the women for scouts.

That night was clear and still. They could hear the voices of the coyotes out in the direction of the area where the multitudes of buffalo were slain. The voices came in great numbers out of the distance, faint but clear, some yipping, some howling. Some seemed to be singing; some seemed to be crying. The beasts could be heard all night. The camp dogs answered them and whined nervously, so that no one could sleep. The old people who were superstitious said it was a bad sign, that when coyotes talked to each other in such great numbers they might cause trouble. "They're up to some devilment," they said.

The next morning the band left off their buffalo hunting and headed west. They traveled two days to Goodwater Creek, then up it into the rough breaks and to a good camping place. The men readied themselves and their weapons while the women established camp.

Tehanita did not want her husband to go, but he said, "I believe Ute Killer may be right. The white hunters may not stop till they have killed every buffalo. I'll go with him." He propped up his shield by the door of the tipi, and she turned it frequently during the day so that it would squarely face the sun.

A war dance was held, but there was little laughter or bragging. They agreed that the warpath they were taking was the most serious they had taken for many years. Spitting Dog was to be left in charge of the camp. He would have the aid of two or three other old warriors and as many half-grown boys. The

war party, fifty strong, rode away one morning just after dawn
behind Ute Killer.

During that time of waiting the children came often to ask
for stories, and she was glad to oblige them. It occupied her
mind. When she was alone, she tended to think not only about
her husband's safety, but about the passage of time. An idea
nagged her: that the two or three winters she had thought
about when she married were past and that her child was daily
growing toward the time when he would be old enough to
travel easily. She did not argue with the idea, but thought it
only fair that it should pass from her and not nag her until its
proper time of fulfillment.

She took the child from his cradleboard so that he could
learn to walk. When no one else was around, she talked to
him often. To further occupy her time she began the braiding
of a halter of horsehair she had been saving; it would be a
present for Burning Hand.

Being in charge of camp seemed to worry Spitting Dog. He
spent a great deal of time in his lodge making medicine. Sometimes he came out and walked along the paths, frowning; if
anyone spoke to him, he responded with a crabby answer. As
days passed, he often came out and stared at the sky, searching for omens in the pattern of rising smoke or in the flight
of birds. He might be heard to mumble, "That's good," or,
"That's bad," frowning at one sign as much as the other. He
would make no prediction about the absent warriors.

When the men had been gone more than half a moon, the
two boys who served as lookouts guided into camp two strange
Comanches. They wanted to see the chief of the band. The
boys took them to the lodge of Spitting Dog, and the women
began to follow along to find whether the visitors brought
news of their men.

Spitting Dog was in bad spirits when he came out. One of
his wives had been combing his hair and had finished only one
braid; the other half of his hair straggled loosely down his

skinny back. He came out, squinting at the sunlight, and said, "What is it? What's the trouble? What is it?" He yelled at the women, "Go to your lodges," but none of them left.

The strangers had stood in silence, holding their horses, until Spitting Dog was brought out. Then the one in front, a heavy man who wore a red cloth shirt, asked, "Where is the civil chief? Is this Ute Killer's band?"

"I'm in charge around here," Spitting Dog said. "What do you want?"

"Are you the civil chief?"

The other stranger, looking around, asked, "Where are the men?"

The one in the red shirt said, "Yes, where are the men? Are you the civil chief?"

Spitting Dog said, "I'm an important man in this band and a holy man besides, and I'm in charge of this camp. If you want to know anything, ask me, and if you want to be made welcome here, you'll have to state your business."

"We don't care about the welcome," the one in the red shirt said. "Is this Ute Killer's band?"

"Yes."

"Where is he?"

"Who wants to know?"

"I do."

"Well, he's away right now. You can't see him."

"When will he be back?"

The humor of Spitting Dog was not improved with the conversation. He said, "Listen, young man, I've got better things to do than stand out here in the hot sun arguing with you. What's wrong with young men these days that they don't show more respect for their elders?"

"I hope Ute Killer's not off on a raid."

"What if he is? What's that to you?"

"I've got a message for him to go east. You ought to be heading east right now."

"You might say an order instead of a message," the other stranger put in.

"Yes, I've got an order for him to go east right away."

"Who's sending orders to Ute Killer? The Great Spirit?"

"It's nothing to joke about or be angry about either. The white colonel says all Comanches must go and camp east of Cache Creek. Then he will know that you don't want to be destroyed. Do you know where Cache Creek is? Go east from Wolf River, past the mountains of the Wichitas, then—"

"Stop!" Spitting Dog said. "Are you going to tell me where that creek is? I hunted along Cache Creek when you were still fouling your cradleboard. What is this? Listen, young man, don't get me angry. What band are you, anyway? Your accent is Kotsoteka, but your words are Penatuhka."

"That doesn't matter. All Comanches must go with the Penatuhka now. You must go and make camp east of Cache Creek."

"So! this is white-soldier business, is it?"

"It is."

"You think you can come in here with that talk, and we won't harm you, because some of the warriors are gone. Is that it?"

The two strangers consulted together in low voices, then the one in the red shirt said, "It's only this, grandfather: The white colonel doesn't wish to harm friendly Indians, but he cannot tell who is friendly. Take these people to the reservation and on east to Cache Creek; let the warriors follow you later. You ought to obey."

"I'm not your grandfather! I'm not kin at all to such as you. I'll give you an order, young man. It's what Ute Killer would say. I would advise him to say it, and I'm sure he would say it. Tell the white soldiers to come out here and camp beside Goodwater Creek. Right over yonder. Then we won't bother them. Tell them to hurry and do it."

The two men consulted again in low tones with one another.

"Go out of camp to whisper!" Spitting Dog said. "You've

got no more manners than two buzzards. Get out of this camp to whisper!"

The one in the red shirt said, "Well, we've made it plain. But I should tell you the direction of the white soldiers so you can watch for them." He began pointing and turning as he spoke. "Colonel Miles. Colonel Davidson. Colonel Buell. Colonel Mackenzie. Major Price." When he stopped naming the strange names, he had turned all the way around and had pointed in every direction. He and the other stranger mounted their horses. He looked at the women and children and asked, "Does anyone know the location of the Kwahadi camp?"

Spitting Dog yelled, "We don't know and wouldn't tell you if we did!"

They rode back down the creek.

The women gossiped about the "order." A few of them were afraid. All of them wished their men would come home.

That summer became extremely hot and dry. Far out on the prairie, dusty whirlwinds could be seen winding their way. Goodwater Creek diminished until water could not be dipped from it except from certain pools in its bed. Then swarms of grasshoppers came through the country. They crawled thickly over the cottonwood trees, which were the only good shade trees, and stripped the limbs bare so that they looked as they had in winter. The women put up shades of hides out in the open places. There, during the Moon of Bulls Fighting, the children played in the sand with captured grasshoppers, putting harness on them made from horse and buffalo hairs, making them carry little packs and pull little burdens.

12. RETURN OF UTE KILLER

THEY BROUGHT Ute Killer back on a robe suspended between
two long poles, carried front and rear by horses. He was badly
wounded, with two bullet holes through him, one in the chest
and one in the bowels. They brought him gently, slowly, carefully over the rough ground.

She saw the procession and saw, without counting, that most
of the warriors were there. Her eyes probed frantically for the
familiar form of her husband. None of the rest of it mattered
until she saw him; he was walking beside the rear litter horse.
Lance Returner and Wide Mouth walked on either side of the
lead horse, Buffalo Bones and Burning Hand on either side of
the rear one.

Ute Killer could not speak. Most of the life that was in him
seemed to be in his dark eyes. They shone out of their sunken
sockets like those of a trapped eagle who has been tied to a
stake in the ground and has flown against his thongs until he
has learned to be still. The chief looked so strange lying helpless on his back that most of the women gave no attention to
the other casualties suffered by the band, which were four warriors killed and one wounded and barely able to ride. Those
were mourned only by their immediate families.

The chief was laid on a bed under a shade in front of his lodge. Talking Woman, his oldest wife, took charge of his care. People brought and offered robes and other unneeded items. Some women brought soups or teas, but the wounded man could take nothing by mouth. Some of the women found occupation in standing back and fanning pieces of stiff hide or in standing guard with long thin branches with a few leaves on the end to drive the flies away. Into the large wounds in his back where the bullets had emerged, Talking Woman and her helpers stuffed fine grass. They gathered quantities of prickly pear leaves and singed the thorns off; of some they made a paste for his wounds; others they peeled and bound whole over his wounds. Sometimes they asked him questions. "Are you too hot, Ute Killer?" "How do you feel?" "Do you think you could take a little water?" "Do you want more under your head, Ute Killer?" But he said nothing.

Spitting Dog began to make serious medicine for the cure of the chief, in his own lodge and in the vicinity of the sickbed. Word went around that he had vowed to abstain from both food and water until it was clear that his medicine had succeeded or failed.

That night and the next day the account of the raid passed from one to another, as such stories pass, until all the members of the band knew it. The men had struck with swift success at two different groups of white hunters, taking them by surprise. Then they had attacked a group of white hunters who could not be surprised, who could not be drawn out of their defense positions, and who owned guns which would shoot a great distance. Ute Killer had stuck his lance in the crest of a small hill above them, had hung his shield upon it, and had stood there in the open to inspire his men, shouting taunts at the whites. A bullet had caught him and slammed him to the ground. He had risen and, holding himself upright by clinging to the lance, had removed his moccasins and thrown them away, then stood, shaking his fist and cursing them, calling them white cowards, worse than Utes, worse than Tonkawas.

A second bullet had laid him flat so that he could not rise. After that Burning Hand had led a charge to draw the whites' attention while two other braves rode onto the little hill and picked up the helpless chief and withdrew him to safety. It had taken four days to bring him home.

The most powerful medicine Spitting Dog had for curing wounds was buffalo medicine. The day after they carried Ute Killer home, he brought his materials and made all those near the wounded man move back. He smoked his long bone pipe and blew puffs to the sun and the earth and the moon and the buffalo. He put on his hood made of the headskin of a buffalo and sang prayers. After a time, he removed his hood, took the dressings from Ute Killer's wounds, and sucked on them by the use of a buffalo-horn instrument. After another chant, he placed on top of the wounds a hard ball from a buffalo's stomach and a magic bone that had turned to stone. He drew the tail of a buffalo over Ute Killer's face. After many passes with the tail and a long period of incantation, he replaced his materials for this medicine back in their bag and allowed the women to come forward and replace the dressings. Through it all Ute Killer remained passive, inert.

Spitting Dog kept up his work, even though he left the side of the wounded man. That evening and night he passed along the paths of the camp, rattling his buffalo-scrotum rattle and mumbling his prayers over and over. Of the medicine man, the people whispered, "If he can save our chief, we ought to forget every mistake he's made in the past." "Well, he's doing his best." "I'm afraid it's too much for any medicine; his inside parts are torn up, and he has lost his blood."

On the second morning, Ute Killer's eyes dimmed. He died without speaking. The older men who were his special friends and kin prepared his body for burial. They dressed him in his finest clothes with his eagle feathers and other war honors and ornaments. His knees were folded to his chest, his face painted with vermilion, and his eyes closed with clay. Around him a red wool blanket was wrapped, this secured by wrappings of rawhide thong.

Without further ceremony they held him seated upon his best traveling horse and proceeded west up Goodwater Creek, the entire band following on foot. Talking Woman carried his shield and lance and bow. Others carried gifts for him. His best war-horse was led carrying no burden. Both horses had been brushed and painted, their manes and tails tied with bits of bright cloth. The procession moved far up into an area of rocks and stunted cedar to a slope so steep that it was difficult to climb. They tied the two horses at the bottom and carried the body up to a place where a rock ledge protruded, with a cavelike hollow beneath it. With hatchets and knives and bare hands they enlarged the hollow so that they could set the body in it, facing east, with the gifts and his weapons. Then, with great labor and difficulty because of the steep slope and the heat, they brought rocks and stacked them so that they closed the hollow. The two nervous horses they tugged and pushed up the slope, patiently; the animals scrambled and slipped. Up by the tomb, they secured the two horses to a gnarled cedar, threw them, and cut their throats.

Most of the band had watched from below. Now they began to straggle back toward camp. Talking Woman and the other two widows of the chief and his sister climbed up to the tomb to lie down and weep.

Back in camp a sense of awe and uncertainty hung over their actions. The young people of the band had always seen Ute Killer as a mighty chief, with great power. Those his age and older remembered when he was young, remembered his short-comings, his coming to power; they had felt it their right before this to think of him as an ordinary man, even to criticize him. But now, having seen his death and burial, they realized that he had been a great chief, like one of those mighty ones of legend. Any one of them who remembered having disagreed with Ute Killer or having argued with him was ashamed of it and wondered at his own audacity. They went about their

activities in camp quietly. Spitting Dog took the medicine bundle of the dead chief and placed it in the creek. They took
down the big tipi of Ute Killer, which had long dominated the
center of their camps, and burnt it along with other of his
possessions. They wandered through the camp or gathered in
small groups, talking in hushed tones.

A group of men went up and forced the widows and sister
of Ute Killer to return to camp. They moaned and sobbed hys-
terically and began to throw off their clothing and slash themselves and throw away their possessions. Later it was noticed
that the youngest of the widows, Sweet Mouth, had disappeared. She had undoubtedly gone back to the tomb. Wide
Mouth, who was her uncle, set out with the intention of bringing her back again before dark.

It was too hot to stay in the tipis even so late in the afternoon. Uncertainty still hung over all the people in the camp.
A few of them ate a little. Some of the men were talking about
the need for a council. They talked or merely waited in uneasy
silence, disorganized, yet together in that their minds were all
on the disruption of the band. Specifically, they waited for
Wide Mouth to bring back the young widow, not because it
was important, but because they had not fixed their thoughts
on anything of importance and because it was the next expected act in the events of the day.

It was still daylight, though the sun had dropped behind
the high ground in the west and the long shadows had disappeared, when he returned, alone. He acted strangely.

The place of Wide Mouth in the band had been peculiar
since he had led the disastrous raid to Mexico. He had changed
from a war leader with considerable confidence in himself to
a bungling, clumsy warrior, whom no one would have followed
on a raid. His place in the band was not challenged, but only
because he never asserted any authority. Sometimes he was his
old jovial self, gregarious, loud; other times he was moody.
For a man his age, he was too anxious to please everyone, as
if he owed a debt that bore heavily on himself. Now, he came

into camp, seemingly disturbed, walking defiantly, yet clumsily, like a prowling bear. He gripped a knife in his hand.

They stared at him. He glared back, jerking his head around at different ones. He stopped where the chief's large tipi had been, near a small group of men. After a moment, one of them asked, "Where's the woman?"

He said loudly, "I've sent her to go with him!"

He looked at the group, then around at everyone within range of his voice, at first defiantly, expecting opposition, then searchingly as if wanting agreement. He seemed to realize suddenly that his knife was in his hand and that blood was on it. A fringe of dry untrampled grass stood up just outside where the tipi had been. He pulled a bunch and wiped the clotted blood from the blade.

"I did it for the great chief," he said. "That's why. For his sake. It's the old way."

They stared at him coldly. He began to stride away, then turned to start to go another way, then stopped, as if he had somewhere to go but had forgotten. "For the great chief who's gone!" he shouted. "That's why! What's wrong with that?"

No one said, "I agree," or "You did well," as he seemed to expect. Many of them, far from condoning his action, were horrified by it, for the sacrifice of a wife on a chief's grave was a practice long discontinued; yet the effect of the loss of the chief bore so heavily on them that they could not reproach Wide Mouth, for any reproach might in some way be critical of Ute Killer. Then there was no kinsman of the sacrificed woman any nearer than Wide Mouth, not any man who might have considered it his duty to demand payment for the waste of her life.

Wide Mouth wiped his knife again and kept looking from one to another of them. He said, loudly but less defiantly, "She wouldn't come on! I told her a dozen times. I said, 'It's time to go,' but she wouldn't come on." At last he seemed to realize that they would not answer him and that he had nothing more to say. He strode to his own lodge and went in.

A WOMAN OF THE PEOPLE # A WOMAN OF THE PEOPLE 202# A WOMAN OF THE PEOPLE 202

That night the spirit of Ute Killer came around the camp.
They sensed it. The spirit looked at them with dark, shining
eyes and said nothing. It did not speak about the bluecoats or
the white buffalo hunters. It did not blame them. It did not
ask any questions or give any answer. As much as anything
else, the ghost seemed merely to watch them to see what they
would do.

Burning Hand said to her, "They'll make your father civil
chief. They ought to consider my father, but they blame him
because his medicine didn't work. I'm glad I have no medicine.
They expect miracles from you."

"What about the others?" she asked.

"Wide Mouth has no support. Buffalo Bones is getting too
old. Who else is there? There's Horse Roper, but he has no
dignity; all he wants to do is gamble all the time. I think they'll
choose Lance Returner."

"What about the younger men?"

"It takes a lot of qualifications to be civil chief, Tehanita.
A man has to be thoughtful and experienced. He must know
the country. He must have a record in war. His name ought to
mean something among other bands. I think they'll come
around to Lance Returner."

But the council had more trouble than Burning Hand fore-
saw, since any action as important as choosing a new civil chief
had to be by unanimous agreement. They disagreed as to what
the policies and actions of the band should be. Many of them
were uncertain and hesitated to commit themselves so far as
to name one chief. They would not even agree upon Lance
Returner, who it was believed would follow about the same
policies as had the chief who was dead. One thing upon which
they were able to agree was that they should keep scouts out,
which they did. After three days of councils they concluded
that the Mutsani should have no civil chief, that if a warrior
wanted to lead a raid, he might induce as many as he could to
follow him, but that general plans for the entire band would

be formed by common agreement between the heads of the lodges.

They were anxious to move away from the sad place where Ute Killer had died, and soon found a good reason. The scouts reported a concentration of buffalo to the north. The beasts were not yet in winter hair, but the New Mexico traders had said they would accept untanned summer hides. It was much too late to meet the traders at the Yellow Houses; they hoped to be able to catch them in Palo Duro Canyon. Also, that canyon would make a good location for the winter camp, far beyond the point where bluecoats had been able to penetrate.

The heat and drought hung on. They moved the entire camp out through the dry, parched land toward the buffaloes. Water was a problem. They could carry enough for themselves, but at times had to water the horses in shallow, gyppy sinks. They found the concentration of buffalo. This herd, or scattered parts of many herds, did not show enough fright at the sight of mounted men; they were too easy game. By now, the men knew that the strange actions were a result of the inroads of the white hunters. It was a convenience for their present purpose, also an ominous thing. They set about the killing under the relentless sun, taking hides and as much meat as they would be able to pack after it was dry.

The child was walking well for his age. She had taken the cover from the cradleboard and put thick straps on it, so that she could carry him easily when she had a good distance to go. While she worked, she turned him loose. At times he would hold to her leg and watch. At times he held to the horn of a dead buffalo and watched it being skinned. She would take a sweet bit of raw meat and give it to him to chew on. She had wanted to name the child Story Teller. Burning Hand had wanted to name him Lipan Striker, because his mother had once struck a great coup on a Lipan. They had agreed that they would give him neither name, but would wait a few years and allow one or both grandfathers to name him. Until that time they would call him Little Hunter; he was born on a buffalo hunt.

They were heavily loaded as they moved northwest through the rough country around the headwaters of the River of Tongues. Every horse was loaded with camp gear or dried meat or flint hides. The horses suffered from the heat. One afternoon they camped on a sandy flat beside a tiny stream. Downstream from camp they watered the horses, with difficulty because of the small quantity of water. Toward the west a bank of clouds, so small that it had been unnoticeable when they stopped, began to build up rapidly.

They grimly went about erecting temporary shelters for the night. The children got relief from the stifling heat by playing in the tiny stream, splashing themselves. The clouds grew to hide the falling sun, and they were seen to be dark and thick; pale lightning winked in them. The wind freshened. They began to look at the clouds with interest.

When they could hear thunder, like a drum stroked with the fingers, their excitement grew. They did not relish a thunderstorm, but the prospect of rain seemed delightful. They began to chatter and laugh like children. The clouds spread toward them and around them and reared over them in an ugly manner. Lightning streaked across the sky, and the thunder grumbled like a giant angry animal. Burning Hand went to check the hobbles on those of his horses which might stray off. Tehanita pointed to the clouds and talked to Little Hunter, that he might not be afraid.

Dusk fell too soon, because of the clouds. Women ran about gathering children. Some of them became aware that where the tiny clear stream had trickled in the gravel now rushed a shallow torrent of muddy water, from heavy rain to the west. While they were yelling, "Look at the creek!" the wind hit. It gusted and jerked, blowing sand and large drops of rain. The smell of the first rain on the dry ground was delicious, but they had no time to savor it; their temporary shelters were blown flat. They ran around in the half light, chasing their possessions which were blowing away, screaming and laughing. As the wind slackened, the drenching rain came down. Water fell on them as if they were standing under a waterfall. Then the creek rose until its swirling muddy water came in a sheet up over the broad sand bar on which they had made camp. They hurried to move their things back to higher ground.

Tehanita carried the baby inside a robe with one hand while she helped to drag the property of her lodge with the other hand. People seemed to be moving in every direction in the dim confusion. Some were shouting, "Isn't this awful? I'm soaked." Others were shouting, "How do you like this, huh? Is this enough water for you?"

When they had moved away from the swollen creek, they began to try to make a place to sleep in the mud and darkness. Their misfortune seemed so ridiculous that they could not be sad about it. They had lived in close awareness of the dry weather for a long time, had said to one another, "Will it ever rain again?" saying it in order to hear the answer, "It's bound to rain sometime." Now the rain seemed like a generous assurance that the world was the same as it had always been, perhaps suggesting that other problems would be abundantly relieved in time and their lives would go on as they always had. Also, after grief they needed a change. Sometimes to move camp was enough. Usually, after the grief of a deep loss, they had to wait for the change of leaves falling or the change of leaves returning. The ending of the drought provided a good change, and they were able to laugh for the first time since Ute Killer was carried home.

The next morning they loaded up and headed due west toward the *Llano Estacado*. Up on the plateau since the rain they would be able to find water in the shallow lakes and traveling would be easier on the flat land. Their way was quite muddy. The horses were overloaded because of the water that had been soaked up by the green hides they carried. Their hoofs would become balled with mud so much that they would stumble. The men carried pointed sticks to clean the mud from the hoofs. Some of the horses were smart enough to understand; when their feet became heavy and clumsy, they would halt until a man came with a stick to dislodge the mud.

For three days they moved up the rough terrain, meeting frequent showers, then came out on the vast mesa. They turned north toward the deeper portions of Palo Duro Canyon, four travel days distant.

When they came to that great red gorge, they found a number of Indian villages already there, Comanche, Kiowa, and those strange newer allies of the People, the Cheyenne and Arapahoe. These camps were identified from high above them on the rim of the gorge. The Mutsani rode two hours west to where they could descend with the pack and travois horses into the deep canyon. They chose a winter camp site beside the little stream, *Kichi-ahkehono,* well upstream of the other villages.

13. THE WINTER OF LIVING IN GRAVES

THE NEW MEXICO traders had been there and gone. They had been nervous about something, had been unwilling to name a time and place for another trading session. The Mutsani men took their extra hides and dried meat to trade at the other Indian villages downstream. They received for them five more precious rifles and a small quantity of ammunition.

The men also brought back speculation about white soldiers. Rumor had it that they were out of their forts and traveling over the countryside. None of the Mutsani believed in the possibility of white soldiers coming to Palo Duro; the distance was too great and the country too rough for them to bring their supply wagons.

Tehanita felt security in the surroundings of their camp site, also serenity. The great broken canyon walls that towered over them promised protection from winter winds. Their vivid burnt-red color contrasted with the deep-green color of the cedars and drew her eyes frequently to them. Up and down the reaches of the gorge a blue mist hung, giving a sense of distance. It gave one an understanding of the size and power of the Earth Mother and her ability to surprise and awe.

She needed consolation, assurance against the idea that was

always there trying to come in and dwell in her mind: that time was passing and the child growing toward the age when he could ride well. Then there was the peculiar message the strange Indians had brought back in the summer. They had pointed in every direction, naming the names of white soldiers. Did it mean that whatever direction she went she would find white people? She found some relief for her uneasiness and confusion in her natural surroundings and also in the things around her that belonged to her husband and herself: the good winter food supply, the tight tipi, the strong lodgepoles. She knew these things in the way a person knows a thing made by his own hands and proved useful.

The first chill of winter was in the air. The men planned a one-day hunt to test their guns and ammunition. They would use one round each of their ammunition up on the high plains to the southwest, where antelope could be found around the shallow lakes. They rode away upstream at dawn on a clear day.

The children came and asked her to tell stories, but she told them she would not as long as the weather was good; they must play games. She straightened up the lodge, put the child on her back, and started out to gather wood. She had crossed the shallow graveled stream and was heading toward a dead, whitened cedar tree when the sound began. It was a faint crackling, like fire burning through dead twigs. It came from far down the canyon.

It was gunfire.

She turned and went immediately back toward her lodge. Women were standing still, telling their children to be quiet, asking, "What's that?" She did not stand with them to listen and speculate, but went in and made a bundle of a small box of pemmican, her husband's shield, a bag of water, a good knife, and two robes. The security of the great canyon retreat was shaken by the possibilities in the faint continuing sounds. She took up the bundle and ran to the lodge of Lance Returner.

Old Woman and Blessed were out in front. Old Woman said, "It's those strange Indians down there. They're shooting, wasting ammunition."

But some of the women, having seen Tehanita, were gathering belongings frantically, screaming for their children, peering down the canyon toward the source of the sound. She asked, "Is Lance Returner here?"

Old Woman said, "No, he's gone with the hunters. I don't think it's fighting down there."

"Why did they go hunting when we have plenty of meat?" Blessed said. "We don't have a horse in camp."

"We must climb out," she said.

Old Woman frowned and considered the matter. Blessed exclaimed, "Climb out?" as if it were impossible. At that moment Come Home Early started pushing an enormous bundle out through the door opening of the tipi.

Tehanita told Old Woman, "We'd better go. If it were the bluecoats, we have no one to hold them back." She had taken the cradleboard off and stood it on the ground to ease her shoulders. She swung the child again to the carrying position.

They had no choice but to go on foot. The main horse herd was in a side canyon downstream, toward the sound of guns. And it would be poor judgment to flee up the narrowing canyon where they could be pursued by white soldiers on horseback. Some of the others were already leaving. Old Woman said, "All right, we climb out." Come Home Early had as much burden as she, as strong as she was, could carry. Old Woman questioned her about what she had in the bundle and fussed at her because she had not made three bundles. They waded the little stream and headed for the south canyon walls.

The walls of the canyon at this point were greatly broken. At some places sheer cliffs stood up, impassable, but they were interspersed with eroded slopes that might be climbed. Much of the way was bare soil, washed by the rain and wind, deep red in color with gray streaks, sometimes sparkling from the gypsum and salt crystals in it when the sun struck it right.

Loose boulders lay on the slopes; rock ledges jutted out. Some places on mounding hills and ridges grass grew, also cacti and Spanish daggers, scattered scrub mesquite and cedar. Far up at the top the rim was a level line. There was no trail.

The flight was without panic. They went hurriedly but deliberately, though Come Home Early staggered under her large bundle. The sounds that had broken their peaceful morning had continued sporadically. Then when they had progressed up the first long incline onto a grassy ledge, a new sound came that confirmed their fear: the notes of a bugle.

The few still in camp now fled in earnest. Old Woman and Blessed began to aid Come Home Early. Tehanita kept up with them, carrying her child and her bundle, looking over her shoulder down at the canyon floor. Their situation was nearly as it had been two winters before, better in that they had received more warning, worse in that they had no men to cover their escape and faced a more difficult escape route.

Bluecoats charged in a line around the bend in the canyon and thundered toward the camp. They were yelling. When they saw the tipis, they began firing furiously as they came. The column broke into three prongs. Some of their horses ran through the stream, splashing the clear water high. When they came among the tipis, they rode around them, firing their rifles and short guns into the leather coverings. Old Woman was saying, "Hurry! Go on. Hurry!" Come Home Early and Blessed, who each now half carried, half pushed some share of the big bundle, were panting with the climb.

The bluecoats seemed to have seen their movements on the south canyon walls. They had dismounted. Some few of them had gathered their mounts and were running back downstream with them. The others flung themselves behind trees and rocks and tipis and began to fire their rifles up the slope. It was the distance of two long arrow flights. Puffs of smoke could be seen coming from their gun barrels, then the cracks of sound.

Crouching, she took the child from her back and carried him in her arms with her bundle. Ahead of her lay a clay slope with a face of rock above it; from the rock water seeped, enough to keep the ground below it wet. She angled across the slope to the safety of a huge, half-buried boulder. She heard the spat of a bullet against the rock face, saw a white spot as big as her hand where the moss-covered rock cracked away. She looked back at the women of the Lance Returner lodge. The two younger ones were rolling and pushing the bundle, while Old Woman, small and skinny but nimble, came behind, encouraging them.

She heard the thud and saw the jerk of the big woman's body when the bullet hit; even so, she could not believe it. It seemed impossible. Come Home Early was heavy and clumsy; it seemed that she had merely lost her footing in the wet clay slope. When her strong arms relaxed on the enormous, robe-wrapped bundle, it rolled away and bounded until it caught against a cedar clump far down near the canyon floor. Her mother and sister grabbed the big woman and prevented her from following the bundle. They tugged at her arms.

She put her child and her bundle down in the safety of the big rock and went to help them drag Come Home Early past the worst part of the slope. The big woman said in a small, protesting voice, "I can walk. I can walk."

Then began the near-impossible task of carrying the woman up the long slopes of the canyon wall. If her bundle had been heavy and cumbersome, she was more so. It was unthinkable to stop, for the white soldiers below might begin to climb after them. Again and again, Tehanita put down her own burden to go back and help Old Woman and Blessed in their struggle. Sometimes her hand came under the back of Come Home Early, and it came away filled with blood. The big woman did not show evidence of pain, but said frequently, "I can walk," though her legs dangled limply. Once as she lay still while they rested, she said, staring at the sky, "Put me down. I can walk."

As they labored upward, they remained aware, through hurried glances, of the activity far below them. The bluecoats seemed to realize that their gunfire was not being returned, and they came out of their concealments. They swarmed through the camp, slashing open tipis, carrying out boxes of possessions, scattering their contents. Distant shouts and laughter could be heard from them. Then they began to pull over the dwellings and pile them. Mules with packs were brought forward, and kegs were taken from the packs. The men scattered what must have been powder from the kegs all through the piles, for when they set them afire, they blazed up quickly.

She stopped looking at the destruction down on the canyon floor and concentrated on the task at hand. It would have been a difficult climb with nothing to carry. At times, the three of them would become exhausted; for a moment it seemed impossible. Then one of them would take Come Home Early's arm and tug on it, and they would struggle upward past the impossible place. Though they had started out near the lead, all the others had passed them.

At last she took her child and her bundle up the final incline to the flat high plains, and left them with a wife of Spitting Dog, and went back down to help tug the heavy woman up. When they laid her finally down on the flat ground over the rim, Old Woman was sobbing. She cradled the head in her lap and said, "My baby! We brought you out. My baby. My baby!"

They could see that Come Home Early was dead.

Old Woman repeated, "My baby," looked up at them with distraught face, and said, as in explanation, "I remember when she was my baby. I remember when she first walked. She was always a good girl."

The tiny figures of the bluecoats moved about the fires, watching them, prodding them until they burned thoroughly and began to dwindle from having consumed the contents of the piles. Then they mounted their tiny horses, formed a column of two lines, and passed back downstream to be hidden by the bend in the canyon.

The remainder of that day they were sad and uncertain. It

was clear that all they had, except for the little they had carried, was destroyed. Besides the first wife of Lance Returner an old man was dead; he had fallen on a steep slope, and his body was not brought out. Two women were wounded, one shot in the leg, one in the cheek. They buried Come Home Early in a crevice just below the rim of Palo Duro Canyon. Blessed put in the silver pin which she wore, and that was all the gifts they had to give her.

As the afternoon wore on toward the time when the hunters would return, they became fearful that the men would not find them before dark. The trail the hunters had taken out of the canyon was far to the west. The women began hurriedly trying to strike fire, and when they had made it, they gathered grass to make a big smoke. Two of the old men sent the smoke signal for danger. Then, at dusk, the hunters rode toward them across the flat prairie, carrying antelopes over the fronts of their saddles.

There was confusion as the women swarmed around them to tell about it. The men held a hurried council with darkness falling. They concluded that the bluecoats must have come in great force, having penetrated past the Indian villages downstream. There was no doubt that the invaders had taken the main horse herd of some three hundred animals. The mounts they had ridden hunting were tired; yet they could not afford to rest them. Here and there the men spoke up with certainty in their voices: "We must get the horses some way." "We've got to try; we can't do without them." "Those devil bluecoats are a long way from home. If we follow them, we'll have our chance at the horses." They dumped the antelopes on the ground and set out east, walking, leading their tired mounts into the darkness.

It didn't seem possible to her that Come Home Early was dead, that she was lifeless and cold over there in a bed of rocks. It was difficult to imagine the Lance Returner lodge without her big, active form and voice. She was not beautiful, but had not a mean bone in her body. And she had loved life, just to simply live without demanding anything. Why hadn't she done something or given Come Home Early something to show her she liked her? If she had just done something special for her before it was too late. The big woman was the kind who would have appreciated it. She would have treasured any gift. But how does one know? It seemed so simple to know it now, so clear. Of all the people to whom she might have done a kindness, this one most obviously deserved it. The others, her sister, her mother, the husband to whom she was first wife, they all must be realizing the same. She felt tender toward them, as she had when Story Teller went out of the lodge.

The women sat in scattered groups on the inhospitable prairie, wondering what went on around them in the dark country. It rained that night and put out their small fires.

She huddled under her robe with the child, the small box of pemmican, the knife, the bag of water, her husband's shield. Every part of her body ached from the unusual work of climbing. The robe held out the rain, but water seeped along the ground so that she sat in mud. When the child stirred in the limited black world they shared under the robe, she sang a small song to him.

Late the following afternoon the men came back, still leading their hunting horses. They were tired and greatly disturbed. Down in the valley of Indian Perfume Creek, whose canyon joined Palo Duro to the east, they had been hidden, helpless witnesses while the bluecoats made certain the horses would not be recovered. They had seen their war-horses, racehorses, packhorses, brood mares, along with four times as many belonging to Indians of other bands, all deliberately slaughtered. The men moved about as if they did not know what to do, saying little, sometimes staring at their own families as if they did not recognize them.

She propped a side of antelope ribs over their small separate fire. Fat smoked from the ribs, and they smelled good cooking, but Burning Hand seemed to have no stomach for them. After an hour's silence he began talking to her. "Such a great, magnificent herd of horses. Killed for nothing," he said. "I'll never forget the sight. It burned into my mind. They smelled their death and became frightened. They screamed and dashed back and forth to find a way to escape. The last ones were covered with blood, and it was thick on the ground; they slipped in it. But none could escape. We could do nothing. Some of the men could hardly bear it. I could hardly bear it myself."

After more silence, he said, "How can we fight them, Tehanita? I have one cartridge left. Lance Returner has three. Buffalo Bones has enough lead and powder to fire his muzzleloader a dozen times maybe. But they! They have a gun called a Gatling gun. It shoots out bullets like bees coming out of a honey tree."

The next day a few of the women wanted to go back into the canyon. They had seen the thorough destruction of their camp, but hoped to find a few copper pots that were unbroken. They were overruled by the rest; it was not worth the risk. The men could not agree on what should be done, but knew that they must move, so in the middle of the morning the band headed southeast. Some wanted to head for the Yellow House, but rumor had it that some other Indians had headed in that direction, and even some white soldiers. They agreed that they must leave the high, bare land of the *Llano Estacado,* also that it was well to move southward before the Moon of Howling Wind. Some thought they should go far south as quickly as possible; others thought they should try for a late meat hunt; still others thought they should search for a place they could make lodgepoles. Any action they might take was limited by their scarcity of horses, of which they had only one per lodge.

They moved slowly, using the precious horses only to make scouting forays, for hunting, and in some cases to pack their few belongings. They allowed the horses to graze often and took care that they were well watered.

The first blizzard of winter struck them on Trading River.

They turned up it, any contrary plans canceled by the immediate necessity for shelter. They came under the lee of clay-
banks and dug into them like animals escaping the cold. They
covered the burrows' entrances with skins or built fires in them
to keep out the winter air. When they had remained in the
place three days, they realized it would be their permanent
camp for the winter.

Sometimes they joked, saying, "Well, if we die, at least we
have good graves already made. We are living in them." They
made light of it to cover the shame of living in holes like animals. But their plight was not a joke. It was the most difficult
winter any of them could remember, with every piece of time
warm enough to stay outside their earth shelters filled with
work. The women went out great distances to dig roots and to
glean scattered grass seeds and half-decayed mesquite beans
from the ground. The men hunted on foot, bringing back,
rarely, a buffalo, a deer, a bear; more frequently, a turkey.
They took turns staying with the horses day and night, moving
them sometimes to a more sheltered place or to better grass.

Some things they had to do differently from their customary way. To cook in water they dug a small hole, pushed a
green hide into it flesh side up, and filled it with water, which
they heated by dropping in hot stones. Their scarcity of axes
or hatchets made wood gathering difficult. The men helped by
dragging in deadwood they ran across in their hunting and
horse tending.

They had no food to throw away. Even small bones they
cracked to make soup. All their dogs crept away and died of
starvation.

Their long-time pride in their ability to endure remained
strong, but an uncertainty hung over the camp. When the men
talked, their conversation always came around to the horse
and the buffalo, though they had nothing new to say. They
spoke about how they must catch horses and about how the
buffalo acted strangely. They would remain quiet, nodding,

then finally would say the same things about the horse and the buffalo.

At times as they warmed by their fire in front of their small cave, she noticed her husband looking at her as if he were seeing her for the first time. If she met his eyes, he continued to look at her as if seeking something in her face. Once after such a searching gaze, he said, without explanation, "You are a good and gentle woman." He was often silent and thoughtful during those hard times.

In spite of the standing joke about being ready for death by living in graves, when the weak ones began to die, they carried them to high places for burial. They gave them respectable resting places, but had no gifts to give and no time for mourning. During the Moon of Babies Crying for Food nine members of the Mutsani died.

In early spring ten of the best hunters, gambling that they would not be caught by a late spell of severe weather, took the ten strongest horses and set out on an extended hunt. In a week they brought back the hides and meat of eight buffaloes. It ended the band's long hunger, gave them strength, and lifted their spirits. They felt the hope that comes with every springtime; it might be that everything would turn out all right after all. Shortly afterward, they broke camp, turned their backs on the place they had spent the hard winter, and traveled into the rolling plains country to the east.

The band was disorganized but determined, diligent in trying to improve their condition. They pursued the scattered buffaloes, pausing in camps long enough to crudely tan the hides they took, looking forward to the time when they would have decent tipis again. They hacked out lodgepoles from every kind of tree; some were not as straight as they should have been; many had to be spliced in order to get light weight with sufficient length.

For a week they followed a band of mustangs and took some of the wild horses daily. It was maddening that they could not catch the good ones. The ones they took were scrubs, still weak from the recent winter, but capable of carrying a pack. They caught twenty-two before they lost the wild band. The newly caught animals were quickly tamed by constant use and care.

They received a rumor of bad news when one of their scouts met two Kwahadi hunters and talked with them. The report was that all of the main bands of the People, except the great Kwahadi, had given up and gone out east to the white man's reservation. All the Indian allies of the Comanches had done the same. The two Kwahadi hunters swore it was true.

Their spirits were lifted again when they had the good fortune to surprise a small group of white hunters. They killed one; the others escaped. From this good luck they gained seven first-class horses, four mules, two axes, some strange food, a metal can of powder, a large rifle, some thin metal for arrowheads, canvas, knives. By this time most of the lodges were housed in skin tipis, and they were beginning to feel a degree of recovery from the severe blow they had received the autumn before. Perhaps because of their improving fortunes they could not agree on what the next move of the band must be. They argued sporadically all one day in a camp near where they had surprised the white hunters; then some of the old men said the argument must stop. They must hold a council.

The council had met early in the morning in the brush arbor near the center of camp. As the day grew warm, the dozen men who sat in council took out bird-wing fans to fan themselves. They passed a pipe, sometimes seemed to sit silently, sometimes were addressed by one who would wave his arms as he sat or stood among them, but no laughter or voices of loud good humor could be heard from them.

Burning Hand was making glue that morning. He seemed to pay no attention to the activity over in the council, though once he said to her, "They'd better quit talking and move this camp. The white hunters who ran off know our location."

In the middle of the day the council broke up, and the men went this way and that toward their tipis. One of them, Bull Heart, the nephew of Wide Mouth, came to speak to Burning Hand.

"I see you're cooking glue."

"Yeah. What does the council say?"

"Can't seem to get together. We meet again in a little while. You ought to sit in the council, Burning Hand, instead of messing around with this stuff."

"I think the older warriors will figure things out. Whenever I go, they do all the talking anyway."

"They talk around in circles. The older warriors are not so sure of themselves as in the past. You're older than I am, Burning Hand."

"I don't think I'll go today. I've got some arrows ready to put together."

Bull Heart hung around in silence a while, then said, "You know, they say sometimes a man gets powerful medicine and at the same time he gets powerful taboos."

"That's what I've heard."

"They say when a man gets such medicine, he doesn't go around talking about it much but keeps it quiet. What do you think about it, Burning Hand?"

"Why ask me? If you want the truth about it, ask my father or some of the men with strong medicine."

Bull Heart left toward his own lodge. Some of the men were already going back to the council arbor.

Burning Hand asked her, "You think he was making fun of me? Why did he bring up that medicine business?"

"No," she said. "He seemed embarrassed to me. I think the men spoke about different things, and your name came up some way. Bull Heart had more on his mind than he said."

The council dragged on. In the middle of the afternoon, old Buffalo Bones left the others and came to the lodge of Burning Hand. He said hello and began to chat about the arrows. Burning Hand had set in the iron heads on a dozen arrows, had bound them in with fine wet rawhide, and now had arranged them by the fire so that the rawhide binding might dry before he glued it.

"We're having a lot of talk in council about a lot of things," Buffalo Bones said. "Why don't you come over and sit in?"

"Well, I'm short on arrows. As you can see I'm pretty busy."

"Couldn't your wife finish the arrows?"

"Well, yes, sir, she could. But I really don't have anything to say over there anyway, outside of what I've already said."

"I've come because we want you to know the older men welcome you younger men."

"Thank you. I want you to know I expect to accept what the older men say and follow it and fight for it."

Buffalo Bones squatted down and was silent, frowning, looking around at the horizon, at the arrows, at the camp. Finally he said, "An idea about medicine came up, Burning Hand. They say some warriors get strong medicine and a strong taboo at the same time."

"Yes, Bull Heart was talking about that."

"What do you think about it?"

"Nothing. You should ask my father about things like that."

"Spitting Dog's medicine is as rotten as an egg that didn't hatch."

Burning Hand squared around quickly to face him. "Are you trying to start a fight, old man?"

"No. Don't get angry. We say what we think in the council."

"You're not in the council now."

"I only left it for a minute."

"Well, keep your ideas about my father to yourself. I may forget you are an honored warrior and knock the *duhktai* out of you."

"Don't get angry. I only . . . uh. . . . They say a man might possibly get medicine and at the same time get a taboo that would forbid him ever to mention the medicine or let anyone find out about it. Do you think it's possible?"

"For the sake of *Kahwus!* What is this, Buffalo Bones? What's going on? With the Mutsani in the fix it is, you council men wander around asking a man like me questions like that. I don't understand it."

The old man rose, scratched his head, and went back to the meeting. Burning Hand went on with his work. She went into the tipi and got the feathers and began to help him split and trim them. They could not guess what went on in the council. She thought he should go, just from curiosity, but he was becoming stubborn.

The sun was touching the trees in the west when Lance Returner came to them. He did not make conversation, but said abruptly, "Come to the council."

They both stared at him. She noticed for the first time that his face was getting deep wrinkles. His scar stood out. His hair was beginning to appear ragged. She knew that Blessed still brushed it. It was becoming ragged because she pulled out the white hairs and wove in black hairs to take their place.

The old man said again, "Come on to the council."

Burning Hand laughed. "What if I say no?"

"Well, I might just tell my daughter to come home and stay for a long visit. How would you like that? But why be stubborn? Why do you hold back? Must we throw a lariat on you and drag you like an unbroken horse?"

"I can be as stubborn as you. I'm busy. My father will speak for me in the council."

"He can't speak for you. Come on."

"Who are you to say he can't speak for me?"

"He says it himself." Lance Returner pointed, and they looked up. There, halfway between them and the brush arbor where the council sat, stood Spitting Dog. The old medicine man seemed to be waiting. He was near enough to have heard all they said. He wore a fancy beaded medicine bag around his neck and his gourd rattles at his waist. He held his skinny body straight, but he seemed uncomfortable. The pained smile passed across his face as they first looked at him, but he seemed to put it away, as if putting away politeness in favor of a serious matter. A moment of silence passed, then he said to his son in a low, distinct voice, "Please come to the council."

Burning Hand rose with no further hesitation and followed the two older men.

He had already cut the three places to mark where the feathers went. She glued in the feather pieces, for she guessed he would not be back before dark. She could see him over there sitting among them. All of them seemed to be asking her husband questions or arguing with him.

Darkness came early, for a bank of clouds had come over the sky. She could see that the men in council seemed not to notice; in the last fading light they could be seen still in session, waving their arms. She took her child and the new arrows inside, fed the child, made ready some food for him, and sat waiting. Lightning played in the clouds. Thunder mumbled. It began to sprinkle. She brought fire into the center of the tipi, and firewood. She waited patiently for him, listening to the flurry of rain on the buffalo leather, as half the night passed.

He came in hurriedly. "Are you awake, Tehanita? We move camp. Get packed."

"Now?"

"As quick as you can. I go for the horses."

"But Burning Hand! In the dark and rain? Who says so?"

"Do you need anyone but me to tell you?" He started out the door, then turned back and touched her and said, "We move because of the rain. It will wipe out our tracks."

She tore into the messy job, first putting the child into his cradleboard and making a quick shelter for him outside. He was two years old, but the cradleboard was still useful. She made bundles to pack on their two horses, singing meanwhile loudly enough for the child to hear. Her main concern was that she might leave something in the darkness. Much of the gear would get wet, but she could not help it. Fortunately, the rain was not cold. She took the cover from the tipi and brought down the poles by the time he returned with the wet horses.

They walked through the rain and darkness, leading the pack horses. She could sometimes hear the voices of the others and could always hear, ahead, the muffled sound of the bell one of the horses wore. Just before dawn they came into a grove of trees against a river.

"This is the place," he told her. She helped him loose the soggy burdens from the horses and place them on the wet grass. The rain had stopped. Before it was well light, he was gone again to take the horses to grass away from the camping place.

She took the binding from one of the bundles and wrapped it tightly around a tree trunk to make a place to hang the cradleboard. It was a distasteful task to erect a lodge in the mud. She went about it, thinking how little her husband had spoken to her on the night move. The move had been a thing he wanted, yet she sensed things in his voice and manner that were unexplained. As she worked, she was only dimly aware of the other women of the band working around her.

Then two women, the sister of Buffalo Bones and Horse Roper's wife, began to quarrel. They each had an armload of poles and had evidently chosen the same place for their tipis. Tehanita went on with her work, pretending not to notice them, though they were struggling for a place not far from hers. They pushed at one another and said, "You move back!" "No, you move back. This is my place." "Move back! I was here first." "But I'm the sister of Buffalo Bones! I have a right—" "No, you don't. I'm—" One of them was caused to drop her poles; she pushed the other and caused her to drop her poles. Then one slipped down; she scrambled up, grabbed the other's hair, and wrestled her down.

The wife of Horse Roper seemed to have got the worst of it. She came over to Tehanita, muddy and tearful. "Make her let me have the place, Tehanita. My husband was close kin to the great chief we had." But the other one was quick to assert her right because of her kinship to Buffalo Bones.

Why they appealed to her, she didn't know. She was ashamed for them both. She said, "I guess you must wait for the men to say."

She paid no more attention to them until she saw Burning Hand coming, walking slowly, looking over the area of the camp. The two women went to meet him, and it was clear that they were carrying their dispute to him. She felt angry at them, but was surprised to see him answer them and point at a location with his finger, then point again, and to see them go get their belongings and start to move to the spots he had indicated. How could they be so inconsiderate as to involve him in their childish fight when they knew it might cause trouble between him and their menfolk? And why should he let them?

He appeared thoughtful as he came to her. Again rose the feeling of certainty that something remained unexplained. She asked, "What is it, Burning Hand? What's happened?"

He laughed a little. "No one told you? I haven't because I only half believed it. Part of me doesn't like it or want to believe it. Then . . . I guess I couldn't tell you quickly."

"But what is it? Tell me what?"

He spoke as if making a formal announcement. "Last night the Mutsani council took important action. They reversed themselves and chose a new civil chief."

There had been a pattern in the new camp that she had seen but had not understood. The tipis were patched and misshapen, with spliced poles, crooked poles, poles of different lengths, with half-tanned hides and even deerskins, but the old pattern, which had been absent since the death of Ute Killer, had returned. On all sides of her were the important and powerful lodges of the band and stretching away behind each were the kin and connections of that family. The muddy, half-set-up lodge of her husband and herself stood in the center of it all. She asked softly, "Is it you?"

"It is I," he said.

The look on his face reminded her of the impression he had left with her that time years before when she interrupted his fast on big Medicine Mound. He said, "You know, I feel strange. If someone had told me when I was a boy that the day would come when I would take that great chief's place, I would have danced and sung with happiness. But now it's different. I argued with them."

"Do they believe you have a strong medicine?"

"Some of them do, but that's not all of it." They finished covering the tipi, and after they had spread their various possessions to dry, after she had cared for the baby and started to prepare food, in the privacy of the lodge he told her: "The council, they don't know what they want. By the time I came, they had decided we must have a chief, and I agreed. Each of us bound himself to accept the choice of the council. Then, Tehanita, it seemed like they took up every man—my father, Lance Returner, all of the ones you would think of for chief —and they talked about how each of them would lead us, and they turned away from each of them. I think they wanted a young man who can fight, but one who can also think of other things. It almost seemed like they turned to me because they don't know what I'll do. I argued with them, but they seem to believe that I'll think about it all and somehow I'll discover a new idea or a new way or something.

"They talked about Story Teller, of all people, Tehanita— how he used to tell true stories of long ago. They tried to remember any story he might have told about a band of the People who were in trouble and danger as we are today, but found a way to save themselves; no one could think of one. You don't remember any such story, do you?"

"No, not where the People were as we are today."

"Most of the men don't know that you own his name. But I thought you might remember something he might have told. You know, like where the People were pressed on all sides and found themselves in serious straits, and perhaps *Kahwus* saved them. What were the ways in which *Kahwus* helped the People?"

"Well, he used magic and shrewd thinking and bravery, but—"

"He never fought the white men, did he?"

"No."

14. The White Banner

It was midsummer when the Kwahadi brave rode into their camp, followed by his two wives who rode a single horse. The wives were crying. The Mutsani scout who guided them in had not spoken much to them because of the embarrassment of the women's unseemly conduct. The strange brave rode to the center of camp and dismounted.

Burning Hand recognized him as a Kwahadi and said, "Welcome."

The strange brave halfway returned the greeting, then said to the wives, "Get down and shut up."

Burning Hand said, "Will you smoke or will you have something to eat? It's past the middle of the day."

"I'd like some food. Those women! I whipped them this morning for crying, and now they're at it again." He added, as in explanation, "They want to follow their kinfolks."

Burning Hand did not seem to think it proper to ask questions or comment on the man's domestic difficulties. There was meat hanging by the fire. Tehanita cut pieces for the women and passed a horn of water to the three strangers. As usual when anyone came into camp who might have news, a crowd was gathering. The leading men of the band were nearest, others farther back. The stranger greeted, and was noticed in return by, three or four of the men he had evidently met before.

He said to Burning Hand, "This is good. We haven't eaten since yesterday."

"Any man of the great Kwahadi is always welcome here."

The stranger said, "There's no great Kwahadi anymore. They—" His face was suddenly contorted as if an emotion inside himself had taken control of his features by stealth. He stopped chewing and seemed to forget the meat in his hand. He glared at his wives as if they had insulted him or tricked him in some way. He frowned and said to Burning Hand, "No Kwahadi. They're the same as dead to me. Worse than dead."

"What?" Burning Hand asked. "Explain yourself. What's happened?"

"They've gone to that place the white man marked out. Would you think you'd ever see the day?"

"What? The *reservation?*"

"Yes."

A variety of protests rose from the nearby men. "What's he saying?" "That can't be true!" "Not the Kwahadi!" "They wouldn't do it. He's crazy!"

"It's true," he said. "I hate to say it worse than you hate to hear it."

"You mean some other band," Burning Hand said. "Surely not."

"I don't believe it myself," the strange brave said, "but I know it's true."

Someone said, "You mean they've gone east to attack the white people."

"I mean they've gone east to surrender their horses and guns and live where the white man says they must."

"He lies!" someone yelled, but there seemed to be no guile in the stranger. He had dropped the meat from his hand without noticing, into the dust at his feet.

"It's impossible to believe," Burning Hand said. "What

about Wild Horse? Do you mean to tell us he has agreed to this thing?"

"And Bull Elk?" Lance Returner said. "Aren't you afraid he'll kill you for telling this slander on the great Kwahadi?"

The stranger asked, "Do you know *Kwaina?*"

"I've heard of him," Burning Hand said.

"I know him," someone said. "He's getting a reputation as a young war chief."

"That's the one," the stranger said. He spoke in a low voice, so that they found it necessary to be quiet to hear him. "All the great chiefs of the Kwahadi, Wild Horse and Bull Elk, all of them, have turned their power over to *Kwaina* so that he could lead them to the white people. I'm sorry. It's all true."

All around in the crowd people were asking, "What does it mean?"

Burning Hand asked him, "Why have you come to us?"

"Because I know Ute Killer," he said. "He'll never surrender. Where is Ute Killer?"

They moved often that summer and kept out far-ranging scouts. Their chief aims were to protect themselves, improve their lodges, catch horses. They came across rotten buffalo carcasses, sometimes fields of bones already picked white, but found enough live animals to satisfy their needs. They planned no raids. The young civil chief would allow no attacking of white hunters except by scouts at a distance of two or three days' ride away from camp.

The child, Little Hunter, was learning to talk. He did not like his cradleboard; she agreed that it had served its purpose and burned it. The child was good company when her husband was gone. He would bring her small treasures—flowers wadded in his chubby hand, colored stones, bugs—and jabber about them. In another year he would be old enough to understand stories.

She took pride in the authority her husband had and in the trust they put in him. He made plans as to how they should scatter if the camp were attacked and where they should come together again. They seemed to believe he was a good civil chief. As if it would make him a better one, or perhaps to satisfy their own feelings, they gave him presents. Three scouts brought in a good riding horse they had stolen; they could not divide it among them, so they gave it to Burning Hand. Another scout gave him a revolver; there was no ammunition for it, but it was a good gun. He was often silent and thoughtful.

One day in early autumn he sat a long time in the tipi, studying the revolver, saying nothing. He cocked the hammer and clicked it, threw out the cylinder and clicked it back together, pointed it up at the smoke hole, sighting. She said once to him, "It's cooler outside," but he seemed not to hear. He was looking closely at every part of the handgun, working the action of it, looking inside it.

"You're wishing you had some cartridges for it," she said.

"Well, I would like to have some cartridges for it. Yes. But I'm thinking of something a lot worse than that." He suddenly held it out in his two open hands and said, "Look at this thing! The way it works! Look at it!"

She knelt and looked. "It's a fine gun."

"No! Think of what it means! It frightens me. Just look at it."

She looked into his face, and he said, "If you ever tell anyone I said something frightens me, I'll cut your nose off."

"I don't gossip about what you tell me."

He smiled a little at her and then grew serious again. "Tehanita, where do all things come from? All things! They grow in the ground, or they are born, or they are made. This short gun didn't grow, and it wasn't born. It was made! I'm sure it was made. That may sound silly, but it's important. Some man fixed this just this way. He thought about it, don't you see? He thought about how each part must work and how it must fit. Then he made it. You'd think it couldn't be done, yet he did it.

"The more I think about it, the bigger it gets, and the less

I like it. You can rub a piece of iron against stone and wear it away. Or you can get a file from the traders, and the file will cut iron. But how in the world would you shape these parts of this short gun, especially the holes? How would you make the holes? It would be hard to make out of wood, and impossible out of iron. Yet some white man made it.

"There's no end to it. If a file cuts iron, how is a file made? Besides that, where does the white man get iron in the first place?

"Listen, a long time ago the Indian saw the white man coming with wagons, and he said there's a fool, because a wagon is too wide to follow a buffalo trail. But what does the white man do? He makes the trail wider and smooths the rough places; then he carries as much with six horses as we carry with thirty. It was the same with the gun. The Indian said there's a fool, because we can draw his fire, then rush forward and put three or four arrows in him while he tries to reload. But what does the white man do? He makes a gun that fires many times, and the Indian who rushes forward against him is killed.

"Tehanita, most people who plant corn, they are weaker than we who ride and hunt. But the white man breaks that rule. It's because of his ways of doing things. He makes things with wheels to carry loads, and he gets iron and knows the secret of working iron. As for that train trail up on the Arrowpoint and the engine that runs on it, I'm not going to think about that. This short gun is already too much to think about. That iron engine moves by itself and has fire inside it. I think if a man tried to put a train engine in his mind and think about it, his head might come to pieces.

"If we only had some way to destroy him and all his medicine. . . . Or, if we had some way to steal his medicine. . . .

"Tehanita, think of all those great, wise chiefs of the Mutsani in long winters past. They were strong and respected. They knew what to do. Is it possible that their office has passed down to such a man as me? How can it be that the People look to me? I see the foolishness of many roads, but no good road. Down every road, I see trouble and death waiting. When I look at this gun and study what it means and see the strength of the white man's medicine, then I come to believe my burden is heavier than that of any great chief in the past."

He became silent. She stayed near him, adjusting the strings that tied the uprolled edges of the tipi, unsatisfied that he had stopped talking after belittling himself as a leader. She wanted to tell him that he might be the wisest chief the Mutsani had ever had. While she was trying to think of a proper way for a woman to say such a thing, he said:

"You used to be white. Could it be that you know any of their secrets?"

"No, I don't think so."

"You should tell me anything you can remember about being white."

"I can't remember anything. You know more than I do about it. You've visited the other Comanches and the Allies more. And you've seen the train engine up near Arrowpoint River." She was thinking about the secret vow she had made the day she married him, even though it surely was not the kind of secret he wanted to know. The thought was painful and made her feel guilty.

After a while he said, "You know, I'm changing my thoughts about Ute Killer."

She chided him gently, "Wouldn't it be better not to speak his name?"

"Why?"

"It might bring back sadness."

"I speak it only to you."

She offered the other common reason for the taboo without being sure that she believed it: "He might come back and haunt you."

"Let him come. I'd have a thing or two to say to him. What did he gain with his death? For himself, honor. But what for the People? What for the People, Tehanita? He couldn't charge me with cowardice. I've risked my life plenty of times. If I could save the People by standing on a hill and throwing away my moccasins, I'd do it before this sun goes down. But thoughts, never dreamed of by Ute Killer, have come to curse me."

He was silent so long that she wanted to think of something pleasant to say: "The scouts haven't seen any bluecoats in a long time."

"No," he said. "They won't come back till the winter. That's when they'll come. When we make winter camp, they'll come."

Early the next morning he was up and about. At sunrise he brought his horse to the door and told her, "Make me a small package of dry meat and fill the small water bag."

"Where are you going?"

"I'll be gone a few days, scouting to the east."

"Please, Burning Hand, where are you going?"

"I'm not sure," he said. "I want to be alone and think. I told some of the council men I would consult my medicine. I might take a look at some white people."

"Take some men with you, Burning Hand. Please. The other scouts don't go alone."

He shook his head.

"I don't understand," she said. "Please don't go."

"You don't have to understand. You can believe, as the old men do, that their chief goes to consult his medicine." He was ready to go, but before he mounted, relented and touched her and said, "I don't know myself, Tehanita. It's just that I've never looked at a white person, a real one, unless I or he was on the warpath."

She watched him ride away eastward and felt unreasonable worry. It might have been the mention of Ute Killer the night before; he, a chief, had ridden away and had come back only to die. Her husband had said Ute Killer's answer was no good, but she knew that the plight of the Mutsani was larger than she could understand. She had grasped her husband's meaning about the revolver, but she would never have been able to figure out the importance of being able to make such a thing; and where such secrets might lie in the land of the whites was beyond her. He knew a thousand things that she did not. Whether he were now in danger was beyond her. A part of her worry was the long deceit she had practiced. It could have no bearing on his important thinking that she could determine, but she could not be sure. How could a white man possibly make a revolver out of iron?

Impulsively, she decided that she would follow him. She took the child and left him in the care of Old Woman and Blessed. She took a halter out and caught her husband's hunting horse, then set out east an hour behind him.

She had ridden about the same distance behind him for two and a half days, getting only fretful sleep because of the fear that he might move on during the night. She had eaten nothing but a handful of sunflower seeds and a few mesquite beans. He had remained within her sight about half the time during the journey. This morning she had begun to notice that the land was slightly different; grass was a little thicker and some clumps of post oaks stood on the rolling hills.

At about midday, he had tied his horse among some small oaks and had walked up along a low ridge. He had sat a while, looking east. Now, he came back some of the distance toward his horse and sat down on the ground with his head on his arms. He appeared quite lonely sitting with his head down, and she felt that she could see the great invisible burden weighing over him. Her original impulse to follow had come to seem foolish. The time had come for her to turn back or else go to him. It would be proper to turn back, but his appearance pulled her irresistibly toward him. She took her horse and tied it with his, then walked up to where he sat.

"Burning Hand," she said, softly, not to startle him. "It is I."

He didn't look around. "Yes. It is you, the most disobedient wife that ever lived."

"Then you knew I followed?"

"I'll never bring the pipe to you when I plan a raid. You travel across the country as easy to see as a white man's covered wagon."

"I . . . came to tell you something. I might have had some thoughts that I never told you."

He had not looked at her, but was still gazing moodily ahead. She followed where his eyes were looking, not expecting anything, filled with the problem of telling him something. But there straight ahead, not an hour's ride away, stood a small flat-topped mountain!

It couldn't be the one. She matched it against the picture in her mind. It couldn't be the one; it was too small. It stood almost like a fortress which had been built from layers of rock and earth of different colors, dark gray and light gray and red. It couldn't possibly be the one. It sat on a grassy, nearly level land. The flat top had oak shrubbery growing on it. It was too small to be the one. As her will refused it, her eyes checked it against the image she had carried and cherished during some twenty-one winters of searching. It was a perfect small replica of the landmark she had seen one time before, when she was nine years old. It had a quality of truth unlike the many other mesas she had seen, yet it had a pitiful quality in its perfection, as a doll compared to a living, breathing human being.

"What is it you never told me?"

She could hardly talk for the hard place in her throat. It was as if two big things had come together, one inside her and one outside. She had come to confess a secret to her husband, and at that same time and place the very Earth Mother had thrust up the flat-topped mountain as if to say, "Here it is."

"I had a lot of thoughts . . . that I might go back to my people."

He was not hearing her. "You certainly should be with the People right now, caring for our son and waiting like a good wife. You came and interrupted me when I was a boy just as I was about to get medicine. Will you also follow me now and interrupt me always when I've got serious problems on my mind?"

She closed her eyes a moment. It seemed impossible that the mountain could be there in front of her. Yet it stood there solidly. "You don't understand. I want to answer the question you asked and tell you the truth. I had thoughts . . . that I would escape and go to the white people."

He was like her husband at once, peering into her face. "Escape? Go to white people? Why?"

She started to answer him but couldn't put it into words. She cast about in her mind. It seemed that she should have a good answer. He was serious now, not sarcastic, and she desperately wanted to explain herself.

"Why would you want to do that? Explain it to me."

"I . . . don't know."

"Tell me whatever was in your mind. Your reasons."

"Well . . . it— I must have had the thought when I was small and carried it with me."

He pressed the question again, and all she could find to say to herself and to him was, "I really don't know. I'm telling the truth."

"All you can say is 'I don't know.' "

"Well, I don't know. Maybe I thought . . . when I was small . . . I guess I thought that white people are good. I only wanted to tell you the truth."

He became silent and stared out across the country for so long a time that she wanted to find whether he were angry. Also, she had a faint hope of finding that the flat-topped mountain was not what it seemed.

"Do you know this country well, Burning Hand?"

"I've raided through here."

"Do you know a river the white people call . . . the *Fork* River?"

"No. Well, the one these draws lead into, they call it the—

What do they call it? Yes. They call it the *West Fork of the Trinity*."

The words pierced through her. They were pointed and keen and small like the sight of the mountain. She knew the names of rivers in a broad land from the Arrowpoint to the Big Salt River. This name was different from them all. It was true and poignant and tiny beside the other names, with a power to pierce like a needle. *West Fork of the Trinity!* The words echoed faintly in her ears, sounding as if they were formed by strange, distant lips, not her husband's, not even her own.

"Why do you ask?"

"From here, a day and a half ride away from the setting sun, beside that river—it's where I lived with the white people."

"What is this thought of going to white people? Do you want to go to them now?"

She realized that she was afraid of the flat-topped mountain and the name of the river.

"Tell me. Do you want to go to them now? It's not a day and a half ride. They have a house yonder just below that rise. They graze cattle all over this country here now. Are you a slave woman who is tied so that she can't go where she wants? Are you a Comanche or a slave? Why don't you go to them?"

"If I wanted to, I couldn't go without taking my baby."

"Suppose I said 'yes' to that?"

"Well, I couldn't go without taking Bird Wing. Sunflower was really my sister."

"I'm the chief. I might be able to say 'yes' to that too."

She was aware of his burden and that she was not easing it any by letting him go on in this jealous way. "I couldn't go without you," she said.

He laughed. "I can see you going to them. You have your son under one arm and Bird Wing under the other; you have a rope around my neck, and you lead me along. But since I am the only chief the Mutsani people have, they follow along too, so you lead us all. Are you sure you take us by the right road?"

"I don't want to lead you. All I wanted to do was tell you the truth."

"You came to influence me."

"No, I didn't, Burning Hand."

"Oh, no, not you. Go ahead. Advise me. What should I do?"

"Please don't be angry with me, Burning Hand. I don't want to go to the whites. I want to go with the People wherever you lead us." He looked out over the land, and after a while she asked, "Do you want me to go away so you can think?"

He ignored her question and asked, "How did it feel when you used to be a white person?"

"I don't know."

"Do you hold anything back from me now?"

"No."

He mused, studying her face, "There must be some good in white people, though it is well hidden."

They ate some dried meat, then took their horses down in a low place and hid them. They put on hobbles of rope he had brought and threw the horses and tied the front legs up to the bellyband so they could not rise. She followed him as he carefully made his way up the high ground ahead. There, in late afternoon, they lay on their bellies in the oak bushes and looked down on a white man's house.

It was a log house with two rooms, open covered passageway between them, a stone chimney at one end. Behind it lay a shed and pens with cows and mules. A man came from the shed to the house with a bucket in his hand and went in. From a tree near the house a line was stretched to a post some distance away. On the line hung clothing and squares of cloth, one a white square as large as a buffalo robe. A woman and a girl came out of the house. They passed along by the clothes, feeling of them. The girl skipped ahead of her mother, testing the clothes and yelling back to her mother. The air was still. The girl's yells came plainly. They were clear but strange: shrill and biting. It must have been words about which clothes were wet and which dry, but Tehanita could not understand a word of it. The two white people went back inside.

Seeing and hearing the little white girl made her feel like crying, but at the same time, lying on her belly beside her husband, she felt freedom greater than she ever remembered feeling. It was not because she had told him the truth, nor was it finding the mountain and the river; rather it was that she had given up escape. Somewhere in their talk her idea of a duty to escape had disappeared, and what she had told him was true: Wherever he led the Mutsani, she meant to follow him. She felt nearer him than ever before, bound tightly to him, but at the same time over these hills where she had ridden as a captive child a part of her now soared like a bird.

"A long time ago," he said, "the Penatuhka had a banner given them by the whites. It had thirteen stripes, white and red, and a blue place with thirty-four stars. It had strong medicine for the whites. Their soldiers carry such a banner. They also use a white banner; it has some medicine too, though not so much."

They lay and watched the sun go down and watched it grow dark. The window was yellow with light for a time. When the window disappeared, he rose. "You wait for me here, Tehanita. If a dog barks, go back and free the horses and hold them ready and wait for me there."

"You won't kill them?"

"No. I won't even take their horses, only the big piece of cloth."

No dog barked. In an hour he came back as silently as he had gone, with the cloth folded under his arm. It was cotton cloth like the traders brought, but not colored, such as was sometimes made by the Yaquis.

They went and got their horses and rode back the way they had come.

About noon on a late autumn day a short moon later the Mutsani band moved across the plains in the southern edge of

the Wichita Mountains. *Puhitipinab,* which the whites call
Fort Sill, lay an hour's ride before them. They could see it on
a low plateau set between them and the great curve of Medicine Bluff Creek with its dark-green foliage. They moved slowly
on their loaded horses, bringing all they possessed, which was
no great amount. Some rode double; some rode travois horses
or pack horses. All were mounted, though their horses were
few and overburdened for a people who were great horsemen
and breeders of horses.

The men wore their war honors, but no paint. The women
wore the best clothes they owned and had dressed their children in their best. No chatter of gossip passed between them.
All eyes were fixed ahead on the place toward which they rode.

She said in a low voice so that none could hear but her husband, "Maybe I should go back and ride with some other
women."

"Ride where I tell you." He spoke without turning his head.
"Close behind me. I might want to speak to you or give you
some orders."

"All right. Do you want me to carry the white banner?"

"No, you're not the chief. I am. You just obey me."

Out to their left the mountains rose dim in the autumn light,
their rough granite points softened by the dusty blue mist of
distance. Over them stood clouds in piles. She looked back at
the straggling procession. She could see Lance Returner and
Blessed, also Old Woman, white haired and bent; the child,
Bird Wing, riding with old Talking Woman; Spitting Dog;
Buffalo Bones; the younger warriors, some forty strong, with
their families. They were all solemn of face. Sometimes one
of the men looked back over his left shoulder toward a hill
where a stone lookout building sat. They had seen flashes from
the building a while ago and had known that the whites were
talking with mirrors to the fort.

They crossed a wagon road and a gully and moved on across
the prairie toward the plateau. The only sounds were the
muffled thuds of horses' hoofs against the sod, the scratching

of travois poles, sometimes the murmur of a few words between the members of a family.

He said, "Tehanita?"

"Yes."

"The closer I come to that place, the more I think the white
man's road will be hard."

"Yes."

"I'd rather go west and fight the Mescaleros than go to the
reservation. I might die gloriously in battle."

She didn't answer. It was a thing that had crossed his mind
a hundred times, that he had already decided upon, that could
not be changed—the answer to which was better given him
by his own mind than by a woman. Ahead she could see the
place, *Puhitipinab,* in the center of which was a high pole,
which looked from this distance as slender as a spider web, and
from its top flew the colored flag he had spoken of as having
stronger medicine than the plain white one he now carried.
Many buildings sat there on the high ground, most of them
long buildings of gray stone. Tiny figures of men rushed
around on foot and horseback between the buildings, and she
could see a group of them in the open on this edge of the high
ground, standing, watching. Some of them held their elbows
up in such a way that one could tell they used looking-tubes,
double or single, such as the white man uses to see long distances.

"Are you there close behind me?"

"Yes."

"I feel sad, Tehanita."

"I do too."

"I'm not afraid. I wouldn't care if the white men kill me.
That's not it. The white man's road is dim to me. When a warrior dies in battle at night and there's no moon, his soul cannot find the way, and it wanders and searches a long time, lost.
That's the way it is to me now."

She said, "I think you should go in smiling."

"Why?"

"To show them we're not beaten. Also, to help all the weak ones among us not to be afraid."

"All right. I guess I'll do that."

She closed her eyes and prayed silently, not trying to find any English words which she might be able to remember, using, rather, the easy, clear language of the People.

"Oh, Great Spirit, our Sure-Enough Father, make those white men treat my husband with respect, and listen when he speaks, and know that he is a great chief of the Mutsani. If any of them laugh at him or slight him, may that one be thrown down and broken like a thin stone. Help my husband not to be so sad. May he find a good road that will be straight enough to follow and bearable to his feet and on which the sun will shine for him all his days. Help our child too. And me."

She opened her eyes and guided her pony close behind her husband's mount. She put her hands on the back of her child, who rode with her, and made him straighten his small shoulders. "Sit up proudly and straight. We are of the *Nuhmuhna*. See your father, how he sits."

AFTERWORD

One of the clearest signs of Benjamin Capps's seriousness as a novelist can be seen in his willingness to take chances. After writing successful novels about the life of white cattlemen on the plains, he was brave enough to undertake a novel about life among the Indians as seen from the point of view of a woman. Unlike the writers of "formula westerns," Capps was willing to forego the sort of novel that celebrates masculine bravery and attempt to see life in the nineteenth-century American West from a new angle. Capps has never been a writer of "westerns," even though his books all deal with the American West. Instead, he has focused chiefly on the conflicts that took place there in the late nineteenth century—conflicts between man and nature and between European culture and the Native American culture that had existed on the Great Plains for centuries.

The confrontations that took place on the Great Plains are almost within Capps's memory. The West that Benjamin Capps was born into in 1922 had been the range of the Comanche for hundreds of years, and it was only with the coming of the whites in the middle of the nineteenth century that the Comanches began to see a threat to their land. Though the issue had already been settled by the time Capps was born, the memories lingered on in the region. On the South Plains Capps first heard tales about the coming of the white cattlemen and the displacement of the Indians. Old residents of Archer County, Texas, where Capps was born, could still remember Quanah Parker, the last great war chief of the Comanches. Capps himself remembers the day in 1929 that Charlie Goodnight died. Goodnight was the most famous of the South Plains cattlemen and trail drivers and one of the conquerers of the region. To be a child on the South Plains in Capps's boyhood was to fantasize about being a Comanche. Children grew up on the tale of Cynthia Ann Parker, who was stolen by the Comanches, bore the great Quanah, and died when she was forced to return to the white civilization she had forgotten.

Sometimes a child on the frontier would side with the Indians, sometimes with the whites. Capps still does both. In his novels one does not see a superior culture displacing an inferior one, but a powerful one exterminating a weaker one. Conversely, there is no propaganda about noble savages being overthrown by dissolute villains. What Capps is concerned to show is that on the plains in the late nineteenth century two authentic cultures clashed and the European one prevailed because of its superior technology. The people in the two cultures were essentially the same. The important thing to remember when red and white clash in a Benjamin Capps novel is that except for differences of language and culture, there are very few real differences between one person and another—even between men and women. As Capps put it in a letter to me, "all peoples are three-fourths the same and one-forth a unique culture and racial spirit" (19 January 1984). In the same letter, Capps implies a similar equation between the sexes, suggesting that a person's humanness is primary and his sexual identity secondary. One of the major differences between men and women is that "women are in charge of . . . immediate supplies of food, clothing, shelter, rocking the cradle, intimate family relations," while men "are in charge of the lesser part, hunting, war, ceremony, diplomacy, geopolitics." Since Capps finds such similarities between cultures and such equality between sexes, it is not surprising that he is willing to write about life not only from the Indian point of view, but from the woman's point of view.

Though *A Woman of the People* falls generally into the genre of the captivity narrative, a form that in the nineteenth century achieved archetypal dimensions, Capps's novel does not fully explore the myths usually associated with the captive maiden. For one thing, Capps does not deal with what Richard Slotkin calls the "salvation-through-affliction" theme so dear to the hearts of the New England Puritans, who, Slotkin says, "reaped the full moral, literary and social consequences of the mythology implicit in the captivity narratives."[1] On the other hand, Capps does not use the motif of captivity to teach moral or literary lessons, though a great deal of social commentary is implicit in his novel. One theme of the captivity narrative that is central to *A Woman of the People* is that of the captive beginning to see values in the culture of the captors. However, since Helen is unlike most of the heroes and heroines of captivity literature in that she is never freed, she never tells her story to the "outside." Instead of seeing her return to "civilization" to proclaim her ardors and teach the lessons that she learned, we see her blend completely into the culture of the captors. She is not regenerated through suffering but is civilized by the humanity of the Indians.

When he wrote *A Woman of the People* Capps had never read books about women captured by Indians but he knew the oral tales about the Comanches' capture of Cynthia Ann Parker (letter, 19 January 1984). In the novel he fictionalizes the Parker story, creating a work of imagination about a young girl growing to womanhood in a Comanche band. It is hard to decide which is more impressive—Capps's rendering of life in the Mutsani band or his depiction of the growth and change of Helen-Tehanita. Certainly his treatment of Indian life is remarkable for its accuracy. There is no doubt that Capps has earned his reputation as an authority on Indian life—his two books on Indians in the Time-Life series and his history, *The Warren Wagontrain Raid,* attest to his expertise. But his reputation as a novelist is equally high. Elmer Kelton, Capps's only Texas rival as a writer of serious fiction about the West, says, "Were Ben Capps writing of urban subjects, using the same skill and insight, he would probably be hailed as one of the country's best writers today."[2] In any case, whether *A Woman of the People* is judged on the basis of its literary quality or its accuracy in portraying life among Native Americans, it is one of the best books to come out of the Southwest in this generation.

One of his finest achievements in this novel is the parallel movement of plot, character, and theme. As Helen grows slowly into womanhood and becomes more and more a Comanche, the tribe shrinks in size and draws closer to its fate of life in captivity. Thematically, the war within Helen between white and Indian values mirrors the war between the Mutsani band to which she belongs and the whites from whom she was captured. As the white girl develops into womanhood as an Indian, the reader reflects upon the theme of cultural equality that is such an important part of the book. This theme is not hammered home—indeed, none of the themes are; instead the reader must bear his share of responsibility in apprehending the full meaning of *A Woman of the People.* A reader who is not sensitive to theme may simply read the novel as the fictional biography of a captured child, and it is certainly that.

In fact, I think the novel's best feature is the characterization of Helen. Slowly and with great subtlety, Capps lets the girl develop into a woman, lets the white become a Comanche. Helen herself does not know exactly what is taking place inside her and is often shocked by the changes. For instance, she has not been with the Mutsani for many years when, on a buffalo hunt, she runs ahead of the other women to a downed buffalo and counts coup by striking the animal and shouting "Ah-heh!" As she waits for the other women to catch up, she suddenly wonders, "What am I doing? Why did I run? Why did I strike the buffalo and cry out?" (p. 65). The Indian girl struck the buffalo, but the white girl wonders why. Capps does not answer the girl's questions, but leaves the reader to *see* what is developing in her mind. The reader is inside the mind of the girl throughout the book and grows in understanding as she does. We first know her as a terrified ten-year-old captive determined to get herself and her little sister away from the savages. Later we see her in a state of indecision—is she a Comanche or is she still a white? Finally, we see her with her husband and young son on the way to surrender. Her last words—the last words of the novel—are to her young son: "Sit up proudly and straight. We are of the *Huhmuhna*. See your father, how he sits" (p. 242). She has come the whole way. She is a Comanche and she is proud to be one.

Helen's gradual transition from white girl to Indian woman can best be seen in her changing attitude about escape. At first it is the only thing she thinks about. She will get herself and Katy back to the civilization that they had known. For nearly half the book Helen plans her escape. Even after Lance Returner and his lodge have accepted her as a daughter (p. 72), she continues to assess her chances of getting away, but her plans begin to dim as the years pass and she begins to forget the white language and white attitudes. Thoughts of escape come less often as time passes, but even toward the middle of the novel when she hears about the Civil War—Helen is now seventeen or eighteen—she thinks of her loyalty to the whites. But as members of the band begin to forget that she is white, as they start to rely upon her good sense and industry, she begins to see herself as a woman and as a Comanche. When Tehanita is being courted by Burning Hand, Lance Returner tells her, "You are a true Comanche as much as any woman that ever lived" (p. 161). He advises her to marry Burning Hand. She does, and after a couple of years gives birth to "a new Mutsani warrior." The transition is now complete. She becomes a storyteller to the children of the tribe, thus fulfilling the vision which the original Story Teller must have had when he gave her his name years before. By the end of the novel, she realizes that she has forgotten what life was like among the whites to whom they must surrender. She admits to Burning Hand that she had once planned to escape and return to the whites. Now, she wants "to go with the people." She feels a "freedom greater than she has ever remembered . . . [because] she had given up escape" (p. 238).

The girl become a woman, the Mutsani band goes to its fate on the reservation, and the novel comes to a quiet close. There are none of the thematic and stylistic hysterics often found in novels about the clash of cultures that took place a hundred years ago on the plains. Capps avoids the sentimentality that characterizes many pro-Indian novels and the blustering heroism that is to be found in tales of the Indian fighters. The book is not a piece of propaganda for either side, but an attempt to tell the truth about a time, a life, and a people.

This truth is reflected in both the dialogue style and the narrative style. The characters speak in a language that sounds normal to a modern reader. There is none of the stilted grunting and halting that we associate with motion-picture Indians. When Helen first meets Talking Woman, the language that we hear from the Indian is stilted and Pidgin-like. But the dialect we hear is not because Indians are presumed to lack fluency in their own language but because Talking Woman has learned Pidgin English from the whites. Once Helen learns the language of the Mutsani Comanches, all the speech seems perfectly natural. Just as important to the stylistic success of the book is Capps's narrative tone, which is simple and un-adorned. When it is eloquent, the eloquence seems to come from the situation. Style, for Capps, is not something to dazzle the reader with; it is an integral part of the theme, plot, and tone.

A Woman of the People is never false, never contrived, never formulaic. Capps has taken the facts of Indian existence, the parts of the Cynthia Ann Parker story that can be known, and the story of the Indian's defeat and woven them into a work of imagination that is greater than its parts. It is not difficult to see, even on the basis of this one book, why Benjamin Capps is held in high esteem by critics of western American literature.

James W. Lee
North Texas State University

1. Richard Slotkin, *Regeneration Through Violence: The Mythology of the American Frontier* (Middletown, Conn.: Wesleyan University Press, 1973). Slotkin provides a full discussion of captivity literature in nineteenth-century America.

2. "The Western and the Literary Ghetto," *The Texas Literary Tradition*, ed. Don Graham et al. (Austin: The University of Texas, 1983) p. 91.

WORKS BY BENJAMIN CAPPS

Hanging at Comanche Wells. New York: Ballantine, 1962.

The Trail to Ogallala. New York: Duell, Sloan and Pearce, 1964.

Sam Chance. New York: Duell, Sloan and Pearce, 1965.

A Woman of the People. New York: Duell, Sloan and Pearce, 1966.

The Brothers of Uterica. New York: Meredith Press, 1967.

The White Man's Road. New York: Harper and Row, 1969.

The Indians. New York: Time-Life Books, 1972. (Non-fiction)

The True Memoirs of Charley Blankenship. New York: Lippincott, 1972.

The Warren Wagontrain Raid. New York: Dial, 1974. (Non-fiction)

The Great Chiefs. New York: Time-Life Books, 1975. (Non-fiction)

Woman Chief. Garden City, N.Y.: Doubleday, 1979.